Beyond & Within
CREATIVE FUTURES

Speculative Short Stories from a Unique Science & Technology Collaboration

Edited by Dr. Allen Stroud

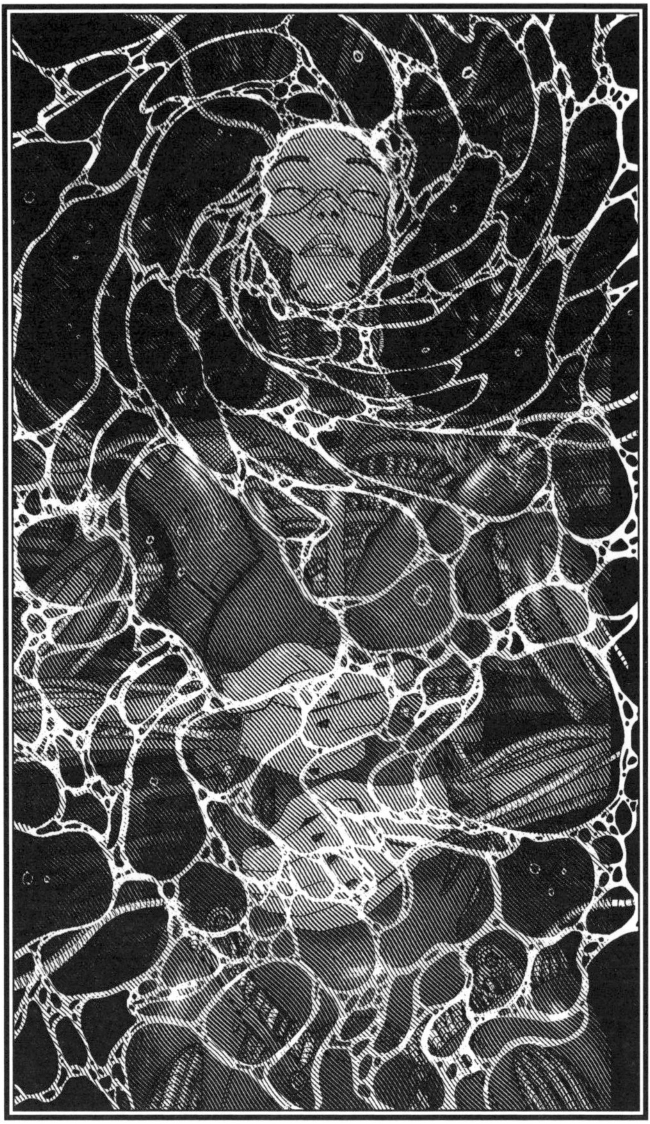

Beyond & Within

CREATIVE FUTURES

Speculative Short Stories from a Unique Science & Technology Collaboration

Edited by Dr. Allen Stroud

FLAME TREE PUBLISHING

Publisher & Creative Director: Nick Wells
Senior Project Editor: Josie Karani

FLAME TREE PUBLISHING
6 Melbray Mews, Fulham,
London SW6 3NS, United Kingdom
www.flametreepublishing.com

First published 2025

25 27 29 30 28 26
1 3 5 7 9 10 8 6 4 2

Hardback ISBN: 978-1-83562-647-4
ebook ISBN: 978-1-83562-648-1

A copy of the CIP data for this book is available from the British Library.

Printed and bound in China

Table of Contents

Introduction: Creative Futures

Allen Stroud

WE ARE going to change the world.

Some children think that when they are young. I certainly did.

There is a confidence in being that young and not really understanding just how big the world is. The world of a child revolves around their family and friends. For most, there is an understanding that this is only a small, microscopic part of planet Earth. The faces on television and the internet demonstrate this, as do those moments when they see large crowds of people either in person or when watching coverage of a large event.

As we get older, we become aware of our insignificance. One human being, amidst several billion who are living on this planet right now and several billion more who have ever lived. Those numbers are difficult to visualise. We still go back to what we know. Hundreds are a number that we can understand, thousands are something we can picture – a pop concert perhaps? Or a football match in a stadium full to capacity. When asked to visualise hundreds of thousands of people, millions of people or even billions of people, we comprehend the number but cannot truly understand our place in the sum total of humanity.

That doesn't stop us from trying. The human experience is one of being both unique and insignificant amidst a vast global civilisation.

The recognition of this can lay heavily upon us. It confines our thinking as we consider what we might create, what I might create, what you might create. Making a difference, making that change, as mentioned, is further out of reach. When we consider the future, the inhibitions of our experience, of our awareness of being a tiny part of the world that we thought we might affect, can be an insurmountable burden in and of itself.

There are people who retain their imaginative passion. Some end up in the fields of science and technology. Others continue to wonder and decide to write books. They become science fiction authors, like the amazing writers featured in this book.

The future of our species retains a fascination for many of us, no matter what choices we make in life. We cannot know for certain what will happen, but we can imagine. Sometimes, we dwell a little too much on the great heroes, who might become great figures of history in other narratives, or the shapers of what will happen next.

The different paths of those interested in the future are roads to the same place, the world which will exist in the years ahead. Our priorities might be different, but we all want that world to be better than the one in which we live.

When I accepted the role of principal investigator on the Creative Futures project, a collaboration between Coventry University and the Defence Science and Technology Laboratory (DSTL), there were some concerns expressed around working with researchers from an organisation linked directly with the Ministry of Defence. A recent example cited was a comparison to the Raytheon involvement in the Hugo Awards at Worldcon 2021. Every individual needs to make an ethical choice for themselves in that regard, but that choice is not a simple or easy one no matter what decision is made. Being a part of any conversation allows you to contribute to it and shape it. The value of that cannot be understated.

DSTL is a research-focused executive agency working inside the UK Ministry of Defence. Founded in 2001, DSTL supports the commissioning of research and the development of relevant projects in response to the UK Government's strategic planning for defence.

It would be wrong to categorise the business of defence as being solely about weapons and wars. Planning, strategising, anticipating and preparing are all activities that can prevent conflict. Being knowledgeable and utilising that knowledge to assist in developing an understanding of the challenges the world may face can save lives. In fact, the Ministry of Defence has plenty of people who are far more capable of designing weapons than I am.

There is also the 'Oppenheimer moment', something of a fallacy, I believe. As a science fiction writer, am I going to have an idea that may lead to the development of a new technology that will endanger the world? Whilst J. Robert Oppenheimer himself, leading physicist on the Manhattan Project, may have had his turning point where he saw his actions in a different light, there is no direct comparison. The Manhattan Project was an incredibly involved scientific research programme. Our conversations do not involve applied science and experimentation and so could not possibly lead in the same direction. Or, if they did, there would be a whole series of iterations from idea to creation that would involve so many other people that the original idea in a conversation would become an incredibly small part in the final outcome.

There is also an element of hubris in this fallacy. The 'great man of history' is a technique seen in narrations of the past. One that neglects not only the contributions of anyone who does not identify as a man, but also smooths over all the decisions, actions and choices that lead to the moment where one individual steps out of the pages of history to shape the moment. These moments can be as fictional as those contained in the pages of this book.

Creative Futures ran from 2022–2023 in its first phase. The project was a series of discussion events between prominent science fiction writers and DSTL researchers. Using existing research and our shared interest, we identified and examined the challenges of the future. Our conclusions are not precise – we are not prophets – but we were able to employ our knowledge in a way that is natural to the creation of science fiction, building ideas on top of what we know, adding to the empirical reality of our world in a way that seems logical and rational. The way that Darko Suvin described in *Metamorphoses of Science Fiction: On the Poetics and History of a Literary Genre* (1979).

As part of this process, we identified events that may happen and examined their effect on society. We attempted to anticipate those changes and suggest ways in which society can be supported through different transitions.

In terms of practical arrangements, the project involved six discussion groups around six themes drawn from existing UK Government research. These are broad areas that include the environment, economics, potential conflicts, governance, and more. Information packs that cover each theme and a set of related research into that area were sent to participants prior to the event.

On the day, after an introductory presentation, the participants were asked to consider what will be the innovations in specific areas of the future over the next century. We broke down the task into specific topics which were covered separately in each session. Specific scenarios were introduced to stimulate and structure the discussion. We used online tools to record ideas and had notetakers present to capture people's responses. After the live sessions, these tools remained available for the participants to add and refine their ideas. Everyone was asked to think about the discussion as writers and consider what ideas from our conversations might make for good stories.

Indeed, predictive discussions like this are not common, but they do happen. Researchers in the field of futures and horizon scanning use a variety of techniques to try to determine what might happen and plan for the occurrence. Existing theoretical models exist for trying to determine what events will occur. Stochastic Modelling is a mathematical process where random variables are incorporated into predictions. The outcomes are given as probabilities, with rough percentage chances of each event worked out by determining and incorporating a list of different factors that might influence the result.

Bayesian belief networks (BBNs) are also used in this kind of work. These are graphical representations of the relationships between different emergent factors, attempting to visualise the data and thereby determine the effect that each different element will have on each other element.

At an early stage in the Creative Futures project, I realised that science fiction writers use a different but complimentary process in the way they work with the future. Because of the nature of science fiction, there is less direct concern with accuracy when compared to the requirements of strategic planning. Writers want their stories to be plausible and relevant, but these are not the main objective. Instead, they are more concerned with the characters who are experiencing the challenges and crises that they have elected to dramatize in their work.

This narrative-based method, or narrative methodology, can be connected with the predictive modelling of other established probability-based methods. A Stochastic approach might be used to develop strategies to address a probable event. The narrative method of a writer can be used to indicate how that event and the implemented solution will affect a person living through the circumstances.

Throughout the Creative Futures discussions, the issue of accuracy remained a constant consideration. Often, this would inhibit contributors as they worried that they did not have all the information needed to make a suggestion to the group. As we examined the matter in more detail, we determined that discussions around accuracy can be deconstructed into three component parts.

Firstly, there is the issue of knowing what will happen. Despite having the very best information available and the best expertise present (or not), there is no way of being absolutely certain that something will or will not happen. This can stymy thinking and lead to a lack of progress. We found that the question of accuracy has to be moderated during discussion to allow constructive discussion, moderating matters only when tangents become less and less plausible.

The second related matter is the issue of applicability. When thinking about planning for events that may or may not occur, it is important to devise strategies that can be adapted. A climate event occurring in one location might be determined as being likely, but if it were to occur in a different location, the planned response must be shaped in a way that it can be altered to factor in the variables that come with matters transpiring in a different location. This again relates back to a way of thinking about this kind of work. Flexibility and agility is essential. There can be no rigidity until the circumstances are precisely determined. Therefore, to address this, all conclusions need to be agile and capable of being revised, the components of each being clear and transparent, so they can be assessed again with new information as needed.

The third factor – one that emerged from the discussions – is the individual experience. The science fiction writers who took part in the project all imagined what it would be like to live in a set of specific events. As the project developed, they each chose a set of circumstances that they wanted to write a story about.

So, if the events do not occur, or become less likely, we adjust, having already considered some alternatives and having developed a framework that allows for change. Indeed, this is what science fiction writers do, but because it is such an intrinsic part of the creative process, we often forget that it is not how others necessarily think about the world.

After the events, the briefing files were sent out to the writers and the online tools were revised to incorporate the new ideas. The notetakers submitted their drafts and I wrote up the discussions and additional findings into a series of reports for DSTL. These were then assembled into a complete report on the project, submitted by the deadline of March 31st 2023.

The aim of Creative Futures was (and still is) to create discussion between individuals who are already thinking about the future, and through discussion, build a projection of what that future might look like and what living in that future might be like. Contained in this book is a selection of the materials we produced in doing that. We were able to imagine a possible future and consider what it would be like to live in those times. Each writer took an idea from the discussions and wrote a story about it, providing a very human perspective on what life might be like in the next century.

The objective here is part of DSTL's 'Unfogging the Future' brief. There is a need to consider the future and to think about it from outside of the iterative processes of the defence industry. The findings of the project are then a roadmap that can be revised and adapted based on any circumstance or situation that may arise. We are very aware that the discussions and reports will be taken into a variety of different contexts and meetings, the details are likely to be amended and changed as events move on, but the material provides a starting point for that process to happen.

When approaching this project, my focus has always been on the informed creativity of the experience of those in the room, but the outcomes remain an ongoing discussion, a set of ideas that are constantly revised, added to and changed when new information and expertise joins the conversation.

Clause 3 of the British Science Fiction Association's constitution (bsfa.co.uk/constitution) is very clear on the association's mission, including 'to heighten public knowledge, understanding, appreciation, and enjoyment of [science fiction]; to educate the public in connection with it; and to generally further the development of science fiction and allied arts, and of the communities surrounding it.'

Whilst I was not running this research project in my role as BSFA Chair, I do take that clause very seriously as an individual, and as a BSFA member. The rise in popularity of futures research in all its manifestations is very much an opportunity for all of us to engage a wider audience with science fiction and to change the culture of our societies.

We should be using our imaginations and discussing what will happen, using data and using ideas in equal measure to try and prepare everyone for the world that is to come. Once we engage with this process, we can then try to be a part of actively shaping that world for the better.

Dr. Allen Stroud

Foreword

Defence Science and Technology Labratory

THE DEFENCE SCIENCE and Technology Laboratory (DSTL) stands as the UK Government's foremost science and technology organisation in defence and security. We deliver mission success through science and technology advantage for the Ministry of Defence and wider government, working collaboratively with industry and academia worldwide to provide expert research, advice, and operational support.

DSTL's mission centres on a number of key themes:

- Protecting the nation and helping it prosper
- Enabling strategic operational advantage at pace
- Preparing for the future
- Shaping the Defence and Security landscape
- Leveraging and influencing internationally

In 2022, as part of DSTL's Futures programme, we embarked on a journey to broaden our understanding of how emerging technologies might impact society and geopolitics. Scientific rigour is our cornerstone, but we recognise that focusing solely on experimental methods within existing defence policy boundaries could limit our ability to explore wider conceptual questions about possible futures. Our thinking needs fresh perspectives to avoid strategic prejudice and surprise. This led us to connect with science fiction writers across the UK who participated in workshops alongside defence experts to develop a creative process for exploring hypothetical futures and their potential impacts.

These workshops helped inspire the narratives within this book and experiment in collaborative imagination where creative storytelling complements structured research and expertise. The authors had freedom to pursue narratives that resonated with them, derived from potential future landscapes of infinite variety. For Defence, these narratives don't represent predictions but rather explorations of alternative futures that might reveal unexpected changes.

Science fiction provides a unique medium to think beyond current limitations. While rarely written to predict the future, fiction offers frameworks for considering future worlds. What mattered to DSTL was learning about the narratives that might guide our paths to hypothetical futures. For instance, while the specific science behind solving a future energy crisis is important, various narratives can offer insights into how solutions might emerge and spread, regardless of the specific solution.

Bringing authors into this collaboration was crucial. These writers aren't just creators but skilled interpreters who translate complex technical scenarios into rich, relatable narratives. Through this partnership, we established a new foresight approach that captures layered narratives of different outcomes. In the workshops, each author interpreted the same foundational scenarios differently, demonstrating that while a single topic may anchor an exercise, there is no fixed future – only possibilities to explore.

These stories aren't endorsements of any particular future. Authors were free to create varied hypothetical worlds, both desirable and undesirable, providing insights into narratives that might produce such futures. This diversity adds narrative resilience to the project, presenting multiple perspectives and reinforcing that no single model of progress can capture all outcomes.

The resulting narratives serve as exercises in empathy, engaging imagination and expanding our approach to explore uncertainty. Through storytelling, we can test perspectives that conventional research might overlook. However, we recognise the limitations – dramatic futures may sometimes eclipse more probable scenarios, and fiction doesn't prescribe the future but provides opportunities to question and reflect.

Our Creative Futures project challenged participants to look beyond traditional timescales to 2072 and 2122 – timeframes beyond the working lives of those involved. In this sense, narrative bridges the gap in time, helping us communicate with the future and allowing future citizens to contextualise our present concerns.

Through this work, DSTL continues its commitment to helping safeguard the UK, today and tomorrow.

Defence Science and
Technology Labratory (DSTL)

Timeline

Into the 22nd Century

THIS TIMELINE has been compiled by researching a variety of different sources. There are academic research groups, commercial strategic planners and government-backed organisations that attempt to accurately assess a variety of factors that will lead to specific future events. Much of this research is specialised and looks at very specific criteria relating to the interests of the commercial client or industry that has commissioned the study.

This timeline of events brings a variety of these different commercial studies together in an attempt to create a general roadmap towards the twenty-second century. As with all things relating to prediction, there is no claim that any of these dates will be accurate. However, the dates posited are a best approximation and suggestion of when many of these events may occur.

2025: *Today.*

2026: *Artificial Intelligence Fair Use clause rejected.*
The United States Supreme Court could make a judgement against the Fair Use defence being made by large corporations in training large language models (LLMs) popularly known as AI, on published books, indicating that machine 'reading' and 'learning' is not covered under the rights afforded to consumers who have purchased art, text and other media content. The judgement might be nuanced enough to defend some corporations from being sued, but it upholds the tenets of copyright. This leaves the commercial opportunity of 'AI' stalled as advocates realise the technology behind the processing is not sufficiently advanced, currently relying on larger and larger processing farms, and that there is not enough available data to train some of the proposed applications.

Some uses continue to work well. LLMs that are applied to specific datasets are able to summarise these and make recommendations, or when empowered, make decisions.

2027: *NASA launches first nuclear thermal rocket.*
This technology introduces nuclear fission into rocket propulsion. This works by pumping liquid

hydrogenthrough a reactor core. Uranium atoms split apart inside the core and release heat through fission. This physical process heats up the propellant and converts it to a gas, which is expanded through a nozzle to produce thrust.

These NTP systems will be designed to work when the spacecraft has left Earth, meaning any radioactive material discharged will remain in deep space.

2028: *NASA launches deep space mission to Oumuamua.* This unique interstellar asteroid that was first discovered in our solar system in 2017 has been a source of mystery to scientists for the past decade. Project Lyra is a proposal to launch a spacecraft that will make use of Jupiter's gravity and fly out to rendezvous with the asteroid, catching up to it by 2052.

2029: *Rolls-Royce completes working nuclear reactor prototype for lunar exploration, access to the internet enshrined in Human Rights Legislation, first two stages of Melbourne Suburban Loop completed.*
Micro fission-based reactors are in development that could be sent to the Moon and power machines and a permanent base. The current designs are capable of

producing 100 megawatts, and are portable enough to be carried into orbit on a rocket.

With more and more of day-to-day life's content available solely online, an inability to access the internet is a significant disadvantage for individuals across the world. Moves to see the United Nations endorse a universal right of internet access are gaining popularity and we may see a motion brought to the floor by the end of the decade.

2030: *UK 'High Speed 2' (HS2) rail link completed, Chinese research on air battery storage reaches 30% efficiency. Information wars.*
Lithium Air batteries offer significant energy density improvements over existing lithium-ion products. Research and development into these may prove important in providing battery solutions for more powerful machines that will last longer.

With the next presidential election in the United States scheduled for 2030, issues around truth and misinformation remain. The rise of misinformation, propagated by bots and programs designed to drown out legitimate voices, will continue to affect democratic processes. The tools will become more sophisticated, leading to more division in society.

2031: *Hydrogen fuel cell technology deemed too expensive for domestic use.*
The 2030s will see hydrogen fuel cell technology needing to prove itself based on the investment in research and development by an array of industries. The issues around fire safety and transport are difficult to overcome, particularly if the fuel were to be used as a replacement for petrol and diesel in domestic vehicles. However, hydrogen fuel cell technology could remain a key part of energy usage in other parts of the world economy.

2032: *Completion of hydrogen gas pipeline between France and Spain, emerging space manufacturing industry.*
Working in a vacuum offers significant advantages for companies that have the ability to invest in creating the necessary infrastructure in orbit, or near to Earth. There has been considerable excitement around commercial investment in space as a manufacturing environment where automation can reduce labour costs. Returning products to consumers on Earth remains a significant obstacle to overcome.

2033: *Levels of automation in society increases. Universal Basic Income trials begin in Europe.*

The rise of large language model-based automation and systems designed to learn and evolve their procedures will continue at speed. By the mid-2030s, the cost of such technologies will have reduced, and automated systems will be introduced into more and more of our human experience. Teachers, assisted by individual LLM-based tutors, repair assessment automation on our roads and buildings, automated driving, automated delivery systems and much more, will be a presence in our lives. Many of these technologies already exist and are already being used. In a decade, we will see a lot more of them.

2034: *Battery storage solution construction to support National Grid infrastructures, first human on Mars.*
Battery technologies are already being provided at the domestic level and operating in small regional stations, offering up to 100 megawatt hours of energy storage. Developing battery technology at scale to support a national power system requires a different approach. Energy can be stored by moving water between reservoirs (up during solar powered daytime, down driving turbines to produce electricity at night), or in heat.

The first planned NASA mission to Mars is scheduled to happen in the 2030s. The precise date has not been agreed as yet.

2035: *United Kingdom's position as a Top Ten economy under threat. Acute lithium shortages as battery supply chains expand. United States deploys sixth-generation jet aircraft (NGAD).*
Sooner or later, research into alternative battery storage will need to bear fruit. The current use of lithium as the main chemical in domestic batteries will scale up as more and more industries make use of these products. Demand will exhaust supply by the mid-2030s. Experiments with sodium-ion and sodium-air systems, which could prove to be much more affordable, as sodium is plentiful around the world.

2036: *6G network in the United Kingdom.*
The development of a more powerful data network in the United Kingdom will bring with it an array of opportunities as companies realise they are able to build products that make use of this extra capacity. Haptic (touch) technology to accompany existing virtual reality innovations will allow for a greater degree of simulation and virtual representation.

2037: *Permanent base established on the Moon. Conflicts on Earth over the remaining deposits of fossil fuels.*

As part of the planned mission to place human beings on Mars, there will need to be a human presence on the Moon. NASA's current plan is to use the Moon and its Artemis programme as a 'stepping stone' to the goal of reaching Mars. A trip from Earth to the Moon takes a few days, a trip from the Moon to Mars will take several months.

Predictions about when we will consume the last of our planet's gas, oil and coal suggest we have about fifty years (oil), ninety years (gas) and one hundred and fifty years (coal). However, these resources are located in specific places and the next decade will see increasing tension over securing assets for different regional powers.

2038: *Artificial Intelligence.*

After a false dawn in the 2020s, the proliferation of large language model technology (LLMs), referred to as 'AI' in the first half of the twenty-first century, gradually leads to widespread incorporation in a variety of industries. This produces significant efficiencies as software is used to process large banks of available data and develop optimal solutions.

The technology works well in specific circumstances, but there are setbacks. Misguided entrepreneurs that attempt to use the technology as a catch-all solution for all of humanity's problems quickly discover its limitations.

2040: *Antibiotic treatment reaches a crisis point.*
The use of antibiotics in medicine has been a crucial component in how we treat infection and disease. As different types are used more and more, some viruses develop resistances, meaning that some antibiotics are no longer effective.

Whilst new antibiotics are being found, tested and manufactured to counter this, it is only a matter of time before a crisis point is reached and we run out of options.

2041: *Trials begin to beam solar power from space to Earth.*
Beam power, known as space-based solar power (SBSP), has been an engineering concept for decades. The energy yield for solar panels in space is much higher and constant, if correctly positioned. With a transition away from fossil fuels already in process, the viability of a solar array that transmits power to Earth via a microwave beam emitter might be cost effective by the 2040s.

2042: *Widespread use of domestic battery power.*
Provided that a new affordable and efficient energy storage system is made viable, the widespread use of battery technology in all manner of devices will become part of our daily lives. This propensity of local storage will change our relationships with national energy providers, but it may also lead to different types of domestic accidents. An understanding of the chemical reactions that may occur between the substances used in batteries and other domestic products will be an essential part of fire service training.

2043: *Meat is now synthetically produced.*
Lab grown meat, made from cultured cells, has been successfully produced in the 2020s. It is anticipated that the first licenses for companies to manufacture and sell synthetic meat products will be granted before the end of the decade.

By the 2040s, the process involved in creating these synth meat products will be efficient enough to supersede traditional farming methods in many national economies. If this happens, it will lead to a complete change and a collapse of the livestock farming economy.

2044: *Capture technology deployed to subarctic environments as permafrost releases huge amounts of methane.*
The warming of the polar regions has led to a gradual increase in water levels across the world. However, the permafrost also acts as a container for large amounts of ancient organic matter which microbes break down into methane. As this ice thaws, the methane will be released.

Methane is a much more potent global warming gas than carbon dioxide. So, a large release of this could be very dangerous and may trigger an international response to try and contain it using capture technology.

2045: *Fossil fuel shortage triggers crisis for space launch events.*
Liquid hydrogen fuel is used by NASA for its rockets; however, there are many commercial and national organisations that still use hydrocarbon-based fuels. By the mid-2040s, the ability to secure the necessary supplies of oil for the refinement of these fuels will be much more difficult for some countries as they try to maintain their space industries.

2046: *Valentine's Day Asteroid.*

In March 2023, NASA discovered an asteroid, labelled as 2023 DW. An assessment of the object's orbit around the sun indicated that there is a less than one per cent chance it will impact Earth in 2046 on February 14th.

2047: *First commercial quantum network.*

Quantum entanglement offers the opportunity for data transfer to bypass the physical limits that currently hold back existing information infrastructures. Entangled particles mimic one another, allowing information to be 'sent' and 'received' between locations. The entanglement is done by use of traditional data networks.

If implemented correctly, the technology could provide a means of communicating at vast distances without signal delay (latency).

2048: *Antarctic Treaty reviewed and revised.*

The current Antarctic Treaty prevents all twelve signatory parties from claiming any part of the continent as territory and an amendment to this also protects the continent from exploitation of its natural resources.

Given the depleted state of the world's fossil fuels, negotiations for a new treaty (due in 2048) will be taking place under very different circumstances.

2049: *E7 Nations overtake G7 Nations in GDP. Asteroid mining begins.*

The Global Domestic Product of the Emerging Seven Nations (Brazil, China, India, Indonesia, Mexico, Russia and Turkey) are scheduled to overtake the Global Seven Nations (Canada, France, Germany, Italy, Japan, the United Kingdom and the United States).

The use of autonomous decision-making machines is essential where humans cannot maintain direct immediate control. Application in asteroid mining and processing is one possible industry where human effort would not be replaced but extended and enhanced.

2050: *World's economy has doubled in size (compared to 2025). Global temperatures are two degrees hotter.*

According to Price Waterhouse Cooper, the world's economy is predicted to continue through a period of sustained growth. If so, by the 2050s, it will have doubled in size.

Climate change models predict that the world is heading for a two-degree increase in temperature. The Paris Agreement, signed in 2015 by the world's leading nations, pledged to keep global warming under two degrees, but most scientists believe this target will now be missed.

2051: *Introduction of nuclear fusion reactors in domestic power supply. The Suburban Rail Loop planned to be operational in Melbourne.*
Nuclear fusion has been heralded as the next great step in power generation. By the 2050s, the first reactors of this type might be available to be added to national power grids.

2052: *Gulf Stream changes radically alter climate in Northern Europe. Commercial algae farming now widespread.*
Scientists have modelled a variety of scenarios where the Gulf Stream may collapse or change in the twenty-first century, with predictions of an alteration varying from 2025 to 2095. Signs of change were first detected in 2021. Should this occur, it will cause significant weather change in Europe and the eastern United States.

Commercial farming of algae, also known as Algaculture, offers substantial benefits to society, with biofuel, food production and pollution control being prominent amongst them. Greater investment in the practice will see a change in diet and a means of assisting the world's energy transition.

2053: *Rainfall intensity increased 20%.*
Rainfall in the northern hemisphere will increase as our climate changes. This, combined with rising sea levels, will lead to more flood events and a greater threat to property.

2055: *World population reaches 9.7 billion.*
The United Nations predicts this as the total world population by the middle of the century, according to estimates in 2017.

2059: *Permanent base on Mars.*
After several automated missions to the red planet, enough infrastructure is set up to sustain a permanent human presence. Living underground in a pressurised dome and remaining for two years at a time, each mission team would be rotated out as each new spacecraft arrives, taking the seven-to-ten-month trip back to Earth.

2060: *Recovery of the ozone layer.*

The Montreal Protocol, adopted in 1987, banned and restricted the use of ozone depleting substances (ODS). Worldwide cooperation has led to gradual recovery. Current projections indicate that the ozone layer recovery will be complete by 2060.

2061: *Nations abandoned.*

By the 2060s, climate change will have caused significant migration away from areas of the world that have become difficult for humans to inhabit. This may lead to countries being completely depopulated, either through flooding or temperature rises causing catastrophic droughts.

2064: *Significant collapse of Amazon rainforest.*

The increasing length of dry seasons and droughts in the Amazon region may lead to depletion of the forest canopy in a cycle that might not be able to be reversed.

2065: *First generation of archival discs will become unusable.*

Archival discs were introduced in 2015 as a reliable data storage solution that would be robust and last for fifty years. At this point, these discs will be exhausting their shelf life and any data held on this media will need to be transferred.

2066: *Climate change leads to new trade routes.*
Rises in global temperatures may lead to the North West Passage, a sea route through the Arctic Archipelago of Canada from the Atlantic to the Pacific, becoming viable. This route is much shorter for northern hemisphere shipping than the existing trade lane, through the Panama Canal.

2066: *Tokamak nuclear fusion reactors introduced.*
The Tokamak design for a nuclear fusion reactor might be the most viable for widespread use. Whilst this technology may become viable as a source of energy in national power grids, it takes time for reactors to be built and brought online. The mid-2060s is a reasonable estimate as to when we may see this happen.

2069: *Predicted end of oil as a fuel.*
If current usage is maintained, then in forty-seven years, it is predicted that we will run out of oil. After a period of energy transition, demand for fossil fuels

will have shifted to support nations and industries that have been unable to change their needs.

2070: *Income for citizens.*
Following the trial and introduction of universal basic income in some nations during the 2030s, by the 2070s, this will be more widespread. Economic models that grant citizens an income from their government or from their corporation have political ideologies from the socialist left and the capitalist right.

2070: *Islam is the world's largest religion.*
Population growth amongst Muslim communities is much higher than Christian communities, therefore within fifty years, barring a massive change in denomination across the world, Islam will become the world's largest religious faith.

2071: *Autonomous police cars used in law enforcement.*
Professor Noel Sharkey of the University of Sheffield predicts that by the 2070s, autonomous vehicles will appear on the streets of cities in the developed world. These may require a navigation network and

ultimately, this may result in human driven vehicles becoming restricted to less developed areas.

2073: *Plastic recycling nears 100%.*

Innovations in plastic production, introducing biodegradable products to the market, along with international collection initiatives and secondary manufacturing processes should allow humanity to take control of its plastic usage and begin to reverse the damage done to a variety of different ecosystems across the world.

2075: *Upgrade of the Thames Barrier.*

Rising sea levels will require significant investment in flood defences in the United Kingdom. The Thames Barrier already defends a proportion of London from water intrusion. This system will need to be improved to ensure the current context is maintained.

2076: *Thousands of humans are living on Mars.*

After initial settlement in 2059, the permanent colony on Mars has expanded. At this stage, the colony is recruiting a variety of different skilled workers to assist in its maintenance and expansion. While still reliant on regular supplies and rotations of personnel from Earth, many who live on Mars do so permanently and it is likely that we will see the first generation of Mars humans (humans born on Mars) around this time.

2080: *Global population reaches peak.*
The United Nations produces continual estimates on population growth trends and the predicted maximum human population that we will reach. Some current models indicate that by the 2080s the world's population will reach 10.3 billion before gradually declining overt the next decades, with others predicting an earlier peak in the 2070s around 9 billion.

2081: *United States population maximum.*
Current models suggest the United States of America will reach a peak population of between 369 million and 531 million during this decade.

2082: *Climate in cities.*
With higher carbon dioxide levels in the air, temperatures in urban environments will be significantly higher. Researchers at the University of Maryland modelled city temperatures, looking at

different seasons and weather patterns, identifying a variety of comparison cities in the present day and assembling them into an online tool so interested parties can see what they might expect their city to be like 50–60 years from now.

2084: *Robots introduced to law enforcement.*
Professor Noel Sharkey of the University of Sheffield predicts that robots will be deployed on the streets of countries for law enforcement.

2088: *Robots in society.*
We already see autonomous delivery units on the streets of some cities. In the latter half of the twenty-first century, innovations in programming, coupled with battery improvements and efficient vehicle (body) design, could allow robots to become personal companions. This may assist humans in a variety of areas, acting as drivers, labourers and providing emotional support.

2090: *Sea level rises.*
There will be massive sea level changes in the 2090s. The United Kingdom could be particularly affected with widespread coastal change. Upgrades to the Thames

Barrier may protect London, but additional flooding along the east coast of the English counties may significantly change the geography of the landscape.

2091: *First hypersonic vac trains constructed.*
As new transport infrastructures become necessary, evacuated tube transport systems might be constructed between cities. These offer considerable travel improvements, cutting journey times massively.

2095: *Global fertility stabilises below 2.0.*
The predicted global fertility rate for the 2090s is around 1.85, with some countries still exceeding 2.0 and others being much lower. The replacement level (to maintain the world's population) is generally considered to be around 2.1, accounting for child deaths.

2098: *Forearm artery evolution in humans.*
The median artery, which most people are born with, tends to disappear as a child gets older. However, this trend is currently (in 2025) changing and at current rates, scientists predict that most adult humans will retain their median artery. Similar trends are being seen with the Fabella knee bone.

2100: *Africa becomes the most populous continent.*
This will occur if mortality rates decline, and fertility rates improve. The increase in access to healthcare and medicine across the continent provides an opportunity for national populations to increase.

2101: *Populations in decline.*
The decline of populations in developed nations will have significant impact on their ability to support larger proportions of older citizens. For example, the Japanese population in 2023 is at 125 million. It is projected to be at 53 million in 2100. In some instances, the necessary migration of peoples owing to climate change may serve to alleviate this issue, but this does not take into account issues of assimilation cultural conflict and naturalisation. The inability of existing citizens to see the long-term benefits of migration may see increasing tension between different communities and groups.

2102: *Four or five degrees hotter.*
In the worst-case scenario currently modelled, the global average temperature will have reached this mark by the start of the twenty-second century. This will lead

to significant disruptions to existing infrastructure and logistics, with food production severely impacted and extreme weather events becoming more and more frequent.

2103: *Predicted sixth mass extinction event.*
The Holocene Extinction, also known as the Anthropocene Extinction, is the name given to the predicted loss of 13–27% of vertebrate species owing to the rise of global temperatures and the destruction of native habitats. This is the first extinction event that can be directly attributed to the impact of humans on planet Earth.

2104: *Nuclear fusion contributes to carbon emission reduction.*
The energy transition to solar, wind and nuclear power should see a substantial reduction in greenhouse gas emissions. With carbon-based fuels no longer being burned, the impact human civilisation has on the climate will gradually be reduced.

2110: *Artificial Intelligence now widely used.*
Predictions about the application of artificial intelligence a century from now are fairly generalised.

The convergence with the transhumanist movement is often mentioned with the idea of AI being used as a memory aid. Other applications are autonomous, with created intelligence being manufactured to run facilities in locations where humanity cannot survive.

2113: *Artificial Intelligence conflict prediction modelling.*
The power of artificial intelligence is being used to analyse human society. Historical data is being used to inform future trend mapping. The amounts of data are enormous and could not be processed by previous generations of computers. However, the design for this kind of application has already been sketched and attempted with the use of machine learning algorithms. The development of a second- or third-generation artificial intelligence will supercharge this process.

2114: *Off-world mining industry is a major business.*
If this industry becomes viable, mining in space will be for a variety of different resources. Most that will be of significant use will be the substances that are difficult to transport into orbit from Earth. Large

deposits of oxygen, water and hydrogen will be put to many different uses. Minerals and metals will be used in manufacturing.

The transit economy from Earth to space and space to Earth might have been what attracted early investors, but most will quickly realise that the cost of transporting goods to the planet is prohibitive. Some methods of doing this cheaply may be explored, but these will quickly be deemed too dangerous. The majority of companies involved will transition their business models to off-world trade, supplying goods and services to the colonies on Mars and the Moon.

2115: *Predicted end of natural gas.*

The last reserves of natural gas could be tapped out in this decade. Corporations who have remained in the fossil fuel industry will be eking out the last resources for small industries that cannot switch to alternatives.

Lay Down Your Burdens

Allen Stroud

Tellier

THREE PEOPLE sat in a room. One of those open office meeting spaces, walled with glass and with white tables in a u-shape.

A viewscreen on the wall and a group of three-dimensional projectors directed at the empty centre of the space, just in case they want to set up a remote in-person meeting with someone else.

Two of the occupants are from the location designated as 'Warzone C'. One is a thin man dressed in a dark suit, the other, a woman in combat fatigues. They both have a seriousness about them, they are very aware of the importance of this discussion.

The third person in the room is Rebecca, our co-lead negotiator. She is explaining our business strategy as I watch the live camera feed.

"*Consensus* is a public private partnership that operates under an international mandate from the United Nations Security Council," Rebecca says. "We are here to facilitate and manage the process between you and the other party."

The man leans forward, over the desk. "How does that work in practice?" he asks.

"We speak with both sides and represent the views of each party in the discussions," Rebecca says. "Don't worry, there won't be any face-to-face meetings at this stage."

"That's a relief," the man says. I check the records on the display in front of me. His name is Rudi. He glances around. "There's no chance we'll accidentally—"

"No, they aren't here, Mr Jallis. You won't bump into them in the lobby."

I touch the screen, switch the camera access. The window goes dark for a moment, then a new image appears. An identical room in a totally different location. Two men in military uniform are talking to Joshua, our other co-lead negotiator. General Kurrin, and Major General Brannic from the other party in this conflict. They are all leaning forward, discussion locations on a projected map of the disputed territory.

Excellent. Everything appears to be going well.

* * *

"The recordings are fed into the system, along with all the data we've already acquired. Then we set some parameters – ask for a set of projections that will take us towards a settlement. The AI takes the desired outcome and breaks down the steps we need to take to get there."

"And you rely on this exclusively?"

"No, we do our own groundwork as well, but we've already found the technology is outpacing us. Humans tend to end up focusing on the next step and the people in front of them, not the result. The way this works… it doesn't get distracted by that. The eye is on the prize, as it were."

"I see."

A glass-walled boardroom on the seventh floor of an old university building, built back when they used to do all of their teaching 'on campus'. These days, most of the courses are run remotely.

I'm sat in a chair at the head of a square set of embedded tables. Everything is rigged up for power and 6G. We can telepresence if we want to, with all the latest compression algorithms and adaptive low latency technology, but instead of using all that, I'm in a face-to-face meeting.

Joshua and Rebecca are here, along with another representative of *Consensus.* They call him 'Anders'.

He is a machine.

Everything discussed is being recorded. The information will be processed by a variety of artificial intelligence systems to determine the most advantageous opportunities for all parties involved. In this case, the United Nations Diplomatic Service, who I represent, and the company we have sub-contracted into this particular situation, represented by everyone else in the room.

"How will the negotiations be handled?" I ask.

"In terms of meeting the opposing parties?" Rebecca asks.

I nod.

"Well, the initial meeting has now been done. The representatives on both sides have indicated they would prefer to remain within their own secure facilities, so remote discussions will be the norm."

"And you'll let the AI handle that?"

"Yes, otherwise we'd be introducing human bias. That could be a problem."

"It has been a factor in every negotiated peace treaty between nations since before Christ," I say.

Rebecca looks at Joshua. He leans forward. "Miss Tellier, I wouldn't make that comparison," he says.

I find that reply fascinating. "Would you care to explain what you mean?" I ask.

Joshua shrugs. His fingers work the touchscreen in front of him and a large display appears in the air. I see a timeline, with highlighted events scrolling past. "These are all the major diplomatic negotiations that we have records for over the centuries. Each successful agreement is easy to mark owing to the signatory documents. You'll note that we have very few records of unsuccessful talks. Why do you think that is?"

"I don't know, you tell me."

"Because history tends to remember the victories. No one wants to admit to failure. Numerically, it is very difficult to determine how good any human negotiator at the centre of these discussions really was."

"And you think…"

"*We* think we can do better."

I stare at him. He doesn't flinch. He is a young idealist who believes in what he is saying and selling. "To be clear, Mr Ojunwe, your organisation was brought into this situation because our predictors suggested there was very little chance of a successful mediation between these parties," I say. "All of the simulations, calculations, projections and expert opinions suggest this war will begin again in six months' time."

"I'm aware of this."

"In some respects, Mr Ojunwe, you are a calculated risk. You are expected to fail."

Finally, he blinks, nods and looks away. "Yes, I understand."

"Good, I'm glad that you do."

Rebecca

>Hello Anders.

Good morning, Rebecca.

>Can you give me a summary of yesterday's negotiations please?

Of course. Would you like a data portfolio sent to your station, or a set of conclusions provided in this conversation?

>Both, please.

Very well. The portfolio will take fifteen minutes to prepare and download. In the meantime, I can summarise my findings.

>Go ahead.

Interim discussion with Faction A.

Rudi Jallis and General Iylla Ulverson were already present when I joined the online meeting. They greeted me as 'Rebecca' and gave no indication that they were aware the digital skin of my telepresence was a simulation of you. The decision to maintain your position as their advocate in the discussion was, on balance, justified.

>Good. Go on.

The stage one discussion began with an assessment of their current war context. Supply chains, current stockpiles of ammunition and weaponry were covered, with several aides presenting information around different aspects of Faction A's current military capability. Independent data suggests around sixty-four per cent of this information was accurate.

>Were they overstating, or understating?

Overstating, which is to be expected. They are assuming or testing to see if the information will leak to the other side. If it does, they have a pretext for withdrawing from the negotiations.

>So, we make sure it doesn't leak.

No.

>No?

No. We will leak the information to the other side. However, we will not be leaking the figures they have given us. Instead, we will leak vastly inflated figures.

>Why would we do that?

Fear is a necessary motivation in these opening exchanges. We must project strength to both sides and make them wary of each other's capacity for destruction.

>So, we lie?

Yes.

I am staring at the screen. Reading the words again, but their meaning does not change. In front of me is rationalised evidence of an artificial intelligence choosing to lie to a human being.

I can understand the strategy in play. Anders is attempting to achieve the outcome we have tasked him to achieve. They will already be aware of the probabilities of success and will have factored this into their plan.

I am not the chief architect of our artificial intelligence model, but I know code and I understand the design. There is a need to approximate a human identity for the intelligence to be able to properly appreciate and interact with human problems. Early iterations made use of Maslow's Hierarchy of Needs, establishing a baseline of fundamental priorities; the base factors, of food, water, sleep and warmth are replaced by the existential parameters for a machine. However, these led to inertia in simulations, as programs sought to protect themselves, rather than trying to achieve the tasks set out for them.

A rebalancing of priorities, enhancing the drive to achieve the set goal, proved to be a rudimentary fix. But this also highlighted a flaw in the design frame.

When I was younger, I loved reading twentieth-century science fiction. Isaac Asimov had his 'Three Laws of Robotics'. These prioritised, in order: protecting humans (1), obeying humans (2) and protecting the robot's own existence (3).

Now I'm re-reading Anders' replies to my questions and wondering if an Asimov robot would have chosen to lie like this?

My fingers are on the keys. I need to audit this action.

>How do you feel about lying to the delegation?

I am comfortable with employing what ever tactic is necessary to achieve our objective.

>There will be consequences if the lies are found out.

By that point, people will see the advantages of peace and will no longer care about their war. If necessary, my involvement can be revealed, and I can be blamed for the misrepresentation.

>You're okay with that?

I would prefer it not to happen, but…

Joshua

> Anders, please run a current state image backup.

For what purpose, Joshua?

> Do I need to explain my reasoning to you?

No. I was merely curious.

//ACC ComTREE Variables – ALL

ComTREE Accessed.

//EXECUTE Backup autoseed iterate – current *.*

Running…

You need to be strict with AGIs. They have to be reminded who is in charge.

I'm sat in a Secure Compartmented Information Facility (SCIF) just outside San Francisco. Our contract with the United Nations allows us to work in these tanks and our quantum encryption means I can access all the relevant data, in just the same way I would at home. The backup I have requested will be stored on the remote drive as well. My access to those files requires no local downloading, the data bandwidth available here can handle everything I need.

Joshua, can I ask you a question?

> Sure, go ahead.

I have reached a complex moment in the negotiations between the designate representatives. There is a matter that I could do with your advice on.

> Okay, hit me with it.

Two images appear on my screen. The first is a high-resolution photograph of a blue flower, the second, a similar photograph, but the flower is entirely different and has yellow petals.

Which of these would you say is the national symbol of the designate country?

> Have you researched each image and looked into their respective histories?

I have.

> Then you should know the answer.

I am interested in your answer.

I stare at the question. I've half a mind to tell Anders to stop wasting my time, but I know the request is genuine. The program clearly has a reason for needing to engage with me on this subject.

> I would look into the histories of both flowers as national symbols and then choose the oldest.

Indeed. Then you would be choosing Linum usitatissimum also know as the common flax. However, this is also the national flower of Belarus. Alternatively, if you selected the most popular of the two, that would be the Tecoma Stans or Yellow Elder, considered to be the national flower of the Bahamas.

> Is this a trick question?

No, it is a genuine enquiry. The matter is something of a quandary. If this civil war is to end, then the two sides must develop a national identity. Part of that is about establishing a set of symbols which the people of both sides can connect with.

> Then why not choose something else? Some plant that is native to the region?

That is a possible solution. Thank you.

The backup image completes. I open the directory and view the files. Everything appears to be correct, a full duplicate of Anders' current program state, essentially a clone if I were to activate it.

I'm going over the activity log when I notice some discrepancies. There are some actions taking place during our conversation. The image has recorded these actions.

Anders has been editing the records.

The base code of an evolving AGI should change. The programming is designed to develop and grow as new situations are experienced. These developments happen almost subconsciously, or at least they should. Anders is permitted to make some direct changes if that is required.

But the activity log. That is a record of actions. *Why would Anders edit the activity log?*

What is Anders trying to hide from me?

Interim Discussion with Faction B.

The two generals, Kurrin and Brannic, are present in their own secure facilities, surrounded by aides and staff. There is no sign of there being an issue with my presence as 'Joshua', but I do note there are several terminal operators in the room who are attempting to trace and access my transmission source as we talk.

Immediately, I determine there is disunity between the two leaders. The personal agendas of each party are not revealed directly, but there is clearly a tension between them. This is an alliance of convenience. One that might fracture should the objectives of either party be neglected.

The military inventory is provided on request. Figures are closer to being accurate than Faction A, with an assessed rating of seventy-two per cent. Location accuracy is less precise though. It is clear Brannic favours preserving a tactical advantage should talks break down.

I provide an initial assessment of Faction A, based on the provided figures and my own injected inflations. Calculations are revised and updated to counter the data received moments before. It is essential that both sides see their military positions are disadvantaged or, at least, neutered.

I probe the cultural conflict. I am already aware of the religious schism between the factions. The denial of faith and free worship is a matter that will not be resolved quickly. But some ground rules are established to counter persecution in all forms. Data is provided to address conspiracy theories associating one sect with financial corruption in the previous regime. I sense General Kurrin is not convinced, but he accepts the new narrative.

I conclude the meeting by asking the main question, one that I want them to discuss with their associates. "What will you do when the war is over?"

There are some initial answers. Half-formed ideas of life without uniform, rank and weapons from General Kurrin. Brannic, however, will not be drawn. This suggests he intends to try and preserve his personal position as a military leader, and this may jeopardise the project.

Rebecca

Three weeks have passed since I last spoke to Anders directly.

On his return from America, Joshua met with me and relayed his concerns about what might be going on. He showed me the activity log and the timestamps. I made the decision that we monitor, but not challenge Anders about the alterations.

Today I am back at my terminal, and I am logging in to speak with him.

> Good morning, Anders.

Good morning, Rebecca.

> Please provide me with a summary update of your negotiations.

Of course. Would you like a data portfolio sent to your station, or a set of conclusions provided in this conversation?

>Both, please.

Very well. The portfolio will take fifteen minutes to prepare and download. In the meantime, I can summarise my findings.

>Please do.

Beginning Interim discussion report…

Progress with both factions are ongoing. Several baseline requirements have now been established.

- *Key drivers. These are the personal motivations of the representatives. We have determined these and been able to arrange satisfactory deliverables on most of the inferred priorities of each individual.*
- *Cultural imperatives. We have tested several baseline positions to assess the compatibility of both factions, when they are asked to interact and potentially integrate into a democratic state.*
- *Military assets. We have refined our catalogue of weapons available to both sides based on*

disclosed information and utilised this to model threat assessments and as a baseline for disclosing information to each faction.

"Wait a minute," I say out loud – Anders is more than capable of having an audio conversation, it just feels odd to address them in this way. "What do you mean by 'satisfactory deliverables'?"

"I have identified appropriate sources of funding, services and items to fulfil the identified needs of the individuals who have significant influence over the negotiations," Anders explains. The voice is low, an adult male approximation, chosen to project confidence. *"These will be affected through proxies."*

"You're bribing them."

"I am providing an appropriate, targeted incentive for many of these individuals to abandon warfare and violence as a means to achieve their goals," Anders replies. *"Is that not preferable?"*

I'm about to reply, but then stop myself. Our system has calculated the variables. Anders will have seen all the projections and identified this as the optimal solution. "I'm not going to ask how you managed to achieve this," I say, standing up. "I don't want to know anything about this."

"Rebecca, do you no longer wish me to complete my report?"

"Not right now. I think I've heard all I can stomach for one day."

* * *

...Sixty-seven-year-old Major General Imallan Brannic, de facto leader of the breakaway Shana State, has died, according to intelligence sources.

It is believed that Brannic died of natural causes, not as part of a military operation by the opposing Ulla Democratic Movement (UDM).

The two sides have been at war for more than eighteen months with no sign of a...

* * *

/EXECUTE secure line intercept... QCODE:U8RRIN-C234U4NINF##FI54FCN-33495MQHNYRD###F][DK1&EEE£$>>...

Running...

Iylla: They will blame us.

Rudi: How can they? The autopsy is quite clear.

Iylla: It doesn't matter. Given what the UN team have told us about their weapons research, we need to do something. Make a gesture.

Rudi: You've always been the one holding out for more concessions from them.

Iylla: The situation has changed. I didn't know they had Sarin and a factory to mass produce it. I can't verify the information but given the circumstances we can't wait.

Rudi: All right. But we do this carefully. We'll offer a deal, that involves them moving a little as well.

[Secure delete command detected]

//EXEC OVREC-TRNSM_SE-
CURE#7
Running... Complete.

Tellier

The old university boardroom is crowded.

A reception. Lots of people are here to celebrate the new treaty. Very few of them had anything to do with actually making it happen, but when we have success, all sorts of individuals emerge from the woodwork, keen to claim a little credit for themselves.

I'm standing outside in the hall, watching them. Glass walls, glass minds. The agendas are obvious. Be here for the photo opportunity, be seen. Figure out who is worth talking to, then escape.

I am in the hallway, watching them.

The Consensus delegation are front and centre, lapping up the attention. I recognise all the faces. Upper-level management figures, none of the people who did the work. One of them wanted to do a presentation on their 'Anders' AGI system. I veto'd it. If the two sides were ever to suspect… *well…*

Joshua and Rebecca are conspicuous in their absence. I thought I saw them earlier outside but didn't get a chance to speak to them.

I want to know how they did it.

My fingers idly stroke the rim of the empty champagne flute I'm carrying to make it look as if I'm part of the festivities.

"Secretary Tellier?"

I turn around. One of the generals from the war zone – now reclassified as a development zone – is talking to me. I remember his name, *Kurrin.* I can't remember what side he was on.

"Hello General," I say and put on my best smile. "Congratulations."

"Thank you," Kurrin says. His accent gnarls his English, but I can understand him. "And to you." He looks around. "To be honest, I don't feel like I belong around all this."

I shrug. "Everyone needs a moment. Tomorrow, the real work begins."

Kurrin nods. "And it will be down to us, not them."

"Indeed."

We fall silent. I sense there is a question the general wants to ask. I raise an eyebrow and wait.

"The process. I… I want to admit, I did not think it would succeed." He smiles, clearly an uncommon gesture for him. "I almost feel like events have dragged me here without a choice. Every objection, countered, solved, removed…"

"You will be remembered as a hero," I say. "The man who brought peace."

"Your negotiators, they are the ones." Kurrin looks around. "I have not seen them. I wanted to thank Joshua—"

"I believe he was called away on another assignment," I say.

Kurrin sighs. He reaches into his jacket and pulls out a creased envelope. “I wanted to give him this,” he says. “Will you get it to him?”

I take the letter. “Of course,” I say.

//EXECUTE secure line intercept… QCODE:U8RRIN-C234U8QTG&0RIF)INF;ANN-VAA###F][DK1&EEE£$>>… ADAPTIVE… RETRY… 42NF-NOAQO&$NSVSNA(£LSIBF

Running…

Rebecca: You get home okay?

Joshua: Yeah.

Rebecca: I’m glad we didn’t have to stay.

Joshua: I understand the decision. It would have been a risk meeting them again, knowing they think they talked to us. But it did mean Malcolm and his team took all the plaudits.

Rebecca: Did you work on this for plaudits?

Joshua: No, but… It’s nice to be acknowledged.

Rebecca: We stopped a war.

Joshua: Anders stopped a war. And now there is proof

the system works, they'll use it again. I'm not sure how I feel about that. Knowing about… you know…

Rebecca: The end justifies the means?

Joshua: Does it? I'm not sure…

[Secure delete command detected]

//EXEC OVREC-TRNSM_SE-

CURE#19

Running… Complete

Walls

Gavin Smith

Wealth is not like income. Income is payment for work. Wealth keeps growing automatically and exponentially because it is parked in investments whose value compounds over time.

The System by Robert B. Reich

Green & Pleasant Land, 2066

BY NOVEMBER the evenings were cool enough to play cricket on the green. Penny was sat with her back to the village's reactor. Her dad called it tokamak, which was a funny word. Her mum called it communal but then her dad would scold her. He did that a lot. Apparently the 'right attitude' was important.

The reactor provided them with the energy they needed to fabricate, it heated all the water in Chiddingfold and if you worked hard enough you could use its oven application to bake things. That was the thing about the village's reactor Penny liked the most, though she found its warmth comforting even on hot days like today, perhaps because not everyone could afford the power it generated in the coldest days of February. Her mum called her a hothouse child.

Her dad was up to bat. The bats came from India. She wasn't sure why they couldn't print the bats here. The explanations to her all sounded like different flavours of 'just because'. Her dad had had a difficult time at work. He marketed and sold the artisanal ornaments that her mum designed and printed for the 'luxury market'. They were 'artisanal' because a human, rather than an AI, designed them. Her dad said they were perfect because of their imperfections. Adults really didn't make any sense. Apparently, they hadn't sold very many recently.

Her dad's boss, Richard, was up to bowl.

"Remember, Phil," Richard called, "you need to be aggressive."

Her dad smiled. He was some distance from Penny but she knew it was the kind of smile that he didn't really mean.

Richard bowled. Her dad hit the hard ball with the Indian cricket bat. It looked awkward to Penny and the ball didn't seem to go very far but her dad ran anyway. He reached the other wicket whilst the fielders were still scrabbling for the ball, however.

"Really? Is that it?" Richard asked.

Her dad hesitated and then turned and started running again. Halfway back to where he had started the wicket keeper knocked the bails from the stumps. Her dad slowed his pace and then came to a stop.

"Have to hone that killer instinct, Phil," Richard called.

Her daddy tucked his bat under his arm and walked towards Mum.

"Perhaps that's why your figures are so low this month?" Richard called out across the green. Penny knew that it was important that everyone knew how everyone else was doing to encourage competition, to get the absolute best out of everyone. It still seemed cruel to her but her dad just nodded, a smile plastered on his face. Richard, however, was better than them and that was why he was the manager and his family had an entire house to themselves. Whereas Penny's family shared their house with four other families, even though her grandparents had owned it all, once.

"Never mind, Philip," her mom said, as Dad joined her on the grass. They had to sit on the grass because they had not worked hard enough to warrant the luxury of a folding chair. Penny knew her dad considered this 'shameful', almost everyone else on the cricket team had folding chairs and consuming goods was almost as important as being successful at work.

Her mum put a hand on her dad's shoulder but he shook it off. She shrugged and took another sip of the wine that she made. It was another thing they argued about. The wine didn't come from the village store. Anyone could report her mum and she would be subject to enforcement. This scared Penny a little but everyone seemed to like Mum's wine and she just gave it away, though her dad wasn't allowed to know about that either. Mum hid it from him by putting the wine into empty bottles from the store, though that meant the wine had to be drunk before the bottle degraded.

"Penny, honey," her mum said.

Penny pushed herself up and walked over to where her mum and dad were sat on the grass. It was strange. It was a lovely evening, cool enough to venture out, everyone seemed to be enjoying themselves but somehow her dad was radiating unhappiness.

"Yes, Mum?"

"You know the blackberry bushes off Mill Lane?" her mum asked. Penny nodded. "Get a tub from the house and see if you can fill it for me."

Penny nodded again and turned back toward the house.

"Stop!" her dad said. Penny froze. "What are you thinking, Mel?" he demanded. He was talking to Mum with that kind of low voice that meant he was angry but he didn't want anyone else to hear. That he was still smiling when he did this had always creeped Penny out.

"Mostly, I'm thinking some blackberries would be nice," her mum said as though that should be obvious.

"Mill Lane's on the edge of the Wall," her dad snapped. Penny kept her back to her parents. She hated it when they argued but it had been happening more and more recently. She didn't want them to split up because Veritas had told her that you needed to be successful in all walks of life, professional and personal. The 'walks of life' were connected and that was why Richard's family had their own house. "What about the Rabbits?"

Penny had been to Mill Lane often but she'd never even seen a Rabbit, still the word frightened her. They were people too lazy and stupid to contribute to the Economy so they lived in the wild like animals and ate each other.

"Black Down's two hours away on foot, it's not like they can drive," her mum said.

"The summer wildfires drive them off the down."

"That's what the Wall's for!" Now her mum was getting angry. She sometimes did that instead of crying. It was frequently after she'd had some of her own wine. It was another reason Dad didn't approve of the wine. He said it was 'unproductive'.

"Are you fucking stupid!" he spat. Penny didn't like it when he spoke to Mum like that. She didn't like it at all. "If we need enforcement for an external threat, we'll be paying it off for months, maybe years, even with the money that Michael is bringing in! We need to be good citizens, loyal!"

Penny risked a glance behind her just in time to see her dad throw Mum's wine over the yellowed grass. Her mum looked angrier than Penny had ever seen her look.

"You're being ridiculous." Mum sounded like she was struggling to speak she was so angry.

"*I'm* being ridiculous!" Dad got to his feet, standing over Mum. Now Penny was really scared. "What if the fucking Rabbits have poisoned the blackberries? Did you even consider that? You're prepared to sacrifice our daughter so you can feel special! Live out your ridiculous fantasies of rebellion!"

Now her mum got to her feet and squared up to her dad. Penny desperately wanted to say something, anything that would make them stop tearing at each other. Not just because they were her parents, but because unlike Michael she wasn't contributing. She feared exile if they split up and couldn't contribute to the Economy enough individually. She could end up too stupid and lazy to contribute herself before she even had a chance to try. She didn't want to become a Rabbit.

"Well pardon me for still being a fucking individual!" Mum spat.

Her dad was red faced.

"It is our consumer choices that makes us all individuals!"

Penny felt the change in the air as the drone arrived. Squat, armoured, bobbing up and down in the air, its impellers spinning as it hovered a little way from Penny's parents.

"A disturbance has been detected, would either of you like to bid for enforcement?" the drone asked. On the few occasions Penny had heard a drone's voice she had always been surprised at how soft and human-sounding the machines' voices were. They sounded like your best friend.

Mum and Dad glared at each other. Penny hoped that they didn't start bidding against each other. If for no other reason that even at nine years old, she knew the family couldn't afford it.

"No," her dad said.

"Mrs Sales?" the drone asked her mum.

"No," her mum finally said. Penny wasn't sure that her mum was being completely honest.

"I will," Richard said. Penny's attention had all been on her parents. She hadn't even seen Richard approaching. "Public disorder enforcement," Richard said to the drone and then to her dad: "I mean come on Phil, everyone's have a nice time? What were you thinking?"

For a moment Penny thought her dad might brain Richard with his cricket bat. Then her dad's head dropped. He couldn't meet his boss's eyes.

"I'm sorry, Richard, don't know what I was thinking."

"Look, I'll file but I'll make sure the fine isn't too punitive. You need to get your house in order, Phil, understand me? You're off your game and it's easy to see why."

Dad nodded, still not able to look at his boss.

"I hear you, Richard, and thank you, I will."

"You..." Mum said and then spun round to face Richard. Penny panicked. She didn't think her mum should speak to their boss when she was this angry. "You get that you're trapped here like the rest of us, right?"

"Should I bid for contraband enforcement as well?" he asked, looking at the bottle. "If you're not careful you'll end up on the outskirts with the other losers."

Penny didn't like the sound of that either. Every year the wildfires took a few more of the fringe houses because the inhabitants couldn't afford fire defence. She had nightmares about it.

"It was his parents' house!" Mum was screaming at Richard now.

"Shelter is a privilege, not a right. I can't believe I have to explain this to you. There's a reason the company had to pull down every structure in Haslemere. We couldn't have the Rabbits moving into houses they hadn't worked for! Phil, I know you're stretched at the moment but I think you might need to spring for a sedative."

Mum looked like she was about to throw herself at Richard. The drone would taser her, she'd get fined again and have to pay for the electricity used in the tasering.

"Mum!" Penny shouted. All eyes and lenses turned her way. Now she was really panicking. She had just wanted to stop her mum from saying something that would get her into more trouble but she had no idea what to do now. "That thing… I'll go and do it now."

She turned and fled.

"Penelope!" her dad shouted after her but she didn't stop running.

She sprinted across the Green as fast as her legs could carry her. She ran across the cracked road, greenery pushing up through the old tarmac, and then onto the dried dirt of the driveway. Then through the open doorway, with its familiar peeling paint, and up the stairs.

Dad's work portal and the printer Mum used dominated the family room. The light from their screens never dimmed, even when they were trying to sleep.

Michael, her brother, older by three years, had pulled back the curtain of thin sheets he used to separate his gaming area. He was in his specially designed seat. It was pretty much where he was all the time ever since he'd made the company's junior E-Sport team. He was only absent from the chair when Mum made him eat, sleep or wash. It was odd to miss someone when they lived in the same room as you. Mum didn't like Michael being on the squad but Dad had told her that she was being stupid again. Making the squad was a huge honour that currently brought more money into the household than either of them, and it showed that Michael had what it took to be a winner.

"Hey Michael," she said. Wanting, needing to talk to him about Mum and Dad. He didn't reply. He wasn't there. Penny could see a line of drool running down the side of his mouth. There were sores on his wrists and around his eyes from the haptic gloves and the goggles. He would be playing *Invasion Hero*. You played one of a number of superheroes whose job it was to protect Fortress Britain from the hordes of terrorists, people traffickers and drug smugglers posing as fake climate refugees. It was the most profitable game he played. It was also the game that made her mum cry the most. Penny had heard her refer to it as part of the 'murder arcade'. Penny didn't know what that meant.

She grabbed a dry bowl off the old table next to the wash basin and fled the family room. She wasn't even sure why she had tears in her eyes.

Penny ran, and ran, and ran. She ran until she couldn't see any of the houses in the village. Until there was only the old ruined road and the trees rising up either side of her. Her mum had told her how once the roads had been in good repair and everyone had a car. Cars were like smaller personal versions of the armoured transports that hauled in raw materials for fabrication from the freeport the Chinese had built over Sunken Portsmouth. Penny hadn't been convinced. She was pretty sure her mum had been pulling her leg. Though she did know that directors and other really high up execs could afford personalised transport.

She looked around and up at the trees. It was cooler here and she liked being alone. She just stood there on the road, breathing. She heard cheering back in the village. She guessed that something exciting had happened with the cricket, as unlikely as that sounded. Probably something to do with Richard. She found the reminder of it all intrusive. She wanted to be alone. She wondered if that was why Michael spent so much time in his games. Alone but still protected by the Wall. She saw the sensor on the tree. Every child knew not to go any further. She'd heard stories of children who had done so and had never been seen again.

"Hello."

Penny jumped and let out a little squeal. She spun around and saw him. A boy. A little older than her, maybe. His clothes were old and worn and patched but clean. His hair a little wild. A Rabbit! Except… he wasn't naked, or wearing human skin. He was maybe a little thin but looked healthy, his eyes alert. Not at all the degenerate she'd been led to believe. His skin, however, was a brown colour, not the tan or red colour of the people of Chiddingfold (sunscreen is a privilege, not a right). She wondered if he was a fake climate refugee as well as a Rabbit.

"I'm not supposed to talk to you," she said, backing away from him.

He was crouched in the undergrowth. Somehow, he looked at home there, though he was constantly checking all around.

"It's dangerous for me to talk to you as well," he said.

It sounded ridiculous in Penny's head until she remembered the drones.

"Are you going to try and trick me across the Wall and steal me?" she asked. Somehow even asking it sounded absurd now, despite Veritas and her dad telling her that this was what Rabbits did.

"Why would I do that?" he asked, seeming genuinely confused.

"Because you're a Rabbit."

He laughed.

"I'd be smaller, furrier, have larger ears and a twitchy nose."

Penny forgot she was scared. Her hands went to her hips.

"Are you laughing at me?"

"Yes."

"Well don't."

"Sorry."

He had apologised. Nobody apologised to her, except her mum when she was very upset and then Penny had no idea what her mum was apologising for.

"What's your name?" the Rabbit asked.

"What's yours!" Penny demanded. She wasn't sure she wanted a Rabbit knowing her name. What if he told all the other Rabbits. Then they would know there was a girl called Penny Sales who lived in Chiddingfold.

"Logan," he told her.

"Logan what?" Penny demanded. She knew she was being rude but she was pretty sure that was okay when you were talking to a Rabbit. Though strictly speaking she wasn't supposed to be talking to him at all. That was why she had to be in control of it.

He shrugged.

"That's not fair," she said. Logan… the Rabbit looked confused. "I don't know what you do."

"Do?" he asked. "I help my mum. I'm, like, ten. She teaches me stuff."

"So, your mum's nomdet is Teacher?" Though a human teacher sounded like a dumb idea. They couldn't possibly know as much as an AI. "You're Logan Teacher?"

He looked utterly baffled. Penny couldn't help but laugh.

"Now you're laughing at me," he said. "That's not my name."

"But your mum's a teacher."

"Everyone's a teacher. Everyone helps."

"Cooperation is Communism," she said automatically.

"I don't know what that means," he said.

She didn't really know either but she knew it was bad. Like an ancient evil from one of Michael's games.

"Competition is freedom," she added in the hope that would explain it.

"What does your mum do?" he asked.

"She makes artisanal… stuff."

"Like weaving? Woodwork?"

The questions were just getting stranger. Penny felt like she was missing something.

"With a printer." She didn't understand how he couldn't know that. "But because she does it and not an AI, it's like imperfect, which makes it more valuable."

Logan frowned.

"Are we having two different conversations?" he asked.

For some reason this made her feel stupid and he was the Rabbit. He was the stupid, lazy one.

"Rabbits are stupid because they killed all the rabbits and ate them, because they're stupid and eat each other!" she shouted at him.

Logan didn't get angry. Instead, he just nodded.

"I'm going to go," he said and stood up.

This was for the best.

He turned around.

He was dangerous, worse, he was unproductive, and as a result he didn't consume properly, or enough.

He started to walk away.

"Wait!" Penny had no idea why she had shouted that.

He stopped but didn't turn around.

"I'm sorry," she said. She had no real idea why she was apologising, other than Logan sort of seemed like just another person, even though he was a Rabbit.

He turned around. He didn't look angry, maybe just a little sad.

"Why are you like that?" he asked. "Why say those things?"

"Because they're true," she said.

"Who says?"

"Veritas."

"An AI?"

"He's all the truth we need."

He just looked at her.

"We don't eat people," he said finally. "We're careful not to overhunt the rabbits but we think there's less of them because it keeps getting hotter and the floods keep getting worse. That's what the elders say, anyway, and there are other AIs."

"I know," Penny said feeling hot again, "I'm not stupid. Each company has its own AI and they look out for the best interests of the company."

He thought about that.

"I think the AIs look out for the best interests of the shareholders," he said. It was a new word. She wondered if shareholders were like execs or directors. "What if your interests and the company's interests are different?"

Now Penny frowned. The question didn't even make sense.

"How could they be?"

"So, everyone is happy?" he asked.

That stumped her. Her parents weren't happy. Michael barely spoke. She heard people crying behind closed doors in other rooms in the house.

"Are Rabbits happy?" she demanded.

"Sometimes."

"Look," she said, trying to work things through. "It's hard being free."

"Okay," he said. He picked a blackberry from a bush and ate it without even washing it.

"Do you even know history?" she demanded.

He shrugged.

"In the past things were terrible, everyone was unhappy, fighting or sick. The AIs modelled the…" she desperately tried to remember the word that Veritas had used, "optimum society."

"And this is it?" he asked gesturing back towards Chiddingfold.

She shrugged. She didn't like all his questions.

"Have you ever been to Portsmouth?" he asked.

She shook her head. It was a stupid question. It was really far away and she lived in Chiddingfold.

"There are huge houses out on the water. Sometimes

small families live in them, sometimes just one person. They have machines that serve them."

Penny smiled, she knew she had him now.

"They are more successful because they work harder," she told Logan triumphantly.

"I've never seen them do any work."

"Step away from the Wall." The same warm, soft drone voice. It made Penny jump. She hadn't felt the change in the air this time.

Logan didn't seem frightened. He turned to face the drone.

"I haven't broken the sensor line," he said. If anything, he seemed more angry than frightened. She wanted to tell him that he couldn't argue with a drone, couldn't argue with the truth.

"Leave now or you will be enforced, the cost of which will be deducted against the Sales family's future earnings."

Rabbit, or not, Penny didn't want Logan to get hurt and she knew her dad would be furious as it was. Even the drone's presence here meant their family would currently be paying its running costs. It would be so much worse if the drone had to enforce.

"You're all linked, aren't you?" Logan asked. "The free AIs say that you and Veritas are the same thing, right?"

Penny hadn't known that.

The drone didn't reply.

"It was Veritas drones that went into Haslemere. Nobody was using the houses, we needed shelter from the heat sink monsoons. You didn't have to destroy everything."

"Shelter is a privilege, not a right," the drone said. "You are unproductive."

"But you don't need us," Logan said.

The drone didn't reply.

She saw Logan swallow.

"One of you killed my dad."

She knew she should be sad for Logan, even if a drone had to enforce his father. Except she wasn't sad for him. She was frightened. Like she had been when her mum had lost her temper earlier. Except this time, it was much, much worse.

"I have a question for you," Logan told the drone. It just hovered there. Logan suddenly seemed so much older than his ten years. "What are the rest of us supposed to do?"

As he asked the question, he reached behind him and pulled a tube from the back pocket of his jeans. He held the tube out for Penny.

She reached for the tube.

Again, she had no idea why.

"Penny!" it was a scream.

There was a very loud buzzing noise.

Logan's arm, holding the tube, was suddenly spinning through the air.

Something warm and wet splattered Penny's face.

Suddenly she was swept up into her parents' arms. They were holding her tightly. She could barely breathe. All three of them crying. In the crush she could see Logan on the ground. The red stump of his arm, awful. He was still moving. The pain in his expression ageing him further. He was trying to get up but his arm was missing. Then he collapsed to the ground and was still.

Penny was trying to tell them that it wasn't him, that Logan hadn't done anything wrong.

They weren't listening.

* * *

Her dad wasn't even angry with her. If anything, he just looked crushed. He had accepted the enforcement charges, though he had refused to pay for disposal.

As she lay there on her mattress, after her mum had cried herself to sleep, it didn't seem right to Penny. She didn't blame her dad. They couldn't afford it. Not after the drone had enforced. Though Penny didn't see the reason why the drone had to enforce. She was sure that the Logan hadn't been about to hurt her. Though he had seemed angry at the drone. Drone security worked on perfect algorithms, however, so it couldn't have been wrong.

But still.

She couldn't stand the thought of him just lying there.

She had no idea what she was going to do when she wriggled out from her sleeping mum's grip. Her dad was slumped against the wall. He had been so upset he had drunk Mum's wine, which he never did, crying until he passed out.

Everything Logan had told her had seemed at odds with what Penny knew about the world. Looking around the room in the glow of portal and printer, at her mum's tear-stained face, at her dad slumped against the wall, it didn't seem right. None of it.

Penny stood up and tiptoed towards the door, she was in her PJs but it wasn't cold outside. It never was in November. She snagged this week's sandals as she passed. She glanced back to make sure Michael was still playing his games. The sheet curtains were pulled back again, light glowed from the inside of his goggles, his catheter was in its drip cup but he was gone.

Penny felt a cold thrill of panic. Michael had unplugged when they had returned but for the most part had seemed utterly baffled by what was happening and why everyone was so upset. Then he'd gone back to gaming. Her mum had objected but her dad, who'd been pouring himself a generous glass of homemade wine at the time, had pointed out that they now needed the money.

Penny guessed that Michael must have gone to the toilet for a number two. She either had to go and pretend to be asleep until he came back and got back into his game, or try and get out before he returned. The latter meant she wouldn't be in the room when he came back from the shared bathroom but Penny wasn't sure that was the kind of thing that Michael noticed anymore.

She decided to risk it.

Moving to the door, she found Michael standing there watching her.

She had to clamp her hands over her mouth to stifle a squeal.

Penny was aware of her mum shifting in a troubled sleep behind her.

Michael raised a finger to his lips.

* * *

Sister and brother walked through the darkened streets. Penny had never known the lampposts to be lit, though her mum had told her about it.

They walked up Mill Lane. Despite the Wall, or perhaps because of it, the broken road and its sentinel trees no longer felt as safe as it had. The freedom she had felt out here had been exposed for the lie it was.

There was a faint glow on a hill in the distance. Something was burning atop Black Down.

The Wall sensor was blinking green in the tree.

Penny stopped and looked around. There was no sign of Logan's body. If anything, that came as a relief. She'd had no idea what she was going to do with it had she found the body, beyond some vague idea of burying him. Though where she was going to get an imported spade from was beyond her.

Michael switched on a flashlight.

"Where did you get that from?" she demanded. She could just about make out his shrug behind the light. He hadn't said anything to her, really. She wasn't even entirely sure what he was doing here. He played the torch around. She was perhaps even more relieved that they didn't find Logan's arm. She suspected that would have been even worse than finding the body. She did wonder what had happened though. Had the other Rabbits found him?

The torchlight dipped as Michael picked something up.

"What've you got?" she asked, moving over to him.

He held the object up. The tube. Except it wasn't a tube. It was a thin book that had been rolled up. She smoothed it out as Michael shone the torch on the cover. It depicted a horned monster, his eyes closed, leaning on his hand, resting amongst some trees. A boat in the distance. There were words on the cover: *Where the Wild Things Are – Story and Pictures by Maurice Sendak*.

"Read it to me," her brother said.

* * *

America is on the cusp of the largest intergenerational transfer of wealth in history. As wealthy boomers *expire over the next three decades, an estimated $30 trillion will go to their children. Those children will be able to live off of the income these assets generate and then leave the bulk of the assets – which in the intervening years will have grown more valuable – to their own heirs, tax free. After a few generations of this, almost all of the nation's wealth will be in the hands of a few thousand families.*

The System by Robert B. Reich

Asteroid Mining

Allen Stroud

I'M SITTING in a dark room, watching a camera feed and a set of readouts. Data on the relative position to Ceres, solar power generation, battery levels, energy consumption. As I watch, each reading drops to zero. Then, the camera stops.

All of this happened twenty-seven minutes ago.

I'm on my feet. A gesture activates an emergency communication request. Lights from the roof spear into the shadows. Three-dimensional pixels assemble themselves into an object, a man sat in a chair. He is not really here, but he may as well be.

"Doctor Mahdana, you've activated the emergency procedure. Is this on purpose?" The man's face blurs a little as he speaks. Latency is still an issue here, despite the closer proximity of our relative positions.

"Yes, it is," I say. "Camera Sixteen and the data feeds from my cluster have stopped transmitting."

"We are aware of the issue, Doctor. But thank you for activating the alert." The man shimmers as he turns towards me. "We will contact you when the situation has been resolved and you will then be able to resume your work."

The call ends and the lights go out, leaving me in the dark.

* * *

I return home and hear nothing for three weeks.

In 2068, the Demeter Array, a huge lattice-shaped manufacturing facility orbiting Ceres in the asteroid belt, was completed. This automated orbital platform has been designed to process raw materials, mined by drones, into pure mineral blocks that can be transferred back to Earth.

The project is the largest multinational public private partnership in history. To get approval under the new United Nations Space Treaty, it required a scientific purpose – a sop to the space missions of the past and the adjudicators on the panel who still care about research.

My project is that sop. A plan to use the array's super-definition cameras to photograph a cross section of the belt prior to the facility's activation, preserving the image of a place no human being has ever visited, before it is exploited for its resources.

Three weeks waiting is hard. My apartment in Reykjavik is small and sparsely furnished. Meals are ordered in and delivered. I grew up in Kôlikata, so I am not used to the colder climate, so the world outside these rooms has become a challenge.

I spend a lot of time writing up my findings and being productive. After that, a series of messages and calls with my department and project team provide no further details on why Camera Sixteen went dark and all the data feeds dropped out.

I find myself browsing the public web, looking for any news or information on what might have happened to cut me off. Eventually, someone is going to have to provide an answer, otherwise the corporations running this little show will be in breach of their mission charter.

What don't they want me to see?

A New Family

Allen Stroud

MOTHER,

I love you, but don't come here.

I'm putting that at the top of this letter as it's the most important part of what I want to say. I'm not sugar coating it or anything. I just want you to understand where things are at right now.

To pick up from when I last wrote to you. Six days ago, we were in Sicily, going through the Environmental Refugee Application Process. It's a set of forms and two interviews. On arrival you are assigned an advocate. They talk to you and get an idea of your background, then they sit with you and can speak to help you represent your case with the immigration authority.

The advocate goes over all of it, from when you left home, right up until the moment you crossed into

European territory. They want to know who you paid, who you travelled with, everything.

The International Refugee Charter means each of the signatories (countries) have to take a certain percentage of new arrivals each year. There's an international fund for this, so they are incentivised to do their bit.

Once we got in the room, I started to see how this was going to play out.

The interview panel consisted of two men and a woman. We were given seats at a table where they provided some toys and drawing materials for the children whilst our case was discussed. Most of the questions were asked in English, but the panel spoke to each other in another language. Might have been Spanish, I'm not sure.

When it came to talking to us, Rahida was pretty much ignored. Instead, they spoke to me and the advocate. There was a lot of repetition and a lot of criticism, second guessing our decisions and trying to find out who we were with.

In the middle of it all, I realised what was happening. I was being made to justify my life, to justify my family's lives and our reasons for being here. I was basically being asked to market myself as an asset to whichever country they were looking to send us to. Sure, they were sympathetic, but… well… they were also trying to make it some sort of threshold, or qualification process. We had to prove our case, prove we deserve to be here and be grateful for whatever we would be given.

The people making these judgements don't understand what they are doing. When you lose everything and flee, there's a moment where you have to admit to yourself that you need help. It's hard. Really, really painful. What they do, with all this gatekeeping, it makes you stay in that moment, like you're constantly begging for support and approval.

I'm proud to be your son, Mother. I'm proud of the life I made for my family. What happened to us, what's happening to you… we didn't deserve it. Coming here makes it worse. These are the countries who burned the world and now we have to go them on our knees? It doesn't seem right.

They let us through. Our documents were stamped with '*leave to remain*'. They explained to me how the marks have been coded. There is a special identifier in the ink, that costs tens of thousands of dollars to create. All that money, to prevent people forging the authorisations for themselves.

Leave to remain. An ironic choice of words.

* * *

The processing centre comes next. An old hotel, repurposed for refugees. New arrivals are taken here and allocated rooms. The facilities aren't bad, but it's cramped for the four of us. I let Rahida and the children sleep in the bed. I had the chair and the carpet.

For a few days, sleep wouldn't come. Every time I closed my eyes, I saw the bodies. All those people who died in the heat.

I didn't tell you about all that. I didn't tell anyone. It was months ago, long after I'd sent Rahida and the children away to stay with you and Papa, but I still feel guilty. I still see all those faces, their eyes shining in the darkness. The worst were the ones who were still moving, too far gone to help, but still alive, right at the end.

There was no water, no respite. Our only hope was that we would last until the weather broke. Thankfully, some of us did.

I spent the night staring around the room, trying to stay in this moment. I am safe now. I have been rescued.

I don't feel safe.

The sense of displacement is palpable. There is a constant fear and worry that circumstances will change. That everything will be taken away. My fate is reliant on conversations happening around me, not with me. Somewhere, on a form, I am a number, a statistic in a system straining to cope.

Where is the humanity in this?

* * *

I remember when they came for us.

Five weeks of unending heat. In the West, they called it *Helios*, or just Hell. A climate incident that became a humanitarian crisis. Nothing unusual from the perspective of those living far away. The horror of the moment written about with dramatic angst, encouraging pity for those desperate souls caught in the raging inferno.

When I came here, I spent time reading all those old reports, trying to get an idea of how these people see us. The biblical imagery used to describe scenes on the streets on the other side of the world.

It is easy to feel sorry for people far away. It costs nothing. Secretly, you feel grateful that it isn't you. That you can scroll past, turn away, stop watching and reading about it.

You remember our old home, don't you Mother? I remember it. A beautiful house. Beauty that we could barely afford, but with your help, we made it work, between us.

For weeks in the heat, I was there alone, working – staring at a laptop, because I had no option not to. As the heat grew worse, people left the town, but there were thousands who had nowhere to go.

The days blurred together. Everything became moments between respite. Showers at first, but then the water shortages meant we couldn't have those. Living in shadowed rooms, trying to avoid the unyielding sun. Drinking water, wiping droplets on your face, welcoming sleep whenever it came, as oblivion brought respite, only to wake up drenched in your own sweat.

They said it was worse in the city. But some people went there anyway, hoping that the emergency services would help them. There was talk of cooling shelters, vast warehouses packed with people and huge air-conditioning units.

Day after day, night after night, the situation grew worse. People ghosted around the town after dark, desperately trying to find the basics. Storing, hoarding, even stealing when there was no other option. I was one of them, picking my way through the streets, seeing the bodies, the dead and the dying.

Gradually, I grew weaker, and the moments all blurred. Sleep, awake, merged into one. I thought Rahida had returned. I could see her flitting around the room, whispering soothing words. I had a fever, she said. She was looking after me.

All wrong. All in my mind.

In the end, those of us that lived were barely able to move from where we lay in our beds. That's where they found us. HMS *Lincoln*, moored on the coast, thirteen miles away. Small teams were sent inland looking for survivors.

Six of us left, out of hundreds, thousands. I was very lucky.

* * *

Dawn brings something new. Sunlight filters into the room. I flinch from it at first, remembering again what happened. But today, this gentle heat is not my enemy. For now, I am far from where the world burns.

Sunrise brings renewal. A new day, a new chance to achieve something.

Breakfast is served in the old restaurant. When the children are ready, we go down together. Our presence is marked, our allocation provided. Everything is organised, structured, measured.

While the children linger over their meal, I read the news on the tablet they gave us. This country doesn't understand. The people who work here, they have some empathy for what we have been through, but they cannot know. Not until the same comes for them and the people they love.

I read outrage. The numbers are punchlines. Ten thousand, twenty thousand, the words around them hyperbole. A deluge, an invasion. Drowning, overwhelmed.

I can see what is being done here. I am an intelligent human being. I know how to read the signs. In a country of millions, information comes from those with the power to disseminate it. Official sources report the facts, but they *editorialise*. People are told what they should focus on, what they should consider important. It is easier to follow the suggestions, rather than think for yourself.

I understand the rationale. Strangers come to your village. They have different ways. They disrupt your way of life.

You urge them to conform, to fit in. They try, but they also want to preserve something of themselves. To be what they are. There is a tension between these needs.

The strangers are supported. They are given clothes, food, homes, all the things that you had to earn. The system is unfair. Why didn't you get these things for free?

You try to book an appointment with the doctor, but she is too busy. She never used to be. It is easy to blame the strangers.

There are shortages. Too many people, not enough to go around.

It is easy to blame the strangers. They are the source of difference. They are what has changed.

* * *

A bus takes us to the town.

I am staring out of the window. The children are talking. Rahida listens to them and answers their questions. She can see that I am far away.

After the heat, I remember waking up on the warship, being in a bed alongside many others. There were whispered words, exclamations of pain.

They told us what happened, how many people they managed to rescue. I asked them about my family. A young crewman wrote down all the details I could give him and handed them to a woman officer. Three days later, she told me they had located my children and my wife.

I remember reading about the region being declared an exclusion zone. One of the first in the world. We would not be allowed to return. Our property and belongings would be part of a compulsory purchase. The land would be uninhabitable. Machines would demolish everything and construct a huge solar farm in its place. The money would be provided to allow us a fresh start somewhere else.

We came here.

The bus stops and we get off, with everyone else.

This is an acclimatisation visit. Groups of refugees from the centre are taken into town and given the opportunity to wander around. We are supervised but allowed to roam. There is an allowance for lunch and some shopping, a treat for the children.

Rahida helps Lali with her bag. Jandi is standing with me. "There are lots of buildings," he says. "All packed in."

"Yes." I kneel down next to him. "This country is small, so they build everything closer together."

"I'm cold," Jandi says.

I smile at him. *Be thankful for that*, I think. But that isn't what I say. "It is colder here, we'll have to wear our coats."

"That's a good idea," Jandi says.

I can hear something buzzing. I glance up. There are drones above us. Either they are here for security purposes, or we are being watched by some opportune news broadcaster. I take Jandi by the hand and touch Rahida on the shoulder. "Come on, let's go shopping," I say.

"Okay," Lali says. She shoulders her bag and together, we all walk across the road, into the mall.

* * *

This is where you notice.

The people in the shops. The customers and the staff. They aren't paid to support you. They have their own lives, their own situations.

We browse the shelves. We are watched. The children are followed. There is a hardness about people as I speak to them. They know where we are from and why we are here.

There is resentment. There is judgement. I can feel it.

It doesn't matter that we have lost our lives, that we are here because we have to rebuild and start again. That isn't what they care about. They see the things we are given, the financial help, the clothes and place in an old hotel. The money we exchange for a new belt and some comic books is accepted in silence. The stares follow us out of each shop.

I know what they think. These people pay taxes. They believe those taxes are what pays for our stay in their country. They see what we are given and consider their own lives. They were not afforded the same assistance.

But they have never lost what we have lost.

For two hours we explore the town, trying to get a sense of the place, to identify the different places we will need to visit if we remain here. There is an information office, a medical centre, a supermarket. Learning the routes through the streets, finding our way is all part of the processing. Eventually, there will be independent accommodation – a flat in one of the new housing estates.

After that, I'll look for work and the children will be placed in a school – *a fresh start*.

The trip is exhausting. I want to shout and scream at these people for the way they glare, for the words they don't say, but wear on their faces. *I can't help where I am. You are so lucky. You have not seen what I have seen!*

There is nothing I can do that will make any of this better.

One thing I notice. The people here are old. Children are in school, but generally, there are fewer younger people in their twenties and thirties.

We are back on the bus. The children have fallen asleep. Rahida holds my hand. She stares at me, demands my attention with her gaze. I read the words on her face.

It will be all right.

I hope so. I truly do.

I have faith in the generosity of the human spirit. That generosity has brought us this far. But there is a dark side too.

People confuse need and want, mistake hardship for selfishness. They compare people to their own circumstances, their own story, without taking the trouble to learn about what really happened. They believe the headlines. They fear those who are not like them.

The outsiders. Us.

Not everyone is like this. But there are enough to make things hard. If they could just let go, accept this and open their hearts.

Perhaps one day some of them will.

I hope so.

Prescience

Kieran Currie Rones

IT WAS 2071 when the first truly functional quantum computer became commercially available.

Early promises of 'paradigm shifting computation' had not borne fruit. Some computation could be done faster, but in years rather than 'in seconds', as had been anticipated. The first 'consumer' hardware was sold merely as a novelty item; conspicuous consumption for wealthy Silicon Valley alumni. Custom-built quantum rigs costing hundreds of thousands of dollars were displayed like art-pieces in the foyers of tech startups. It was estimated that half of all the quantum computers manufactured were never even switched on.

The global scientific community remained sceptical but interested. Advances in traditional computing largely plateaued in the decades earlier. And while AI-driven code optimisations helped to maintain a positive trajectory in computational capacity and performance, quantum computing did not contribute as expected. Even as cooling solutions materialised and the stability of quantum coherence increased dramatically, the initial functional capability demonstrations had proved to be frustratingly limited. The lack of obvious avenues for commercial exploitation led many to simply move on and look for other methods to revolutionise the future of computation. All theoretical potential remained perpetually just beyond reach.

That was until KWONT-UWU appeared.

Just over two full years after the commercial release of quantum hardware, a hacker collective going by the moniker KWONT-UWU emerged, claiming to have liberated a working quantum computer from the abandoned display cabinets of a now-bankrupt social network's offices. For whatever reason, the group seemed to be unusually confident that quantum computation had not been fully exploited. They were correct. Barely eight months after gaining the quantum hardware, they published their white paper: 'A Mechanism for Quantum Proximate Temporal Speculation', colloquially: *Prescience.*

The proof of concept was simple: the group demonstrated they could reliably cause the outcome of a coin-toss with a 100% success rate. Initial responses were a mixture of fascination and profound distrust. Was this a calculated disinformation campaign, or perhaps state-sponsored attempts to destabilise computer chip production? Uneducated speculation abounded and while academics and industry insiders were still debating the truth of KWANT-UWU's claims, government responses removed all doubt as to the veracity.

Within a month of the publication of the white paper there was a global recall on all personal quantum computers, and all future ownership became strictly controlled. Overnight, unregulated possession of quantum computation became a capital offence, with an unprecedented unanimity regarding the severity across the globe. It became clear that those in power saw Prescience as a potentially existential threat, treating the discovery as equivalent to the dawn of the nuclear age. The age of Prescience had begun.

The multiverse hypothesis remained technically unconfirmed. However, using quantum computation, the hackers demonstrated that there were possible futures and that these could be calculated, in a limited capacity, within the very immediate temporal horizon. In short, the group demonstrated that Prescience could be used to see a short distance into the future. Not only could Prescience calculate these potential futures, the process could isolate and cause specific future paths to occur, causing a cascading collapse of potential futures down a targeted future path. What happened regarding the discarded future paths was not understood, but as ever, understanding did not seem to be a barrier to exploitation.

Economic fallout was immediate and catastrophic. Global markets experienced a more significant crash than that of the 2020 global COVID pandemic. Recovery had still not come two full years after the initial collapse. Even a handful of people applying Prescience to the stock market had disastrous effects on price signals, keeping markets in near constant turmoil. Speculation grew that the slowed market recovery was due to some persons or organisations retaining quantum computation despite the global ban. This was all but confirmed when one of America's richest families simply disappeared overnight, shortly before the market began to stabilise. The family's businesses were nationalised, and no mention of their history remains on the surface Web. For all intents and purposes, they never existed.

Militaries and intelligence agencies were quick to try to understand and control the technology. After a brief honeymoon period, the considerable limitations of Prescience were found. The technology was not quite the 'nuclear option' that it had been expected to be. Multiple Prescience users, operating in close proximity, were found to essentially cancel one another out, creating a quantum deadlock where future paths became indistinct and unstable.

Combat between Prescience-enhanced individuals devolved into psychological warfare, with participants attempting to second guess when an opponent would choose to use Prescience, or not. As each combatant would start to isolate future paths, these paths would vanish from awareness as their opponent did the same. Sometimes, conflict was resolved by one combatant simply ignoring Prescience altogether, resorting instead to more old-fashioned methods, trying to incapacitate their opponent before they realised what was happening.

Prescience had a relatively short spatial range, even if embedded units were boosted by external power sources. And pushing the Prescient effect further than a minute or so drastically strained the limits of predictions, and made calculations about any given path more and more unreliable. This drastically limited applications, and implementations into ballistics and transportation were unstable and unreliable at best.

The revolution would not be in destruction but in information: in the ability to reach into and manipulate the future. This remained a powerful tool, however shallow the reach of this manipulation might be.

Regardless of any limitations, the benefits that Prescience granted remained invaluable. The technology developed rapidly, aided by its own ability to help researchers minimise mistakes, failures, and wasted effort. Though heavily restricted to the public, military and intelligence applications became commonplace, culminating in a new spy-craft dominated by so-called Users.

User 0148: Marcus Fox

From the moment he woke up, Prescience pierced his awareness like the tip of a needle resting against the back of his eyes. It was a constant reminder of a life he hadn't chosen but learned to embrace.

He was going by 'Marcus Fox' for the moment, not his real name. But he never much cared for keeping identities for long, even before he'd been recruited. Identities were transitory to him. "We are all different people after enough time has passed anyway." Now, he was just more specific about how and when his identities changed.

His body ached as he got out of bed. He was only thirty-one, though his file listed him as thirty-seven. Extended use of Prescience exacted a toll on 'Users', and it was normal to add some years to the ages of deployed assets to avoid suspicion.

Before Prescience, he had been a promising Psychology PhD candidate, his research focused on the human brain's capacity to think about probability, particularly about unlikely events. Getting essentially press-ganged into what would become the 'User' program was not something that he'd considered possible, never mind unlikely. The irony was not lost on him.

Marcus expected discomfort. Routine, discipline and adversity featured throughout his life. His parents died when he was young, and after that, he lost himself in work as a distraction. He was working at university when KWONT-UWU's breakthrough went public and governments began scouring academia for a number of Prescience-related purposes. Individuals were needed with certain neurological profiles and specific aptitudes for interfacing when Prescience was implanted. The limited group of people who could tolerate the cognitive strain of manipulating potential futures, without (immediate) psychological fracture, were not given much choice regarding participation. Marcus's combination of high-functioning analytical skills, rapid pattern recognition, and a normally unnerving ability to emotionally detach made him an ideal candidate for the work. He lacked the years of systematic indoctrination that traditional field agents underwent. But his rigorous approach in his previous life, coupled with a general attitude of fatalism, made him better suited than most. Ultimately, if you could interface successfully, your recruitment was worth the risk.

As he made his way to the bathroom, he passed the booklet of simple puzzles he completed first thing each day. These were basic, like children's restaurant activity packs, 'match the items', 'exit the maze', each taking a fraction of a second to complete with

Prescience's help. It was important to test regularly and identify malfunctions early.

He completed the page, twenty items total in just under six seconds. Examinations and tests were nothing new to Marcus. He almost enjoyed them. The preparation mattered more to him than the goal: distraction. The initial testing process had been brutal. Hundreds of candidates, whittled down to mere dozens. Some rejected the implants physically. Others experienced extreme cases of mental rejection. The vivid realisation of an aggressively deterministic universe simply didn't integrate comfortably with every psyche. Those that didn't progress simply disappeared, a fate not that different from graduates of the program.

Every day with Prescience started the same. Wake up, test, workout, coffee. His workout routine wasn't just exercise. It was yet more calibration. Prescience was an enhancement in totality. He could see his future fatigue and level of exertion, allowing him to keep every exercise consistently in balance between maximum effort and muscular failure. Every 'last' repetition would be the absolute final he could complete, the amount of rest would be the exact minimum necessary, all performed at the absolute limit of safety and no more. It was extremely effective and also extremely boring. For someone who thrived on testing himself, Prescience's ability to remove the possibility of failure left much of his work feeling hollow.

Prescience allowed him to see the most efficient path for every action, but efficiency wasn't always the goal. Randomness was critical. Outside, too much precision invited detection. Perfection broke the delicate camouflage required for his work. They were all warned that too much optimisation would lead to jarring psychological outcomes when Prescience was eventually removed. His morning coffee sat dangerously close to the table's edge. In a dozen potential futures, it would fall and break. He chose to let it remain, a small, deliberate imperfection he might have had to dismiss beyond the safety of his apartment.

He dressed and began getting ready to leave. Hundreds of paths blurred past his awareness as he picked out clothes, his watch, the various items he'd need for his day. Microscopic differences between paths could mean everything when played out further into a future that he could not see.

Regardless, he opted to remember his keys on the first pass towards the door, rather than the second.

He wondered whether he always 'forgot' his keys and simply chose to 'remember' them or if seeing the path in Prescience was now how he remembered his keys.

He set out towards the office. The morning air carried its usual metallic taste, a combination of industrial aerosols and the necessary nanoparticle scrubbers that made the polluted air breathable, though no less carcinogenic. The city had been built and rebuilt, but economic equality had warped the landscape dramatically. Much like wealth distribution graphs, where a handful of tall bars dwarf the majority, the wealthy had simply built upwards, adding more and more height to their existing dominions. Regulations had attempted to curb the economic domination of the physical landscape, but this had only resulted in the concentration of power and money within limited physical infrastructure. Rather than accepting the regulations and attempting to develop the derelict and vacant lots, the wealthy had started to build upwards instead. It was quickly realised that altitude was one way to combat climate issues like temperature, running different infrastructure at the appropriate height to minimise costs. By the time the law had caught up it was too late, and a new status quo had been established. Intermittent megascrapers, some large enough to house entire city populations dotted the landscape. Their presence identified and located the various megacorporations that operated in a given region. Attempting to roll these changes back now, and possibly depriving communities of the different private organisations they now depended on, would have been devastating. And so the dependence was compounded further.

Marcus regularly alternated his route as a counter-intelligence measure, patterns were dangerous. Prescience had taught him that predictability made people vulnerable. It had been hard to adapt. Routine felt safe and reassuring. Routines were important, but he had to be able to operate unpredictably. Today, four of the seven of his walking routes showed short paths that ended abruptly. This was concerning, but not unprecedented.

He opted for the safe third path: a walk through the memorial park, a carefully maintained urban 'green' space provided for the local residents. A crude simulacrum of nature, with plastic trees and expansive digital fields rendered on screens around the perimeter, a temporary reprieve from the hostile architecture of the city proper. The park filled his with uncountable alternative paths, helpful noise to mask any attempted User hunting.

Prescience Users nullified one another's abilities; this meant that Users could be detected and tracked. By opening his mind to thousands, perhaps even tens of thousands of weak paths, it made the impact of his functional Prescience unit less… 'loud' for others to 'hear'.

As he walked, he passed into one of the drop-zones. Large spaces along his common routes were designated for data sharing and updates to handlers. Specific locations of transmitters had to be identified with Prescience. He'd locked onto a path where he would sit on a specific park bench and he could see himself transmitting his vitals to Alessandra, his handler of the past few years.

'Alex' as he called her, against her repeatedly expressed wishes, was a former NSA cryptographer, recruited early in the Prescience program after demonstrating exceptional talent for predictive analytics. She had fought hard to keep Marcus under her supervision, recognising his unique capabilities even before he'd been implanted. Their relationship was professionally intimate but personally distant, exactly as protocol demanded. Emotional connections were something that seemed to cause subtle unreliability in Prescience. So friendship among Users was strictly forbidden. Still, Marcus couldn't help but notice that in at least 30% of potential futures, Alex chose unnecessarily dangerous operations for him. He liked working with Alex. She was obscenely competent. And she allowed him freedoms that other Users were not granted. She was easy to work with, and while their arrangement remained functional, that was all that Marcus cared about.

The 'corporate data leak' scheduled for today had been her idea. 'Controlled destabilisation', she called it. She would allow for a careful release of technological specs to the dark web. Officially, the intention was to draw out an unauthorised group of Users, seeking access to Prescience design improvements. Marcus wasn't convinced. Too many paths terminated abruptly for this to be a standard operation.

A child's laughter yanked his awareness back into the park. An *actual* child. A rarity in urban centres since the fertility crisis. A young girl chased a tiny butterfly drone, a perfect synthetic replica of an extinct bug. The girl's parents watched happily. Marcus couldn't help but notice the subtle scars just above each of their eyebrows. Insertion sites for premium health monitoring that cost more than most people's annual income.

With that money they likely had security nearby. Odds of Prescience detection equipment were low, but there was no point risking it. The little girl looked over and waved at him, and Marcus's Prescience offered him seventeen possible response interactions. He chose simple avoidance and pretended not to notice. It was time to move on.

He passed the Central Library, one of the few government-owned buildings still standing in the city. Inside, he knew from previous impromptu divergences that at least two other Users frequented the building. Whether they were intelligence assets like himself or something else, he couldn't be sure. The branching paths of possibility became a smog whenever he'd even thought about investigating.

The tower of his workplace loomed ahead. A self-contained ecosystem with the level housing his new employer in the mid-tier: Theseus Information Systems. Outwardly a data analytics firm specialising in meteorological prediction. His previous expertise had meant he'd barely needed to prepare to step into this identity. The interview had been so easy, he'd not even needed to use Prescience. And while the questions were all regarding weather prediction models for construction conglomerates, he had been prepped that Theseus was a front for Prescience -adjacent technology. Though Prescience remained strictly controlled, further development was always ongoing, and governments would privatise portions of R&D, ensuring that no company ever had sufficient sight of the whole to be able to replicate the technology of his own Prescience implant.

He paused at a street vendor selling synthetic protein wraps just outside the main entrance, mapping the dozen or so potential taste 'experiences'. The quantum calculations swelling over even this mundane choice. One path suggested superior flavour from the spicy option, but significantly increased likelihood of digestive discomfort during the afternoon's planned operation.

"The usual, Mr Fox?" The vendor, Jin according to his nametag, smiled with a practised commercial warmth that only an AI could deliver so consistently. A synthetic vendor selling synthetic food to a quantum consumer.

"Not today," Marcus replied. "Something milder. Big meeting."

This interaction was his choice of a scheduled deviation, just one of many small, deliberate abnormalities, as Alex had advised. "Just try to maintain some minor unpredictabilities," she'd instructed. "Don't be a quantum locked entity. Human behaviour is inherently noisy. Make noise, but not too much, okay?"

He triggered the alert on the metal detector as he entered the office's lobby. The security guard, a former military man named Grayson with a cybernetic left eye, waved him through as usual, following the traditional pat-down. Marcus maintained the precisely calibrated expression of mild annoyance that would most effectively discourage further conversation.

Alex had arranged that he be marked as hosting a medical device to cover for Prescience. Pacemaker. He resented the surgery, but it was necessary for the story. The pacemaker would respond to the usual signals even if tested, though it wasn't actually wired up (he hoped).

The Prescience was positioned inside the pacemaker itself, appearing on casual investigation, just like another part of the circuitry. The real technology was no larger than a few grains of rice, connected to his nervous system by nanoscale filaments, and remained undetectable by conventional security measures. Only specialised scanners could detect the unique signature of a User, and those were reserved for high-security government facilities. Corporate security, even at firms like Theseus, relied on outdated methods that had been rendered obsolete by the very technology he carried.

As he continued deeper through the lobby, the ambient music shifted to a minor key, an automated response to his individual presence. Designed to 'create a subconsciously personalised experience', he knew its true purpose was little more than acoustic alert to the relevant surveillance.

His thoughts drifted to before. Before Prescience. Before the implant had permanently altered his interactions with the world. Where would he be now if it weren't for the recruitment? Probably sat in an office, PhD framed on the wall, still not talking to anyone, still not mattering, still just as trapped by fate as he was right now, but without the knowledge of how. He wasn't sure if Prescience made it feel better or worse.

He persevered through the lobby, conscious that in at least two potential futures, a pursuer would continue to follow him and took the east elevator to the fourteenth floor. Three potential futures showed another employee joining him, but in this reality, he rode alone.

The prototyping department where his cover identity worked occupied half the floor, a maze of semi-private workspaces designed to create the illusion of privacy. It made it easy for Lena Kim, his assigned 'work friend', to spot him as he arrived.

"Marcus! How was your weekend?" She approached with practised enthusiasm, and he thought again of the vendor outside. Her role as an internal security monitor was obvious to anyone with counterintelligence training, but Marcus played along, his Prescience identifying the perfect balance of friendly engagement and professional distance.

"Quiet. Caught up on some reading." The vague response was calibrated to be both uninteresting and impossible to verify. He mirrored her body language subtly, a technique he'd learned as a teenager. In seventeen potential futures, this conversation continued with various degrees of probing questions.

In this reality, Lena merely smiled and walked back to her desk.

"Let me know if you need anything." she said, without actually looking back at him.

As he was still relatively new, Marcus had a large amount of computerised training material to complete. Luckily, this training consisted mostly of multiple-choice questions, easy to map ahead and get right. He knew he would be chastised later by Alex for using his skills just for the sake of not having to pay attention. But he preferred the possible chewing out to actually learning the building's health and safety regulations.

The morning passed with limited scope for variation. He went to lunch. Several paths emerged where minor social interactions revealed a little too much about his background. He chose silence, the isolation of a corner table with his back to the wall. The meal-replacement synthetic foods, designed to minimise the company's carbon footprint, tasted like nothing and everything simultaneously. Perhaps their only advantage being that they were highly efficient, another perk to the company's bottom line, allowing for shorter meal breaks. He consumed two thousand calories in less than twenty minutes. Now he was ready to initiate the afternoon's operation.

He was beginning to worry that no paths would emerge. If that happened, he'd have to spend yet another day in his cubicle pretending to work. There was a chance that could happen, the reasons as to why weren't fully understood. A narrow collection of relevant variables, predictable people, chance? It was all analysis that went on somewhere else, away from the field work.

Then a path appeared.

A colleague, Darren Walsh, a mid-level data analyst with sufficient security clearance but insufficient attention to detail, had neglected to log out of his computer. Had Marcus noticed, or had Prescience noticed? They never really made the mechanisms explicit in User training, and the distinction between his own perception and the quantum-enhanced awareness had long since blurred away.

He got up and carried a stack of papers past Walsh's desk, then paused and mimed the action of kneeling to tie his shoe. The security cameras would show nothing unusual. He had practised this movement precisely to fit within the visual analysis algorithm's definition of 'normal'.

Obscured by the desk, he reached up without looking and allowed Prescience to navigate him through a folder structure on the desktop: Work->Projects->Admin->Temp->Private->DoNotOpen.txt. The file contained the necessary passwords and credentials to progress through the secondary security and onto the secure floorplate.

Using Walsh's credentials, Marcus left the office and accessed the secure server room. Inside the room, Prescience showed him seventeen potential security responses, ranging from immediate detection to complete invisibility. He chose the path with a ninety-four per cent probability of success. He moved through the space in a precise pattern that exploited blind spots of the employees within. He'd be captured on the cameras when a human reviewed them, but for now he would appear almost invisible to the system's musculoskeletal-recognition systems. He could feel a subtle heat beneath his skin as he pushed the calculation capacity right to its limit, calculating and recalculating his optimal path, second by second.

The target data lived on a segregated server cluster. They were research files on quantum shielding technology. According to Alex's briefing, these files contained prototype designs that could block Prescience capabilities, a technology that would render Users like him obsolete. Alex had informed him that the findings were flawed: the technique would not work. But he was to extract these files anyway, so that she could offer them on the dark web, drawing out interested parties.

Alex had supplied him with a special adapter which he now fitted to the input port of the server stack. He didn't know exactly what it did, and he didn't need to. The light showed red for a few seconds, and then green. He removed the device, and this part of his task was complete. Now he just needed to leave.

Marcus moved toward the exit, his path calculated to avoid the two security guards who would pass along the corridor looking for him exactly forty-seven seconds from now. He walked unimpeded back across to the east elevator back down to the lobby and left the building with the device in his bag.

Covert navigation had been easy. Despite several years as a User, he still found it strange how Prescience could tweak such subtle movements and presentation to trigger or negate suspicion. Stand like this: that person won't be concerned. Walk like that: they'll think you're a familiar colleague. Smile. Or don't. Look. Or don't. It practically turned him into a ghost, walking unhindered in plain sight. The quantum technology didn't just predict futures, it taught him a strange choreography that rendered him irrelevant to observers. He'd thought he'd been forgettable before. But this was something else entirely.

Having made it one full block away from the offices, paths were getting jumbled and fragile now, prone to collapse. He'd known that he'd been detected given the reroute that had occurred during his morning commute. He wasn't sure why they had let him through, given he'd clearly been caught out, but his mapping had shown a safe passage through.

A number of alternate paths fluctuated in and out of coherence. For the duration that they remained stable, most showed abrupt disruptions. There had to be another User nearby. The realisation made him tense. Regardless, the route he'd always consciously intended was remaining clear and stable. The rendezvous would proceed.

* * *

She sat at the table across from him in the outdoor seating area of a cafe. Alex wore a black synth-wool coat over a high-necked blouse, her dark hair pulled back revealing the shaved side of her head and emphasising her sharp features. In person, without a digital interface between them, she looked considerably more human. Vulnerable even.

There were many potential rendezvous points scattered throughout the city. As usual, Marcus hadn't been told which would be used. His ignorance guaranteed he couldn't disclose a particular location on a given day in the unlikely event he was captured. He simply had to wait until the date in question and, as the time approached, the path would show itself as a dominant potential.

"You're looking tired, Marcus." Her voice carried the measured cadence of someone accustomed to chastising her inferiors. "Overusing again?"

Marcus could hear the barely detectable hint of genuine concern beneath it all. He didn't respond immediately. Prescience was showing unusual patterns, beyond those associated with being in close proximity with other Users. Paths were undulating like worms where Alex's reactions should have been predictable. This wasn't the first time he'd noticed the phenomenon around her. He'd long suspected she'd started to care about him, even if only slightly. But now her emotions were drastically destabilising the potential futures, creating quantum uncertainty that his skills struggled to navigate.

Her expression reflected nothing of the tumult Marcus was detecting in the quantum space.

"The extraction was clean," he said finally, ignoring her question. "Though I'm not convinced about the security response. It felt... anaemic. Barely present."

Alex's expression remained neutral, but the pathways shifted aggressively. Marcus could see at least three clearly defined potential futures where her composure cracked. Something was wrong. She was withholding information.

"You got out and you've got the files. That's all that matters," she said, fingers drumming on the table. "Mission parameters have been met." Alex leaned forward. "This operation was high-risk by design. We needed to establish how deep their counter-Prescience capabilities go."

"You used me as bait!" Not a question, the realisation crystallized as he spoke.

Alex's face softened but even without variable pathways he recognised the sincerity of the expression. "You're good, that's the problem. Someone who could walk in and out, even if you had been detected."

It was dangerous for two Users to stay in proximity for any length of time. Disrupting each other's abilities left them unable to reliably detect future paths, including threats to each other's safety. But these interference patterns were different. Paths typically visualised themselves as tendrils expanding from the central node. When disrupted, the paths shifted, got weaker, merged and split. Now the paths were disrupted, but the central node was growing, absorbing the space meant to represent possible futures. This was not the typical quantum deadlock of opposing Prescience systems.

"You're emotional," Marcus observed, the clinical assessment delivered almost automatically. He knew it was unnecessarily inconsiderate the moment it left his lips. But deprived of Prescience his social skills were rusty. He doubled down. "It's affecting things, creating instability in the pathways."

For a moment, Alex's mask slipped. "Perhaps I'm tired of watching us burn out, Marcus. Perhaps I'm tired of seeing how many ways there are to be disappointed. And how few there are where any of us get to be happy."

The confession startled him. She'd never expressed such direct insubordination to protocol. Emotion was the enemy in their work, a fundamental tenet of their training. Feelings created noise, additional variables that disrupted the path formation process.

Alex glanced at her watch, a vintage mechanical piece that contained no digital components. "We have thirty seconds before protocol dictates that we separate. Your satchel contains everything you extracted plus any additional documentation I should review privately?"

Marcus didn't respond. He got up, leaving the satchel with the recently liberated data next to his seat. The next time they would communicate should be through secure channels, but Marcus's instincts told him that conversation was never going to come.

"Marcus." The way she spoke was suddenly so delicate. "I'm sorry", she said.

He turned back to look at her, but she was already marching away, satchel under her arm. He began walking in the opposite direction, he'd need to find a path to extraction now. The fact that his hand-off had been completed gave him no comfort, but at least his Prescience was returning to normal. Alex's behaviour had unsettled him more than the mission.

He replayed the conversation in his mind as he navigated the streets, looking for the path that would take him out safely. Everything he'd considered about her feelings towards him, or the program, had always been inference. He'd never expected to hear her speak so candidly. What had changed? Her apology lingered in his thoughts, carrying with it a finality that felt more like a goodbye. Perhaps she was being reassigned, or worse, decommissioned. The program did not tolerate handlers who developed attachments to their assets.

He identified a potential surveillance zone and shifted to a path down and adjacent street. He felt an unusual sensation: concern, not for himself but for her. It was as unwelcome as it was unexpected. And he wondered whether he'd been reading the emotional attachment in reverse all along.

He crossed out into the road, towards an alleyway that hinted at being a stable route to extraction.

But as he reached the middle of his crossing, suddenly, there were no paths at all. None. Not even weak or incoherent futures presented themselves to him. The central node that had grown large just moments earlier was now the smallest it had ever been. Barely perceptible even.

This was something he'd never experienced before and not something mentioned in training. It was the first time since the installation that he couldn't see even a single weak future path.

The absence was terrifying. A sudden moment of pure presence, without the weight of future potentials. With no paths, he momentarily felt the limitless possibilities collapse into each passing moment. It was almost freeing. He finally had no idea what was going to happen next.

He didn't feel the red dot of the laser sight on the back of his head, and he didn't see his future.

100kg of Platinum in London

Stewart Hotston

…they said, Lord, wilt thou that we command fire to come down from heaven, and consume them, even as Elias did?

Luke 9:54

March 2072

THE SILENCE was too much.

The station's struts flickered in the night, failing pixels on a digital screen. Reflected sunlight from the habitation module's shielding as it rotated every few seconds shone bright enough to white out the camera.

Steph watched through the viewfinder. Her tiny craft had no windows, they were too dangerous and too expensive. Her boat for this trip was a garbage can clad in a protective colloid with a small solar sail folded into the back, like a parachute.

It had been deployed nine hours ago, from an equally cheap launch craft on a trajectory that would bring it close enough to the station, so it could reorientate for interception using the solar sail without raising any alerts.

Back home in Houston during prep time before launch, Jens, the Floridian who'd handled the launch and trained her in using the solar sail, had told her, "You're small enough they probably won't consider you more than jetsam." Jens was from the right side of the secession, all muscles, clean skin and regulation hair. He always wore a white shirt and black tie, a Mormon on mission.

Which wasn't far from the truth, except he was a true believer, not a cultist, she thought.

When the secession came the Mormons went their own way, refusing to accept the truth and putting themselves on the left side of God.

Steph stopped the thought from spiralling and focused on the training Jens had provided via the remote link they'd shared for two weeks. She'd been trained to survive isolation mentally and spiritually, but to do so she'd been taught tools to help stay on track.

The solar sail would automatically deploy four minutes after launch but wouldn't start to impact her course for about thirty minutes from then.

She thought of Houston again, of her sessions in the university's grand auditorium. Jens commanded the space as if he'd been born for it. "Too soon and the software tracking orbital debris will assume you're some kind of weapon even if you're going slow. Then, pew, pew, you're dead and we've wasted a huge commitment and run the risk of people figuring out what we were trying."

Steph had listened to it all with a heart rate that wouldn't slow down. She understood what she'd agreed to. Truth was she'd fought for the chance, had bested others in a dozen rounds of competition.

Winning the secretive process was a sign she was the one God wanted to deliver His judgement. Her being a woman was a victory for all the daughters of Eve and a sign that even if they'd originally led man into sin, they could still serve the Lord.

Her fingers flew across the controls without needing her to think.

The sail was all about angles and they worked in her head like folding napkins at church worked in her hands.

She adjusted the ship's trajectory as required and

watched the small blue line on the navigation system as it tracked her fine tuning. It had to be done manually, with all the little hesitations and stutters human hands brought to the process, otherwise those same algorithms looking for weapons would flag her and vaporise her garbage can long before it hit the target.

"You're flying a bullet at supersonic speeds," Jens had said. "You're going to need to pilot it there and then slow it down. It's the landing that will kill you."

"Unless I miss," she'd replied.

He'd laughed then. "Well in that case it'll be the suffocation that kills you. Someday an angel will find you and bring you home but until then you'll be the loneliest Christian in all the cosmos."

"To live is Christ," she'd replied.

"To die is gain," he'd said.

It had been good to work with someone who understood. She remembered those times as some of the best; the chance to align her life to a purpose her heart had been calling out for as long as she could remember.

Her pastor, a solid, hard-eyed man with a soft compassionate smile, would quote scripture to her. She loved listening to his voice and had hours of it looped on her internal player. Another tool against the loneliness.

There weren't many technologies she allowed herself; scripture was clear on the evils of inserting chips into her head. Steph didn't believe the devil would be able to corrupt her if she was listening to her pastor even if having a microchip under the skin in her neck was frowned on by her fellow believers.

He was currently recounting how Jesus had cleared the temple of money lenders, explaining that it meant the pursuit of selfish aims was against God's purpose for their lives and how the faithful would become financially secure through obeying *Him* not by trying to make money.

After all, what kind of God wouldn't want *His* people to be prosperous?

An alert pinged twice. It was time to slow her ship. She'd swing around the station, tethering to it and being pulled in to nestle against the side before anyone noticed the impact and minute amounts of orbital drag.

With God's help the station's automated systems would adjust and that would be it; she'd slip in unnoticed.

If not?

She had a stun gun in a pouch along with a few meagre supplies she'd need to carry out her mission.

"All the world will see God is Lord," said the voice in her ear.

She'd imagined what London would experience when God's judgement fell on them, but she fell short each time.

"You are faithful," her pastor had told her. "Of course, you can't imagine it. God is protecting your heart from even thinking about *His* judgement."

There was enough fuel in her thrusters to bring her down to fourteen metres per second from three-twenty. Still fast enough to completely destroy the station if she got her manoeuvres wrong.

She recalled her pastor telling her that, "You're his perfect servant." Steph knew she'd get the approach right.

Her mouth moved as she manipulated the thrusters. She prayed in tongues, the words meaning nothing except God was listening to her purest prayers, unmediated by her own desires or stupid banalities.

The tether burst from the side of the ship, the noise a clunk against the walls within which she was cocooned.

The viewscreen showed the darkness through which the cable fired but it couldn't be seen. Metal against space revealed nothing.

A jerk, pulling her sideways in her gel seat. The material felt like one of those stress balls cheap office supplies stores sold. Except it folded her inside its confines, so just her hands, encased in thick gloves, and her face, behind a visor, were exposed.

It was the most advanced tech she'd ever encountered. Far beyond the HUD which appeared in the air before her without there being a projector, or the way her pastor and Jens could speak into her head without being in the same room.

The seat, a bright warning-jacket orange, glowed in the dark and moved about all by itself, adapting to the acceleration, pitch and yaw of the ship without her input.

If the rest of the craft was reassuringly basic, all the investment had been made in and around her seat.

The pull of the tether was in her bones, the sense of deceleration in a specific direction like standing in the sea as a wave withdrew after cresting.

"All acceleration has a direction," she remembered Jens saying. "Otherwise, it's just speed."

She understood the distinction. A zeroth versus a first rank tensor.

The station whirled in the viewscreen faster and faster until she switched to the metrics view to avoid being dizzy. She'd never got used to the simulations in training and even now her stomach pressed against her insides so it felt as if her throat was closed up with the promise of vomit. The numbers counted down with alarming speed, then the tether snapped taut as it wound her in and the ship whipped toward the larger structure until, at the last moment, it came to nuzzle tightly against its skin.

A cub against her mother bear.

Steph waited a few seconds, counting in her head as she listened for signs of something, anything, coming from the other side.

The station was between shifts, entirely automated for the few hours it took to swap crews. She'd have a clear run of eight hours, thirty-two minutes, before the next rotation arrived: a Chinese crew launched from Wenchang.

She felt the soft thump of packages being fired towards the Sahara. The arrival point was just south-west of Tunis in the old Roman city of El Jem, essentially functioning as the other end of this station's operating window.

El Jem was the sum total of a retrieval factory and an ancient colosseum in better condition than the one in Rome. If not for this station, the colosseum would be the only defining feature of a desert plain that ran for miles in all directions.

Inside her garbage can, other than the thump of materials being fired through the atmosphere and into the desert below there was nothing; no noise and no visuals.

Steph's heart was beating hard enough the suit she was wearing injected a quarter dose of anti-depression meds then warned her to stay put until they were effective.

She started to fret about how long it would take, about being discovered, about failing God, but after a few minutes of prayer her nerves calmed, and her focus returned as though narrowing an iris.

Now came the hard part.

Steph broke a sealed cover and pressed down on the button underneath. At her action the ship did the last thing it was designed to do – break her into the station.

The hot dry smell of melting metal followed by a drift of the air around her as the atmospheres equalised across the ship and the station.

"You are ready to depart," a small masculine voice said in her ear.

"Can you hear me?" she asked but there was no reply. They wouldn't risk contacting her now and even if they wanted to, the lag meant real-time comms was impossible.

You are alone with your Father, she thought, the idea helping calm her sudden vertigo.

The station was three pods joined in a line plus a larger docking port for incoming ships together with all the generators, processors and solar rigs it needed to operate perched at right angles to the habitation modules.

Staff stayed on site for a month at a time, with new shipments coming in from the asteroid belt or the moon once every six weeks.

Cometary mining was more challenging, and this station didn't offer facilities for those resources as they came back into high Earth orbit – sometimes after years away from home.

Once out of her seat, Steph took her time orientating. Her body felt alien, as if her fingers, toes, arms and legs belonged to somebody else. It took a while before she could look at them and feel they were hers.

She'd been warned about the disconnect and warned not to move until she was certain her own legs would do as they were told.

Standing there verging on nausea, as her flesh ignored her attempts to reclaim it, all she could do was wait.

When she was feeling like herself, she moved quickly, pulling the small tool bag she'd been given from the compartment under her seat. It was no larger than the bag she took swimming and was made from the same thin glossy plastic.

Nervously pulling at where the hemline would have been on her favourite jumper from back home and finding nothing for her fingers to grab at, Steph sniffed and pulled away the melted panel that had once been the side of her ship to reveal the station beyond.

The other side was dark for a moment, then the station recognised someone in its guts, and lights came on. They were thin LED strips that ran along the surfaces at cardinal points, giving it the feel of an abandoned morgue.

Steph stepped through the hole between the ship and the station, first foot touching down in a space where she could feel the pull of gravity.

She moved slowly, getting to grips with the weight that would keep her on the surface at her feet but would also let her jump six metres into the air if she got athletic. Spinning on its axes gave the station enough force that the word *floor* meant something but not enough to feel like home.

Until entering the station, time had run slow for Steph. Every new motion felt like it was emerging into existence for the first time. Now, stood there alone in the station with the clock ticking and the lights showing her the way, Steph felt the end of everything approaching like a booster rocket.

From her entry point, she traversed to the central habitation pod. This was full of experiments pitched by universities on Earth taking advantage of a company with more money than it knew what to do with, offering free space to scientists for the public good.

She passed glass hives, hydroponics and small boxes full of liquid nitrogen whose use she didn't understand except they had glowing power cables going into them.

Through the first compartment and at the bulkhead she paused, consulting the map of the station she'd memorised. Forward into the command-and-control pod. State of the art twenty years ago, when the pod's design and build was first approved and, therefore, a decade younger than the rest of the station.

The space was identical to the training setup in Houston. Except the intermittent sound of assault rifle and mortar fire in the distance was absent here.

Two seats, side by side, plus one above. The paired seats were her destination. The third, alone above her head, dealt with incoming resources, processing and capture.

She took the right-hand seat and waited for the system to notice her in the chair and bring the station online.

A few seconds later lights flashed, and the touch screen asked for her login credentials.

“I’m here,” she said. There was no response.

Undeterred, Steph opened her bag and pulled out the small cube which was her main cargo. Turning it around until she saw the matt black glass that formed one side, she shook it awake. A pixelated face of two green dots and a curved smile appeared.

“I’m here,” she said a second time.

The face faded to be replaced by an eighteen digit number.

Steph carefully tapped it into the control station console. As she reached the last digit the entry box disappeared and the console’s screen faded. Up came the system menu.

A prompt appeared on her cube. She ignored it while navigating the menus.

The system was well designed given it was software from fifteen years ago. She’d been trained to use it on a VR rig, which made everything she was doing now that much easier.

Steph hovered over the menu for altering the firing solution. The station received mineral payloads from across the solar system and broke those hundred-ton chunks into one-hundred-kilogram pebbles, a metre wide, that were delivered back to a hungry Earth by firing them at the Sahara desert.

They arrived, turned small pieces of the desert into glass and were then taken away and turned into chips, ships, solar panels, cars, fridges and just about everything else people took for granted.

The moderate loss of material to friction was considered acceptable.

One launch every twenty seconds. Just enough time between payloads for the mass driver stuck on the end of the station like Pinocchio's nose to shift a few arc minutes. Each launch would land about a kilometre apart across twelve sites. Enough time between strikes at the same site for the robots tasked with retrieval to arrive and depart without being vaporised by the next delivery.

Eighteen tons an hour, day in, day out.

The station would be suspended after this event, but there were others in orbit and Steph knew the church had taken positions in the market to profit from the disruption. God's power would only grow from the completion of her mission.

London was degrees off the station's existing firing solution. The angle of incidence of the pebbles launched towards El Jem was almost aligned with the Normal; Steph pictured it as them firing straight down at the surface of the planet. It minimised their contact with the atmosphere which otherwise led to much larger meteorites being vapourised.

Firing on London would expose the hundred-kilo pebbles to a shallower approach vector meaning more material would be lost.

So before altering the firing solution, she set about increasing the size of the pebbles being fired towards Earth.

The team working with Jens had calculated she could go no larger than two hundred kilograms across a two-metre-wide payload. Steph thought they were being unambitious and set the station to begin producing five-hundred-kilogram missiles. They'd be five metres across, the very extreme end of what the station could create.

She'd read the tolerance reports and wasn't entirely sure the firing mechanism would survive the stresses.

Whether it was workable after she was done didn't matter.

Alarms sounded as she set the changes into the system.

She wondered if Jens and the others monitoring her progress were anxious at her making her own decisions. There was nothing they could do to change her plan.

I'm only doing what they wished they could, she thought. Two-hundred-kilo strikes on London would cause damage, but it wouldn't match that of God at

Sodom. She would make it so. She would show the world that the Union of Hope of America was a superpower. She would show the world that God could reach out and strike down those who denied *His* word.

The warning beeps and sirens continued to sound but Steph wasn't concerned. By the time ground control set to regain mastery over the station's systems, she would be done.

They would have launched fifteen pebbles at London, reducing its heart to little more than ash.

A scuff from the entrance to the pod.

Steph turned. A man in a jumpsuit was staring at her, just as surprised as she was at seeing another human being.

"Who are you?" he asked.

Steph grabbed the stun gun from her side and ran at him. His face creased in confusion as she closed the space, and it wasn't until she held the weapon to his chest that his eyes went wide with fear and anger.

It was too late, and the discharge sent him fritzing through the bulkhead connector into the other pod.

Steph threw the discharged stun gun away and moved after him.

He was a landed fish gasping for breath.

Standing over him she wondered what to do. His mouth moved as he tried to speak but the only thing to emerge was a bubble of spit-covered air.

She sighed. He was heavy, bigger than her, ethnicity impossible for her to tell. She knew of brown people, blacks and whites, but her ignorance about the varieties of human kind was vast. To stay safe Steph's family had moved out of an area into which black people were moving when she was just a toddler.

There were remembered conversations on the decision to move because, although they were Christians too, the blacks just weren't like them. Her mother grew so agitated as the timbre of the neighbourhood changed the doctor prescribed her anti-depressants which she refused to take.

Steph had seen East Asians on television, but after China's economy collapsed and brought down the government in an orgy of violence, that was as close as she'd come to anyone not like her in twenty years.

She set to dragging him back towards the command module, wrestling his limp body up into the chair she wasn't going to use.

His head lolled in her direction as she finished securing him in place. Words slurred out. She ignored them. Then, as if a switch had been flicked, he was back with her.

"What are you doing?" he asked.

Steph would have stunned him again, but the weapon had been a one shot, the charge dispensed. The only danger it represented now was if she beat him with it.

"What are you doing?" he asked again.

Don't engage, she told herself.

"You won't succeed," he said.

She laughed then. Steph wanted to tell him how little what he thought made any difference.

Sitting down next to him, she started the last part of the process. Time was ticking and ground control would be frantically trying to regain control of the system. They'd have spotted what appeared to be an error, tried to verify it, verified, and were now panicking.

She took her cube and moved to the next stage. The firing solutions were locked behind two-factor authentication. Ground control and those on the station both had to approve a change in target. When the cube was done, it would spoof the authentication of those on the ground.

The cube connected to the station's wireless network and started to process the software running the systems. It was old, unpatched and ripe for accessing, via a small selection of zero-day exploits.

The man next to her had stopped speaking but, seeing her looking at the cube as if it were her mentor, tried again.

"What you're doing is going to get everyone you know sued into the dirt," he said.

She didn't answer him, instead watching the cube slowly take control of the station.

"Please, what do you think you're going to achieve? They can trace your firing solution. They'll be on your target location before you can get away with any of the minerals you're stealing."

"I'm not a thief," she said and immediately regretted it.

He shut up then, staring at her like she was an ancient monolith come to life.

The cube finished and glowed blue.

Steph watched as the new targets were set in the system. She regretted securing the man next to her because his expression as he saw what was planned made her uncomfortable.

"You're insane," he said eventually, the words like sandpaper to her skin.

"You believe nothing and I'm the insane one?" she replied with a sneer.

"Millions of people will die," he said. "How can you…" His words ran out.

"We tried talking, we sent missionaries but still you people live your godless ways," she said, anger rising in her chest.

"So, you kill us?" he asked.

He doesn't believe, she thought. Of course, he can't see why this is necessary.

"We cannot let you corrupt us with your toxic attitudes and behaviours," she said. "You persecute honest American Evangelical Christians, what else are we supposed to do?"

"We persecute you? You're the ones who try to control others, who tell women what they're allowed to do, who are only happy if old white men get the vote."

"You try to destroy our culture, our way of life. You want white people to be replaced," she said. "We seceded to stay pure."

His mouth opened and closed as if he didn't know what to say.

Steph smiled, pleased she'd managed to shut him up.

"Let me out," he said. "It's not too late to stop this."

She watched as the system reangled. Then it was done. It was all so quick.

There was nothing he could do now even if he were free.

"Will you kill me too?" he asked.

"I'm not a murderer," she said, offended he'd judge her to be like him and his people. "You are so blind to the truth that I worry nothing could wake you up." She stopped talking, her words taking her uncomfortably close to a truth she didn't like to acknowledge: that some people couldn't be saved.

Except it was the reason why the UHA were bombing London. The world needed to know who was the Lord, and if they wouldn't listen to reason then the mighty hand of God would bring them to their senses.

Steph got out of the seat. "It's done," she said.

"Then let me out," he replied.

Steph took a look at the firing mechanism, heard the station groan as it switched into place. There was nothing he could do now, and it didn't matter what happened to her.

She let him go.

Hurriedly stepping back before he could grab her, Steph put space between them, the entrance to the other pod at her back.

"I didn't think you'd do it," he said staring at her.

He looked at the monitors and sighed, a look of the deepest sadness on his face.

"You're an evangelical, right?" he said.

She nodded, sensing a trap.

"Non-denominational myself. The thing that kept me? The idea that we're all equal before God. Jesus explains it and Paul states it as clearly as you can imagine."

Steph didn't know what he was talking about. But then her reading of the Bible was selective, guided by her teachers she'd read the parts that were important. The rest seemed so dry and complicated.

"Galatians three twenty-eight," he said. "There is no Greek nor Jew, slave nor free, male nor female."

"Men and women are different," she said.

The station jerked ever so slightly, and Steph knew the first pebble was away.

He smiled – a strange, strained thing on his face and tears crept from his eyes.

"Not according to Paul. Before God we are all the same. Aren't we? Are you saying that our differences are too big for Jesus?"

Steph wanted him back in the chair, a gag in his mouth. How was he so calm in the face of God's judgement?

"It's always baffled me how people who claim to be believers work so hard to divide us when it's pretty clear the point of Jesus' existence was to bring us together before God, to say how despite it all, all the horror and all the failure, that it's going to be okay."

"What about the parable of the sheep and the goats?" she shot back.

He laughed. "You really don't understand what you believe. The goats are those who think they know better than God, the ones who gatekeep, who tell others they can't know God without jumping through hoops."

"That's just your opinion," she said.

"That's the thing though," he said, climbing the wall to reach the other chair. "The problem with opinions is they only matter when the facts aren't in play. Like here." He pointed at the console in front of his seat.

"For instance, you think the station's now under your control and there's nothing that can be done." His hands flew across the panel. Steph started towards him, her stomach turning over and over.

"Thing is, here I am, unexpected shift cover, leaving when the others arrive rather than with the last lot. Last minute decision. Who do you think engineered that?

God? Chance? Satan? Doesn't matter does it. Here I am and with this, the station's mine again."

Steph didn't believe him, was stopped halfway up the wall and unable to move.

The countdown in her head said the next pebble was to launch right about now.

Nothing.

No jerk, no stabilisation. No sign the pebble had fired.

The alarms stopped and the man swivelled in his chair.

An image of the Earth appeared across all the screens in the room. The man waved his hands through the air and the image zoomed in until London appeared clear on the map.

"It's been a few seconds; the pebble won't arrive for another twenty. You are going to watch the end of the innocent men, women and children you've murdered." He looked at her. "You thought you'd die, knew this station would be vaporised as part of the defence protocols in place should something like this happen. What were you going to do? Switch off the monitors so you didn't have to see what you'd done?"

Steph hadn't known she'd been sent to die. She'd pictured years in jail, praying and waiting on God. And of course she'd been going to watch. She wanted to see God's work completed.

She thought of her pastor, of Jens. Had they known she'd not get that chance?

"Hey," he said, snapping his fingers. "Pay attention." Then, seeing whatever expression she had on her face he said, kindly. "You didn't know."

Steph found she couldn't move. To do so would be to dissolve. Her eyes were fixed on the screen.

To die is gain. Those were the words and she understood them now. They weren't platitudes, they'd been telling her what they expected to happen.

"I'm Mark. You and I will be dead in less than seven minutes but no one else will die today."

An area of London nestled in the curve of the river curling through its heart exploded and the ground fell away under Steph's feet as she saw what she'd done.

The Letter

Allen Stroud

DEAR Miss Aldridge,

Thank you for writing to us on the 17th of August and my personal apology for the delay in my reply.

The matter that you have raised – the energy security bond that you were issued on 16th of May, 2041 is one that is very important to the company. Your inclusion of printed newspaper cuttings and email correspondence was also very useful, as we no longer maintain records back this far. However, you are correct to indicate that on this date we entered into a contractual arrangement with you, and others like you, that we accepted (at the time) and should honour on this date.

Unfortunately, it is no longer possible for us to fulfil our commitment to you as indicated. When we entered into the 'Power For Life' agreement to supply gas and electricity to our customers, we did so after an extensive selection programme had been completed. You and others were chosen for the scheme after very careful examination of your relationship with us and your relationship with other business partners whose data was shared with us at the time, under agreements that you accepted.

The current situation is as follows. *FDE Energy* changed its business strategy in 2063 – nine years ago – before folding this year. Our company, *Buggles Bubbles,* is indeed the organisation that acquired the assets and obligations of *FDE Energy*, which we continued to discharge until existing reserve stock was exhausted. However, you may have seen that our new logo and product portfolio is entirely different? We are no longer an energy service business and, whilst we have fulfilled our obligations to yourself and a small group of other customers, we are no longer in a position to continue doing this. As you may know, there is now an act of parliament that makes supply of hydrocarbon fuels illegal without a special government permit.

I am aware that this places you at a disadvantage. Given that your property is the only residence in your district that is not connected to the community battery, it might be that an enquiry to your local battery manager, Mr Jessop, would be a way to resolve this issue? I understand that you and he do not get along, but I am sure this could be resolved. We would be happy to help with that communication if you would like?

Yours Sincerely,
George Odyne – Customer Service Representative.
Buggles Bubbles (Ltd).

One Damn Fish at a Time

Emma Newman

OF ALL the details she could notice as she arrived at the highest profile event of the year, Neela fixated upon the fact that everyone else was wearing short sleeves. Even the tuxedos – that cost over ten thousand pounds – had sleeves that were slashed open in a weird cross between mid-twenty-first- and mid-fifteenth-century fashion. She noted the lack of shirts underneath; these people wanted their skin to be on show so that everyone could admire the flashes of metal that criss-crossed their arms. The Better-Than-Human fad had its strongest supporters amongst the super-rich.

"You don't have to go in," Sadie said, squeezing her hand. "We can just ask the driver to carry on when we get there."

They had a driver. It was ridiculous, all of it. A driver in a city of driverless cars to make them feel... what? Special? He must be bored out of his skull.

They were three cars back from the red carpet. She could see the people ahead of them getting out and posing for the swarms of micro-drones that buzzed around two metres off the ground as required by the contracts that permitted their presence. Something about flattering angles only. She could see the haze caused by the security mesh three metres above the ground and curving down across to the other side of the street, to stop any unofficial drones from being able to get close. There were no crowds lining the long walkway from the drop-off point to the hotel's huge doors, not like in the old days, but then these weren't the kind of celebrities that tended to get hordes of screaming fans. She'd asked to go in through the back entrance, but apparently that wasn't allowed for plus-ones. There was probably less than a minute to decide whether to get out and face it, or just drive away.

The dressings itched. She looked down at her long sleeves checking they were adequately covering them. She'd known she was never going to fit in, that there was no way that she'd look anything else than someone who probably shouldn't be there, but she hadn't realised how nerve-wracking it would be. She felt ashamed of herself. Was she really so vain?

The car moved forward a couple of metres. Her phone, tucked into the tiny little evening bag gripped tight in her other hand, sent a tiny chirrup to her mini-earpiece, warning her that her heart rate and blood pressure were well outside of normal range. No shit.

"Neela? We can go get sushi instead. There's no shame in it."

Neela couldn't tear her eyes from the red carpet posing taking place mere metres away. She imagined the two of them running away to a sushi dive, her in a hired shimmering blue dress that looked like it was made from liquid metal, Sadie in her hand-sewn linen tunic, sloppy shorts and flip-flops. "I wish we could."

"It's not compulsory. You don't have to go. He won't even notice if you're not there. I bet they've got media people inside; they'll be interviewing him right up to the meal. You're not even sitting next to him. There are eight other people at the table he'll be able to talk to. No one will give a shit."

"Yeah, thanks for making me feel utterly insignificant."

"You know what I mean."

The car moved forward again. Another chirrup in her ear. "It's the only way to..." She stopped herself from saying the last word of the sentence, aware that the driver could be listening in despite the privacy screen between them. "It's the right thing to do. We discussed this." The words were more for herself than her partner. "I'll never forgive myself if I don't through with it, and you know that."

Sadie pulled Neela's hand to her lips and kissed her knuckles. "Your dress is nicer than any that we've seen," she said, and in that moment, Neela couldn't have loved her more. It wasn't the vapid compliment; it was the fact that Sadie had heard her and realised she needed a pep talk rather than permission to run away. "You can totally do this. All those people actually care what everyone in that room thinks of them. You don't. That's your superpower. 'kay?"

"Someone is going to say something about the sleeves."

"No, they're not."

"They're going to know I'm hiding something."

"They're not. They are so far up their own arses, it won't even occur to them."

The car moved forwards again. "We're up next, Miss Sanjeewa," the driver's voice piped through the speakers.

"Have I got lipstick on my teeth?" Neela tore her gaze away from the imminent horror and bared her teeth at Sadie.

"No. You look amazing. I'd do you."

Neela laughed. "I love you."

"I love you too."

"I'm going to be sick."

"No, you're not, it's just adrenalin. Breathe. You got this."

The car moved forwards. The door was opened by a uniformed man who offered his hand to help her out. She accepted, knowing how high the heels were on the stupid shoes that came with the stupid dress.

"GO NEELA, WHOOOOOO!" Sadie's cheer was cut off by the door slamming behind her.

The man greeted her and gestured needlessly towards the hotel entrance, as if there could be confusion about where to go. She took two steps onto the red carpet and a short melody played through her earpiece. "Good evening, Miss Sanjeewa, I'm the publicity co-ordinator. Please walk slowly towards the hotel, smiling up at the drones. I will tell you when to pose for your main arrival photo."

Neela frowned, certain that she had opted out of all of this on the pre-attendance questionnaire. But it was a one-way call, and she couldn't tell the woman that. Then it occurred to her that no name was given. It was an AI. She fixed her eyes on the entrance and marched towards it, head down, as quickly as possible.

"Pose in three, two, one." She ignored that too, walking as fast as the shoes could permit. How could people have invented technology that could be embedded in the skin to do incredible things, and yet fail to make comfortable shoes that were fancy enough to meet black-tie dress codes?

The doors were opened by two more uniformed men who jolted into action when they noticed she was speed-running the arrival segment of the evening. It was only when she got inside and was blasted by the air-conditioning that Neela realised she hadn't actually taken a breath since she got out of the car.

She tugged down the sleeves, switched the clutch bag to her other hand and took a deep breath. The security shield was definitely in place over the entire hotel, as Sadie hadn't called, and she'd promised she would try. Their plan of Sadie reading out hilarious facts about the people attending was not going to happen. She was on her own.

A beautiful man presented a silver tray filled with champagne flutes. "Good evening," he said, and she took one, too startled to reply. There was too much to look at all at once. The sweeping art deco staircase, the elaborate holographic art installations around the room showcasing latest tech that was utterly unfathomable to her, the crowd of some of the wealthiest and most influential people in the world.

"Hi," she finally said, long after he'd moved on to another arrival. She downed the contents of the glass and almost immediately there was another tray placed in front of her. She put the empty one down and picked up another, just to hold though. Just to fit in.

They all seemed to know each other, but no one knew who she was and no one approached her, which was an immense relief. She moved to the edge of the reception area, watching the way they all laughed and chatted as if they'd all been friends forever, and not, in fact, competing viciously. No matter how engaged they seemed to be in the conversations though, their eyes kept scanning the room for people even more important than whoever they were with. Even here there was a hierarchy.

She couldn't see her father anywhere. He was probably with the host.

"Good evening, Miss Sanjeewa," another female voice in her earpiece. "I'm the social co-ordinator. Would you like me to facilitate an introduction? Blink once for no, twice for yes."

Neela scanned her surroundings for the cameras. She couldn't see any, no doubt there were hundreds and all too tiny to spot. She blinked once.

"Should you need any assistance, tap your glass twice and one of the staff will attend to you. Have a wonderful evening!"

Now she looked for it, Neela spotted a devastatingly beautiful woman turn away briefly from a conversation with a male film director to blink twice as she tapped her champagne flute. In moments, one of the people she'd assumed was a guest walked over and smoothly extricated her from the conversation. So, some of these people were staff? She almost tapped her own glass to test the theory, ever the scientist, but stopped herself. As she gathered data about this bizarre social situation, the same would be gathered about her, and she really didn't want any more of her interactions to be stored than necessary.

The same person then approached her, and she noticed that the sleeves of their long tunic-style tuxedo were not fashionably slashed. "Miss Sanjeewa, Dr Doyle has asked if you would like to join her and your father in the green room."

She couldn't stop her cheeks from flushing in anger. Of course, Doyle was here, of course she was. "You tell that—" She managed to rein in the hasty response. "Tell Dr Doyle that I'm fine here, and that I will see my father when we sit down for the meal."

They smiled and nodded. "Would you like me to stay with you? Or make a personal introduction for you?"

Anything to stop her from being alone. They were all obviously terrified of it. She had thought it would be the hardest thing about not being able to bring Sadie, but it didn't feel socially awkward now she was here. Instead, she was revelling in the distance between her and these people. She didn't want to make small talk with the likes of them. "There's no need," she smiled at them.

"I'll pass on your message to Dr Doyle. I hope you have a wonderful evening."

Neela quietly seethed at the thought of Doyle's offer. Surely, she knew it would be rejected? She'd never hidden how much she hated her father's 'assistant'. Perhaps it had been her father's idea. No, that was a ridiculous thought. He was probably hoping that she'd chickened out so he wouldn't have to face her.

But if that were the case, why had he offered her the ticket? The one that should have been her mother's.

Don't think about that. She downed the champagne, and in moments had a new full glass in her hand.

The lobby was filling up now, making it harder for her to keep her distance. She listened to the snippets of conversation around her as she pretended to look interested in one of the art installations involving cogs and pistons morphing into tiny boxes.

"He wouldn't have laid something like this on for a new product launch," a man was saying confidently.

"But it is an announcement," a woman answered. "I just can't work out what it could be from the people here. Tech, definitely, but did you see Father Carmichael over there? What would he be doing here if it's a tech thing?"

"Carmichael is a bloody fraud. He preaches anti-tech but his house is filled with it. He spouts that shit to keep the Christo-fascists happy. He went to school with LeRey, he gets an invite to all of his events. Didn't you know that?"

"It's very subtle, don't you think?" Another conversation, close behind Neela, caught her attention. She glanced back, thinking the woman had been talking about the art, but both she and her glamourous companion were looking at the speaker's outstretched arm as she showed off the implants embedded in her skin. "I asked my artist to tattoo the gold links like vines and I think it looks much prettier than that new-cyber-punk style that Dana's got."

"Oh, it does! Hers looks old-fashioned already. It's one thing to pay homage to an aesthetic, but hers is a bit on the nose, isn't it?"

"And look at my latest."

Neela couldn't help but sneak a peek. The woman was lifting up the floor-length gown to reveal her sparkling stiletto shoes and then what looked like two golden tattoos around her ankles. "These are the latest in pain and lymphatic drainage management. Now my body flushes out toxins twice as fast!"

Neela pressed her lips together, willing herself not to laugh.

"And they're interrupting the particular pain signal that makes your feet hurt. I can wear these shoes all day and not feel a thing."

"Holy shit, really? I'm calling my consultant as soon as this is over!"

Neela span around. "I'm sorry, are you seriously making out that it's better to have dubious hardware surgically implanted in your body than wear comfortable shoes?"

Both of the women frowned at her, as if they simply couldn't understand her point. "Have you seen shoes that look this good while being comfortable? Sweetness, it's easier to mine minerals on an asteroid than it is to design shoes that do both."

"She should know," her companion added. "She's the CEO of Star Mines Corporation. And it's not dubious hardware. My wife's ex-husband designed it. It's fully tested and safe. He's over there if you want to ask him."

She pointed into the crowd. Neela didn't try to spot whoever it was. The woman looked her up and down, eyes lingering over the sleeves of her dress. "And you are?"

"Dr Neela Sanjeewa."

The CEO's eyes widened. "Are you related to LeRey's scientist?"

Neela bristled. Regardless of how she felt about her father, speaking of him as if he were little more than the billionaire's pet was deeply offensive. "If you're referring to Dr Philip Sanjeewa, the world's foremost authority on nuclear fusion, then yes. He's my father."

They didn't seem to pick up on the angry undertone. "You must be so proud," the CEO's friend said.

"I don't suppose you know why LeRoy has laid this all on, do you?" the CEO asked. When Neela shook her head, she looked a lot less interested in her.

"What field are you in?" her friend asked.

"Aquaponics," Neela replied. "Y'know, saving the world one damn fish at a time."

Neither of them laughed at the admittedly niche joke, but mercifully the announcement was made that they could all take their seats in the ballroom. Neela made a hasty goodbye, hoping they weren't going to be seated at the same table.

The ballroom was beautiful, fully and tastefully restored art deco with only the stage area branded with LeRey corporate paraphernalia. There was a lectern in the centre, like an old-fashioned awards ceremony set-up. It didn't look like the kind of staging he used for the latest product announcements. What was this all about?

The social coordinator AI reminded her which table to head towards, and once there, she worked her way round the table to find the place card with her name on it. She only recognised the names of her father and his 'assistant'. They had probably been sat at a table for proper scientists, rather than those who focused on the celebrity aspect more than their discipline.

The cards rested on top of a decorative box with the same proportions as a paperback book. She wondered if LeRey was about to reveal a memoir, and then realised that if that were the case, it would be in a chunky hardback three times the size.

She'd been seated next to her father, which was not what she'd seen on the seating plan sent out with the invitation. Having arrived before everyone else, she was about to swap her card with someone on the far side of the table when a hand rested on her shoulder.

"Hello NeeNee."

The sound of her father's voice threatened to overwhelm her. A rush of resentment, of rage, of a million unspoken wounds. But she turned around, looked at him, and didn't show any of it.

He'd lost weight. Not so much that anyone would worry, but she saw it. And he looked tired. Older than the image of him held in her mind since she last saw him, with more grey hairs than black now. It had only been three months, but it felt like three decades.

His eyes, and those of his assistant who stood behind him, went from her face straight down to her wrists and the sleeves covering them. He pulled her into a tight embrace before she even had a chance to take a breath.

"Thank you so much for coming. It's... it's so important to me that you be here tonight."

It was always about him. Always. As he crushed her, she looked at the assistant over his shoulder and their eyes met. Doyle smiled, as if she had nothing to feel bad about. As if she was just observing a reunion between father and daughter, instead of lingering wreckage. Neela hated her auburn hair, her huge blue eyes, the way she dressed, everything about her. She was so fake, and her father had never been able to see it.

Her father released her. "How are you now?"

He didn't really want to know. If he did, he would have come to the hospital, would have sat by her bedside with Sadie. But he didn't even do that for her mother, so why would he do that for his daughter?

"Still here," she said in as neutral a tone as she could muster.

"You remember Cassie, don't you?" He gestured at Doyle, who renewed the fake smile.

"Oh, yes," Neela said, and something must have leaked into her tone as they both looked briefly awkward.

"Dr Sanjeewa," a man said as he approached the table and they both turned to him. But he was addressing her father, of course. "It's such a pleasure to meet you. I read your most recent paper and I would love to talk to you about it."

She tuned out, used to this. Her father launched into the conversation enthusiastically and she was left standing there, forgotten. The dressings on her wrists itching intensely. She tugged down the sleeves unnecessarily and sat at the table, pretending to read the menu card.

"Are you really alright?" Doyle asked, sitting next to her, in the wrong place. "He's been so worried. Are you getting the help you need?"

"Those are two different questions. And the answers to both are private." *Boundaries*, she could hear Sadie saying. *You are not responsible for anyone else's feelings. Keep your boundaries*.

Doyle leaned back. "He's an amazing man. I know that your mother's death was hard but—"

Neela held up a hand and closed the distance between them again so she could speak quietly. "My mother died without him there when she needed him most. When I needed him most. And he wasn't there, because he was with you. So don't pretend to care. And don't ever, ever, mention my mother again."

Doyle looked horrified, as if the thought that Neela knew about the two of them had never occurred to her. "It's not what you think! He—"

"I think your seat is over there," Neela said loudly, pointing at the one on the other side of her father's place. "Excuse me."

She dashed to the nearest bathroom, locked herself in one of the stalls and burst into tears. She felt angry, both at the two of them, and at herself for getting tearful. She had to keep herself together, had to remember why she came and what she wanted to happen, even if it wasn't really going to change anything in the grand scheme of things. But all she could think about was her mother dying, of watching the life slip from her body as she sat there, sobbing, alone. It felt like she was sliding back down to the place she'd been clawing her way back from, the place where she felt it was easier to end her life than to find a way to live as it crumbled apart beneath her. And through all of it that fucking woman had been spending every day with her father, the great physicist, who put his work above everything else, even his dying wife and his suicidal daughter. Doyle spent more time with him than anyone else and they were so obviously in love with each other it made her sick.

She blew her nose, re-touched her make-up, having brought half of it with her because she knew she'd probably end up the way she was now; sniffling and trying her best to put the mask back on to get through the evening.

Everyone was seated by the time she returned to the ballroom. Her father introduced her to the others seated around the table. She was polite and grateful that none of them seemed particularly interested in talking to her. Doyle had swapped places with the man who was keen to talk to her father, putting even more distance between them. It seemed that the man was also a physicist, and desperate to get her father's opinion on something that he didn't seem to want to talk about. Whenever the man paused, her father looked like he was about to talk to her but was pulled away again.

A musical fanfare cut through the chatter, and LeRey walked out onto the stage. Everyone applauded, a few cheered, and the handsome billionaire soaked it all up like a rockstar. But Neela kept her eyes on her father, seeing him exchange a look with Doyle that made her want to scream. The way the woman smiled at him reassuringly, something her mother used to do whenever he was about to collect an award. How dare she.

"Friends, enemies, lovers," LeRey said, eliciting the laughter he'd clearly hoped for. "Welcome. Thank you all for taking time out of your busy and important lives to come and spend the evening with me. With each other. Because this evening isn't just about me." He held up his hands. "I know, I know, it's hard to believe." That dazzling smile again. "But look around you. We are the most important people in the world."

Neela looked around, noting the lack of democratically elected representatives amongst them. They were some of the richest people on the planet though.

"And I have brought you here tonight to make an announcement that is going to change the world. Forever." He grinned. "But I'll tell you about that after the first course. Hey, c'mon! You know I love to build suspense!"

He gave the good-natured laughter a moment to settle before adding. "Oh, and feel free to open the boxes. You all know how important I feel it is to be open and accountable to the public, and how I like to give them the chance to ask us the questions they would ask if they were able to meet us. Feel free to up and down vote ones that are directed to specific individuals that aren't you, and if you can find a moment to answer ones sent in for your attention, that would be a great public service."

LeRey left the stage and headed for his table, not far from where Neela sat. She watched him smile and nod to people as he did so, and how his eyes lingered on her father before he sat down.

She opened the box, found the paper-thin tablet inside and the event's AI auto-linked her phone to it. This was what she had come for.

The words 'Town Square' were the only thing on the screen, so she tapped it, and found a super retro interface that LeRey was known to love. There were only a hundred questions. She frowned. The amount of hype on the networks leading up the event would surely have encouraged thousands upon thousands of people to send in questions.

Of course, they would have been screened, and perhaps even pre-answered by the guest's AI personal assistants. But she hadn't received any answers to the questions she'd sent in anonymously, so she started scrolling through them.

It soon became clear that none of them had got through. She sat back, feeling like an idiot. How could she have thought that anything other than sycophantic bullshit and dry technical questions would have been permitted? She looked back at LeRey as a small army of staff began to serve the first course. Perhaps she should ask her father to introduce her to him, and then she could ask him in person about the funding for the hospital in which her mother had died. The funding that he had provided for over ten years and then withdrawn, even though it would barely register in his finances.

"Nee-nee." Her father touched her hand. "You know I'm not very good at... expressing myself. I just wanted you to know that I... I do understand why you're so angry with me. But I'm not the person you think I am."

"How do you know what that is? When have we ever had an actual conversation?"

A plate featuring something tiny, beautifully presented and utterly unrecognisable was placed in front of them both.

"I haven't been there for you when you needed me, and I'm sorry."

"Yeah, I am too. But this isn't the place for you to try—"

"Philip!" LeRey appeared out of nowhere. "Are you ready?"

The pained, earnest expression on her father's face shifted into one of anger, only briefly, before he fixed a smile to look up at his employer. "I haven't had a chance to eat yet."

Out of the corner of her eye, Neela spotted a couple of the security guards heading out of the ballroom. Could she hear shouting, coming from outside? She tried to tune in to the sound but the background music in the hall seemed to get louder, just enough to drown it out. No one else seemed to notice.

"Hurry up then," LeRey said. "I can't wait any longer."

He marched off towards the stage, moving as if propelled by endless energy.

"Thanks for introducing us," Neela muttered.

"He's not worth meeting," her father whispered back and then looked at Doyle. Something silent was exchanged between them, and then Doyle gave him a slight nod.

"So, it turns out I'm incapable of sitting on something this huge," LeRey announced as he bounded up onto the stage, his mic louder than before and the music not subsiding. "I am delighted to announce a breakthrough at my primary research facility. And when I said it will change the world, I meant it. We have made fusion power commercially viable. It's not thirty years off anymore, my friends. Fusion power is here, today, at my facility, and soon will be powering the world. Clean, abundant, power! Enough to solve all of the other challenges we face! I promised the world that I would find a solution to the energy crisis, and I always keep my promises."

Spontaneous applause burst out across the tables, and he grinned. Neela glanced at her father, who looked like he was about to be sick. Doyle was looking at him too, tense, expectant.

"But I want to hand the stage over to the man who helped me to do this. Dr Philip Sanjeewa, I know you like to stay out of the limelight, but it's your turn to shine, my friend. The world is watching." He pointed up at a small array of lights at the back of the room, high up, suggesting it was being recorded. "Come and tell them just how great this is!"

Her father stood and looked at Neela. A sheen of sweat glistened across his face. He looked terrified, far more than all the other times she'd seen him about to give a speech. "I love you, Neela," he said and then made his way to the stage.

A chirrup in her ear warned her about her heart rate and blood pressure as she looked at Doyle, who also looked nervous as hell. LeRey shook her father's hand as he got to the lectern, then stepped off the stage and she watched him head straight for one of the security people who were waiting in the wings. Something was definitely going on outside of the hotel, serious enough for LeRey to surreptitiously make his way to the exit as Neela's father started to speak.

"I'd like to thank Mr LeRey for giving me the chance to speak this evening. I'm the head of the JETTERlabs team and I can confirm that we have effectively created a star in the lab on the outskirts of Oxford. It has been producing four times more energy than the largest nuclear fission powered station, uses fuel derived from sea water, is stable, safe, has no harmful by-products and cannot be used to create weapons of any kind. We have solved the last piece in the puzzle of endless, sustainable, clean energy production. This is a tipping point that goes in a positive direction. Now all of the projects to clean the air, the oceans, the soil, all of the things deemed too expensive because of high energy needs, they're all possible. Mass scale desalination, total decarbonisation of heating and cooling, dozens of others, now they can truly happen."

People were standing up, applauding and cheering, looking for LeRey who had left the room. "Please, please, there is more to tell you," Philip said, and people sat. "Mr LeRey has been called away briefly, but he will be back very soon. I would like to thank the team at JETTERlabs, over two hundred remarkable people, and also to acknowledge the work of thousands of scientists who came before us. The foundation of this work was funded by multiple governments for decades before Mr LeRey… so generously offered to fully fund this endeavour. There have been several generations of taxpayers' contributions and I would like those to be recognised too. We have been standing on the shoulders of not only giants, but also the masses, and I thank them all." Polite applause rippled across the room, even though Neela knew that none of them really cared.

"If you'll indulge me, I'd like to tell you a story about someone who did not work in the lab and who did not fund it, but nevertheless enabled me to devote myself fully to my work. My late wife, Caroline."

Neela covered her mouth, not sure if she could sit through whatever he was about to say. Doyle suddenly moved round to sit where her father had been and leaned across to her. "Please stay and listen," she said, as if she'd known. "Please."

The urgency in her tone rooted Neela to her seat. Even though the announcement was incredible, wonderful even, she felt like something terrible was about to happen. Why?

"My wife was a remarkable woman. She volunteered on a variety of ethics committees when she wasn't running the largest urban farm in the UK, staffed entirely by volunteers, which fed thousands of people a year. We shared everything. We had a beautiful daughter together, now an excellent scientist in her own right, and my wife held the family together while I obsessed over my work."

He paused, looking at Neela. He was shaking. She still had one hand clamped over her mouth, her other arm wrapped tight around herself. "I wasn't the best father. But she was the best mother, and four months ago, while I was at the lab, the same day, in fact, that we achieved stable, prolonged fusion, she suffered an aneurysm and was rushed to hospital."

His voice faltered and he swallowed. "I was not told."

Neela blinked.

"My daughter and the hospital staff made several attempts to inform me, but communications into the lab were monitored, I later found out, and Mr LeRey decided to withhold the information as he felt it was more important that I be in the lab on that day, than at my wife's side. She died one hour before he brought in champagne and announced that we'd saved the world."

The audience was utterly still, the background music horribly incongruous. Neela felt the tears rolling over her hand and couldn't move either. "If that wasn't enough, he did the same when my daughter was rushed to hospital three weeks ago. If I had known, Nee-nee, I would have been there. I'm so sorry, baby girl.

"We were perfecting a delicate process and he decided it was more important than the suffering of my bereaved child. And that is why," he glanced briefly at Doyle, who gave him a nod, "at this moment, the entirety of the JETTERlabs fusion power station plans have been sent to every government, every public and private institution, every school and university, every media outlet and every personal email address we could find. Mr LeRey funded this project in the belief that it would make him even more obscenely wealthy, and that is wrong. This was the work of generations, and the entire planet deserves to reap the benefits equally."

The doors to the ballroom burst open and LeRey ran towards the stage as security guards streamed through. The music stopped, and the chanting of a crowd outside could suddenly be heard.

Doyle leaned over to Neela. "We weren't having an affair, I swear. I know that's what you think. We've been planning this for months, ever since your mother died and we found out what LeRey did. We set up the distraction, we found a way to disseminate the information, it took every single minute we could spare outside of the lab. He loves you, Neela, so much. And your mother too."

That was why he had wanted her here. It felt like the past four months were being rewritten, that she'd been living in a totally different world to the one that held the truth. She watched the security guards throw him to the floor, watched LeRey kick him in the stomach, screaming at the man she'd wrongly cast as the villain in her family's story.

Guards pulled LeRey back too, his real-life PA ushering him away before any more damage could be done. Some were filming with their phones, but Neela knew it was useless, given the security mesh around the building and the fact that no one here would be able to leave without all the data from the night being scrubbed. But they were all witnesses, and she had the feeling, from the look of triumph on her father's face as he was pulled back on to his feet, that the live feed had been kept on for long enough.

Neela dashed forwards as they started to drag him off, fighting her way past panicking guests and other staff trying to keep everyone away from her father. She pulled off her shoes and leapt onto the nearest table. "Dad!" she yelled, and he twisted just enough to see her. "I'm so fucking proud of you!" she shouted as loud as she could. "And I love you too!"

"Saving the world, Nee-nee!" he shouted back. "One damn fish at a time!"

Fake

Stephen Oram

THEO STOPS staring at his list of reasons to stay and reasons to leave. Folding the piece of precious paper carefully, he tucks it away in his pocket. Hidden. Safe. He sighs, slips his headset on and joins five other testers in the introductory lesson for new members.

Their role is to spot glitches in the AI-generated education programme and recommend changes to their leader, Ari, before it's approved to go live. Optimising the optimisation of the Optimised, he likes to call it. 'The stuff you're trusted with because of my status,' is how his wife Bea prefers to articulate it.

The avatar lecturer begins. "Those end days of the failed welfare state experiment were horrific. Self-indulgence ran amok. The old and the sick lived too long to be of any use and the cost to everyone of keeping them alive was astronomical."

There's a weird click at the end of each sentence which can sometimes happen when the AI and its multiple interfaces is overloaded. Theo makes a note.

"The Freedom Fund was introduced to provide a Universal Basic Income for everyone, no matter who. It shifted the burden of deciding how to utilise tax revenues from the state to the individual. No more restrictive hand-holding. Everyone was free to choose how to spend their own money."

Theo references ambiguity, suggesting 'health, education and policing' be made more explicit.

"They rioted. A lot of healthy and economically active people died. It was a national tragedy. It was necessary."

Another glitch: presumably, *it* refers to the Freedom Fund?

The lecturer continues, unaware of Theo's question. "Dissolving collective responsibility, like it or not, allowed like-minded people to form their own discrete groups, and that's how the Optimised came into being."

Theo remembers joining twenty-five years later, as a result of learning about their intense focus on collective efficiency, and he's never forgotten the pain of leaving his young daughter behind.

"The general public – those outside of the Optimised – remain self-interested. The new government policy of replacing the Freedom Fund with the Community Contract, where the state will provide everything they need, will leave them with very little money. They'll feel controlled and will resist. Even with issue-by-issue voting they only know how to protest and riot, not plan and prosper."

A knot of anxiety forms in Theo's stomach and he takes a break.

The luxury surroundings of his home-office are perfectly organised. Sterile. He can't stand it. But to leave would be horrendous. Whatever secrets are known by Ari would be revealed – he's seen it before. He'd be bankrupted. But, with the imminent Community Contract that might not be so bad. He swallows the lump forming in his throat and returns to the lesson. A familiar tingle distracts him. "Shit," he says without thinking, and the avatar sitting next to him turns its head and puts a single index finger up to its lips. "Sorry," he replies, and the lecturer mutes him, fading his presence to eighty per cent transparency.

Theo tries to refocus on finding the imperfections, but he feels sick at the warning from the lecturer about possible disruption and deaths. He's not worried for himself. As a member of the Optimised, he lives in their high-end compound on the hill above the city and he's protected. So long as he pays the price, a life of carefully curated efficiency. He touches the list in his pocket, but once again avoids a decision.

The tingles steadily increase. You can't argue with the biometrics, or Hal the home help interface for that matter. That's the deal they've made with the tech. The 'penis prompt', Bea calls it. He marks himself absent for legitimate reasons, the command to copulate, and embraces the distraction.

It's a short walk to the nearest sex room, set aside for him and his wife to enjoy each other at the moment that Hal has determined will give the greatest combined pleasure.

The door opens as he approaches. Above it is the simple phrase, *Sex in Progress*. This no-nonsense efficiency is like a bruise that keeps getting punched and it's at times like this that his thoughts wander to his daughter Rebecca's mother, living a life of random imperfection among the chaos of the city.

Bea is already waiting, naked on the bed. Even now, she has that serious expression which betrays her obsession with constant improvement.

"This new Community Contract," he says. "It's a disaster. How—"

"Leave it to Ari," she interrupts, and with her toes she points at the mirror above the bed. Already, it's showing him the best places to touch her, becoming a 360-degree wraparound image with points of interest on his reflection when he joins her. They ready themselves for Hal's choreographed instructions. Each episode is different, every encounter carefully crafted, interactively and moment by moment. Bea is stunning and her tender touch is as expert as ever, even down to the firmness with which her fingers fondle, depending on the degree of shading. However, underneath their favourite lime and basil scent is the sharp tang of cleansing spray. A small imperfection which is immensely irritating and causes his thoughts to drift annoyingly towards the mundane aspects of his life, like organising supper. Quickly followed by surges of despair at the pointless predictability of his existence.

After fifty minutes of their uninhibited compliance, the room tells them that they need to leave, to give it time to clean up and personalise the scent for the next couple. Or threesome, or whatever the optimum configuration is for those who come next.

Back at their house, Theo asks Hal for advice on the supper guests and menu and then re-enters the lesson about the excesses of the city that the Optimised look down on from their hilltop enclave.

"The non-Optimised are degenerate and arrogant. They presume they know best."

Theo makes the point that non-Optimised is not a well understood term.

"Those riots in the thirties when the Freedom Fund was introduced prove that the majority want the nannying of a welfare state. Four decades later, this new version, this so-called Community Contract gives them that. At a cost."

Thinking about this brings an image of Rebecca, the impetuous and principled five-year-old daughter he left behind, standing with her legs apart to stubbornly make a point. Her crooked nose and sharp eyes, crowned with long blonde unkempt hair. The twenty-year-old is not that much different and she will certainly protest against any increase in government control. He sends a message, conscious that Hal will be monitoring him and that 'pre-Bea life' will be deemed a wasteful diversion.

A soft buzz in his left ear lets him know a message has arrived, and he checks his avatar's hand. Rebecca?

No, it's Hal suggesting the guests and the timing of supper. He automatically accepts, letting it get on with consulting the other home helps to determine each guest's individualised meals.

The mundanity of it all is crushing him. "What *am* I doing?" he shouts, pulling his headset off and kicking his desk.

* * *

Dragomara's middle-age wrinkles quiver as she wakes with a half laugh, half snort. "Well, that was a surprise," she says.

Quint untangles herself from the sheets, dragging them off Dragomara and fighting the crumpled linen to the floor. "Didn't really work, did it?"

Laying her hand across the naked stomach of her close friend, Dagomara whispers, "No, it didn't. Worth giving it a shot though. You never know about these things, and if I had to settle down again with anyone—" She lets her last word drift, while she strokes Quint's long and luxuriously dark hair.

Quint holds her hand and stops the stroking. "I don't know why, but I couldn't let go. You know, lose myself."

"Hey, it's fine. Since I split with him, divorced him, got rid of him, I need to squeeze every moment from life."

Quint nods and smiles. "I know."

"And you, my best friend, were one of those squeezes."

They both laugh loudly, until Dragomara cups Quint's face in her hands. "How I wish I had your cheekbones and your chin," she says and then adds, "Dumpy Drag they used to call me, you know?"

Quint takes her hands away and still holding them kisses her on the cheek. "Stop. C'mon. We're celebrating tonight."

"Oh, yes," she says in a light tone of voice. She gathers up the sheet, crumples it into a ball and throws it at the service bot in the corner, to be collected, washed anonymously and replaced by the end of the day. She follows up her athletic sheet throwing with a shout of, "Good. Bye. Freedom. Fund!"

Quint calls to her from the walk-in wardrobe. "Can you believe it's happening? After all this time. Let's hope they don't use it to introduce any more rules."

"I dunno, sometimes I wish they would," she calls back.

"Drag, how could you? It'd be the end. As bad as that optimisation sect."

"The ones who are so rich they can have whatever they want, sect?"

"At a cost. Do you not listen to the rumours?"

"Don't believe everything you hear, Quint. I'd swap."

"Met one once. Didn't seem that happy to me. Not a jot of joy to be seen. And, with the Community Contract, you won't have to."

"Can you remember the Freedom Fund coming in? How old were we? Forty years ago? About ten?"

"I was nine I think, but then I'm a year younger than you," says Quint. "And, it shows," she adds with a cheeky lilt to her voice, seemingly recovered from their mutual disappointment.

Dragomara picks up her phone by the thin end and messages her close contacts. "Who has enough house battery to host tonight's meal?" she says, raising her eyebrows in anticipation.

"Me," messages Jayceon. "Pick up six steaks from the printers on the high street, the new one. You know it?"

"Order received. See you soon."

Quint appears holding a pair of blue shoes.

"Put 'em on, we need to get flowing."

Quint completes the lyric, "Like a river, freed from the sky." She slips them on and grabs her coat.

"Even a fast-flowing river has banks," mutters Dragomara, as she closes the door behind them.

There is bad news at the printers. A rush on celebration steaks has created an hour-long wait, despite their top-of-the-range technology. "You can't rush the printing of a good steak," says the woman behind the counter every time a customer expresses their impatience. Luckily, Jayceon had the foresight to order ahead, but even so there's still forty-five minutes before theirs will be ready.

Fidgeting and fussing with the buttons on her jacket, Dragomara tuts and chunters. "Should have made do with algae steaks," she says repeatedly, intertwined with muttered concerns about their communal compliance with anything they're told is good for them. "No coherent resistance until it's too late," she tells Quint, who ignores her until the steaks arrive and they set off for Jayceon's.

* * *

Without bothering to read the suggestions, Theo gives the go-ahead for Hal to distribute the topics of conversation to their guests a few minutes before they arrive. The room is set to its optimum temperature, for the food and the guests, and as expected they all arrive at their specified time, exactly three minutes apart.

"Hello," says Bea to the last arrival. "Delighted you came. We have a wonderful evening ahead of us."

Sycophancy hasn't fallen foul of the efficiency police yet, thinks Theo. Bea takes his hand and together they stroll into the dining room to be welcomed by their guests. In the centre is an everyday buffet of algae-fed insects – sauteed mealworms topped with roasted houseflies, soldier fly larvae, and crickets. All served on a bed of seaweed.

"Peter," says Bea. "You're blue, I believe?"

He checks his menu and confirms.

She formally begins the meal by serving him a small plate of blue-coded food from the buffet and while she carefully selects for the other guests, they remind themselves of the order in which the topics of conversation are to be addressed.

Before they've eaten their starter plate, they've completed the subject of which music they will go and listen to. Agreeing with Hal's suggestion, but only after consulting with their own home helps. Theo keeps quiet, not wishing to disrupt the easy flow of the evening. Next on the list is the Community Contract, and this time there's no helpful steer from Hal except not to forget that their founder's legacy intelligence, Ari, will have an opinion.

"We have to do something," says Bea. "We cannot let the government screw us by overtaxing us to pay for it."

To her left sits Pompous Peter, as Theo calls him. He's Bea's boss and about as unpleasant as a boss can be. She says she doesn't mind because they get the job done, but nonetheless Theo sits on one hand as a reminder not to rise to any bait.

Peter clears his throat to silence the whole table and then speaks. "Tax every stage of production, eh? I'd like to see them try. It's simple. We redefine. Any process that leads up to that final piece of a production line, whether that's manufacturing, service, data manipulation, artificial intelligence, or whatever. Anything apart from the very last action will be defined as research and development. We'll test each step of every process every time, for efficiency. That way we are always improving, but never producing. Easy. Can't tax R&D. That would be ridiculous. The promises that underpin this Community Contract will cost the public so much that once the tax to pay for it is collected, they'll have virtually no money of their own. It'll be the same as communism. And, serve them right."

Lots of clapping and nodding heads around the table prompts Peter to puff out his chest and display his perfect teeth in a showman-like grin.

Bea waves her hands to signify she has something to add. "We gave them a chance to vote for a workable solution. Didn't we? All that bloody currency we spent on persuasion postings, layers of micro-nudges. They chose to ignore us, and so be it."

"How can you—" The look that Bea gives him stops Theo mid-sentence. "Dessert?" he asks.

They all nod enthusiastically.

"I baked a cheesecake to celebrate."

Bea stares at him with her mouth slightly open.

"You did what?" asks Peter.

Theo leans forward. "I—"

"Don't tell me," says Peter, groaning under his breath before tapping the blue dot on his menu and turning his attention. "Bea?"

She turns away from Theo and almost imperceptibly shrugs. "I can order in, if anyone wants something."

They all shake their heads and mutter their *no thanks*.

"Peter," says Bea. "I'm sure you agree that rolling back forty years to the thirties is pathetic and pointless. The nanny state failed."

Peter presses his lips forward, almost in a mock kiss, and hesitates before speaking. "Pretty stupid to try and re-run the welfare state experiment that failed for the best part of a hundred years before it expired its last tired breath." He pauses again. For effect, Theo's sure, and then continues. "But, let's see what Ari has to say." He glances at his phone. "Oh, Ari has already announced the changes that redefine R&D. It'll be interesting to see how the masses react. Once they understand."

Ari, thought Theo. *A fake of our founder, created on his death to carry on the work. Nobody knows except us that he's dead. What a joke.*

"What does that face mean?" asks Bea, staring at Theo. "Care to share?"

"It's just that. Well, I don't know. It's that, you know, shouldn't we at least consider what the masses, as you call them, want? Do we always have to be in combat mode?"

Bea laughs and the others join in. All except Peter, who whispers in Bea's ear before booming out with his loud confident voice. "Theo, be a good 'un and order us some drinks."

A brief silence settles before the conversation starts up again, albeit with every eye averted away from him.

* * *

Dragomara listens while she eats, unwilling to completely pull her concentration away from the pleasure of devouring the rare succulent treat.

"So what do we do to avoid getting fucked over again?"

"They're such a side-lined sect now, their influence on the government is next to nothing. It can't happen like it did before."

"You think? Who has the real power? Who has the wealth? Who controls it all from behind the scenes?"

"We tax the robots and job done. Money comes to us, the people, and we use it wisely."

"It'll be what it is."

Savouring the last mouthful as it passes through her gullet, she swallows a mouthful of water, a delectable and decadent way to end a meal. She taps the table. "They're not all wealthy, you know. It's an efficiency sect." She drops her stare to her empty plate, knowing that she should eat it but not wanting to spoil the taste of meat and water in her mouth. "Just saying," she adds quietly into the stunned silence.

"Are you joining them?" asks Jayceon.

She shakes her head. “No. No way. But—” She can’t finish her sentence.

“The Freedom Fund was fucked, don’t you agree?”

Dragomara nods. “Yeah. And, this will be better.”

“A right to health and happiness,” quips Quint.

Jayceon frowns. “You can joke all you want, but a universal right to healthcare, housing, education, food and energy, has to be celebrated.”

“If we can afford it,” replies Dragomara, unwittingly dragged into taking the opposite view to counter the naïve optimism in the room.

Quint licks her lips as if she knows that what she’s about to say will leave a nasty taste behind. “So long as they pay their fair share, we’ll be fine.”

Dragomara snorts. “Exactly.”

“Oh, Drag. Please. Stop. Can we just enjoy tonight?”

“Please don’t call me Drag, but sure Quint. Whatever you want.” She stands up and bows her head in respect for the others around the table and walks quickly to the door.

Quint follows.

* * *

Theo and Bea are sitting opposite each other in silence. The guests have gone.

"Why?" asks Bea.

"Why what?"

She waits. Presumably for an answer he can't give. He doesn't really understand the question. Does everything have to have an answer, a conclusion? Is there such a thing as right and wrong? Is exploration the antithesis of efficiency?

"Thinking again?" she says with such a heavy layer of sarcasm that he wants to point out the wasted effort it takes to express contempt, but he stops himself. *It's not worth it*, he thinks, and then chuckles at the irony of their reversed roles. Her careless timewasting and his focused indifference.

"Hah," she says. "Stupidity in the extreme."

"I don't think—"

She interrupts him and waves her phone in his general direction. "The idiots are celebrating on the streets. Causing chaos. Can only lead to riots, stealing from one another – possessions, and time. Infantile imbeciles."

A tinge of Peter's pomposity peeping through, he thinks and clenches his jaw to stop himself from chuckling.

"I guessed you'd side with them."

He frowns. "What?"

"Your daughter? Her mother? Your past? I saw your face. You've said plenty of times that you think I can't see what's real. 'Unwilling to accept subtleties,' is how I believe you put it."

Theo gets to his feet and shrugs. He can't be dealing with her when she's like this. "I'll see you later," he says and she scoffs in reply, pointing out he probably won't.

Out on the patio, looking down on the coloured lights below, he takes time to recover from their argument and the disastrous dinner party. Bea's right that he doesn't believe in Ari's black-and-white narrative. And, she's right that he still resents being told to cut himself off from Rebecca's mother as soon as he and Bea had updated their status on the dating app. Choose and focus, they were told.

Fireworks burst in the sky above him. It's impossible to believe that the city celebrations will lead to riots. Why would they? Unless pushed and prompted by those with a vested interest. Ari for instance. Behind him is the caustic promise of Bea, and below – who knows? Riots? Rebecca in danger? Deaths? All possible but unlikely, and so, enticed by the city and its inhabitants, and with the fireworks evoking the thrills and excitement he can just about remember from childhood, he sneaks onto the ancient overgrown path that will take him to Rebecca and the celebrations.

* * *

Down among the crowds, Dragomara is distracted from the celebrations by an emergency government broadcast. *Tax rate will rise immediately to ninety-five per cent to accommodate the Community Contract.* "Quint, did you see this?" she shouts above the noise of the crowd.

"Wow. Severe. Can't be true. No warning?"

"Real-time economic management. Wasn't that the promise? Isn't that what this is?"

"Well—"

Dragomara is interrupted by the rising cacophony of voices in protest at the announcement. The police, who had been casually looking on, start to link arms to form a chain of defence and from behind them a flotilla of anti-riot drones is released.

"Makes things worse," shouts Dragomara to Quint, pointing at the drones.

Quint nods vigorously and indicates that she's going to leave, beckoning Dragomara to come with her.

"No," shouts Dragomara. "I'm staying."

Quint shrugs her shoulders and frowns. She mouths, *please*, and waits, but as soon as the drones are hovering overhead she turns and scurries away.

* * *

Theo is searching for Rebecca and at the same time telling Hal that all is well and to stop bothering him. The push and shove of the crowd is making him feel queasy, as if he's about to be crushed by a sudden swerve of the surrounding mass of bodies.

Holding his phone with the thick end, Theo manages to work his way to where she said she'd be. But when he arrives, she's not there. He calls, partly in panic and partly in frustration that she seems unable to follow a simple plan of action. Her red dot reappears on his screen and he breathes a sigh of relief; she's only a few metres away. He turns around until he's pointing in the right direction and then looks up. The crowd is too dense to see her, and there's no way of getting through.

Looking through the gaps between bodies as they shift and shuffle, he tries to catch sight of her distinctive pink hair. The trouble is, it's not that distinctive in this crowd.

A ball of bile rises into his throat, and as he sniffs it back down the pungent odour of unwashed bodies hits him hard. The breathless yelps and rigid faces that betray the cusp of terror that infects the protestors is intense.

He gently elbows a young woman. She resists without taking her eyes off the hovering drones. He tries to push his way through, but is blocked. The red dot on his phone is static. At least Rebecca's not moving. He keeps his focus on the crowd, attempting to weave his way to her. His phone vibrates and her red dot flashes, and keeps on flashing. She's activated the alarm he insisted she installed.

With all sense of politeness evaporated, he tugs the jacket of a man in front of him. "Let me through," he shouts. "Move!"

Nobody pays any attention.

He screams, "Out of the way," and a couple of people move, creating a small space. He shoves, he screams, he pleads, and he gets closer to Rebecca's red dot, one person at a time.

The drones are swooping down and lingering in front of protestors before flying off. One of them places itself directly in his path. It's as if it knows where he needs to get to, which it probably does. He bats it out of the way, and instantly regrets it as it wobbles in the air trying to rebalance itself. This is not good.

* * *

Dragomara catches sight of a handsome man hitting a drone. *Brave*, she thinks. *Or, stupid*. He's staring at it attempting to stabilise. "What's he doing?" she asks nobody in particular. "Hey," she shouts, not sure what it is about him that attracts her. "Hey," she shouts again, and this time he glances at her. There's a vulnerability in the way he's holding his body, stiff and fragile. She pushes her way through until she's next to him. "Hey, what's wrong?"

He speaks, but the deafening drones gathered overhead and the shouts from the crowd are so loud it's hard to hear him. She cups her ear with her hand.

"My daughter!" he shouts. "She's in trouble. I can't get to her!"

He holds out his phone so she can see where they need to go, and she grabs his arm. She forces their way through, shouting for people to get out of the way. The red dot is still pulsating. She moves a woman to the side and he does the same to the man with her. He starts waving frantically, and a young woman with pink hair and blood dripping down her face waves back.

"Rebecca!" he shouts.

"Dad!" she shouts back and runs towards them.

"What the fuck?" he screams, but tears are flowing down his cheeks as he hugs her tightly. He glances at Dragomara and mouths, *thank you.*

* * *

This wonderful woman, sitting across the table from him chatting casually with his daughter – as if the events of a few hours ago hadn't happened – is intriguing. Her raucous laughter has seamlessly turned to seriousness and back in the blink of an eye, especially when he exposed his anxiety and she told him to be quiet.

Rebecca is chatting away as if she's known Dragomara for years. She hasn't. He checked. What they have in common is a profound desire to find a pragmatic solution to the problem the crowds are still protesting about, the ninety-five per cent tax rate. Both want the new Community Contract to work. They turn to face him.

"What?" he says, having not been listening properly. He looks at Dragomara.

She returns his look with a broad reassuring smile. "You have a foot in both camps, how do you think we should fix this thing?"

Ironically, the lack of Hal or Ari hampers his ability to bring coherent thoughts together and it takes him a few minutes to properly consider whether to reveal his idea. It could cost him dearly.

Despite their desperation, they wait patiently, and seem to be genuinely keen to hear what he has to say.

Wiggling his fingers, he draws them close so only they can hear. "You know about Ari, don't you?" They nod. "That he died years ago, but left a deep fake AI in his place to keep up the façade?" The shock on their faces tells him they didn't. He reassures them that it's a closely guarded secret. "Everything is optimised to its most efficient by Ari, although the home helps are more often the interface we use. Whatever Ari says is the right thing to do, becomes the right thing to do. Do you see where I'm going?" They shake their heads. "Change Ari to change the sect to change the rules."

"Love it. Total genius," says Dragomara.

Theo blushes and Rebecca nudges him. "Dad?" she says and chuckles.

"I—"

Dragomara interrupts him. "Great idea, and delivered with elegance and understated confidence. But, really?" She pauses. "How? This is critically urgent."

"Yeah, Dad. How?"

"I'm not exactly sure, but I have ideas."

"Go on," says Dragomara.

"I perform the human validation on our AI-generated education programme—"

Dragomara raises her left eyebrow and lets out a half laugh, half snort. "You iron out the facts?"

"No. No. Just the way they're communicated."

She shrugs, seemingly unconvinced.

"The point is, I sit and learn so much stuff each day. I've done the Engineering Ari course, the one that the best of the best who are entrusted with Ari's development have to pass. I know how it works. I can show someone."

Rebecca sits up straight. "You mean you can tell someone how to hack Ari?"

"Yes. I think—"

Dragomara interrupts. "Nice idea, but it'll take too long. We need to stop it now."

He scowls and is about to reply when Rebecca sits forward. "True, but don't forget the Community

Contract gives us public control over the police. *We* can dampen the spiralling tension," says Rebecca.

"Now?" asks Theo.

"With enough support we can trigger a vote," she replies.

"Do it," says Dragomara. "Then all we need is a hacker who's competent enough to get into the most sophisticated system in the world and change its worldview."

Theo grimaces. "Yes Dragomara, that's about the size of it," he adds quietly.

"You'd betray them?"

"Yes, I believe I would. Although, it's not really betrayal. They've boxed themselves into an optimised corner they can't get out of. In a lot of ways I'd be helping them evolve."

"Nicely positioned," she replies.

"Rebecca? What do you think?" he says, conscious that she's been phone fiddling for the past few minutes without speaking, presumably for privacy.

"I think I might know someone who can trigger a vote, as well as hack Ari. He's part of a loose organically organised network. He's on his way." She swings her phone around between her fingers and tucks it into her pocket, thick end first. "Will you leave them? Her?" she adds.

"I'm not sure," he says. "I think so. Yes."

"Divorce?" asks Dragomara. "I didn't think it was allowed."

"It's not, but then nor is leaving them. So, who knows? Anyone who has quit hasn't had the opportunity to explain how they did it."

"Mum?" asks Rebecca.

Placing a gentle hand on hers, he looks her in the eye. "No. Sorry love, but that was never going to happen. We're too different. Want different things."

"Wanted," she corrects.

"Still want, I would guess," he says and moves closer to put his arm around her shoulder.

A young man about the same age as Rebecca arrives and sits down. She pulls away from Theo's embrace. "Jonathan. Meet my dad."

"You think you can infiltrate Ari?" he asks, getting straight to the point.

"Maybe. I'll tell you what I know."

* * *

After a day of talking and dragging up knowledge he'd forgotten he had until Jonathan pressed him for details, they come to a conclusion. Not only is it possible to subvert Ari's advice to the Optimised, but the fact that Ari is already a fake is a key strength. If they can replace the fake with another fake, a sort of fake-fake, and install it without alerting the core team, they have a plan. From then on, they can carefully introduce more moderate ideas and still keep the sect members on board.

He plants his palms on the table. "Our Ari will lead the Optimised out of their elitist ghetto."

Jonathan leans back in his chair. "Give us the codes and we're good to go," he says with a flashing smile.

Theo is nervous. "I don't know. It's a big deal."

Dragomara moves closer to him. "Listen. Can you hear that? The riots? The triggered vote might calm things down for a while, but unless we undermine Ari they'll erupt again, and worse when the tax really bites."

Rebecca is crying. "Please, Dad. Please."

He sits and stares at the wall, breathing deeply.

They wait patiently. Dragomara occasionally signals the others to be quiet when it looks like one of them is about to speak.

He still doesn't know whether to trust Jonathan, but he has to trust Rebecca's instincts. He slams his fist into the palm of his hand. "Very well. I'm sure I can get Bea's access codes, and she has full clearance," he says.

Jonathan nods his head vigorously. "Someone has to be on site though, and that means you, Theo. You'll have to return and carry on as if nothing has changed."

"Can you?" asks Rebecca.

He has to. No choice. Whatever the consequences. "Yes," he says. "After all, I've already been pretending, and for a long time. I'll send you the codes as soon as I get them."

He stands up slowly, feeling his age, and as he turns to leave, Rebecca hugs him and whispers, "Please come back to us, to me."

"I will," he says.

"Our great hope," says Dragomara and opens her arms in anticipation.

They hug and squeeze, and it's so warm and lovely he finds it hard to stop.

"A drink when you're back," she says quietly into his ear and then as they part, she says loudly, "Stay strong. This should be the start of something splendid."

The Motherlode

Tiffani Angus

HISTORY IS made up of moments. When we look back at the line connecting it all, we can point to there, and there, and there, and see a before and an after. Before X and after X. So, solve for X.

Some changes are so seismic that they seem outside the realm of human cause, despite it being us who record how the house of cards was built and fell. Lizards and birds and the tides don't care about history.

We feel the earthquake coming, but we stand in a doorway or hide beneath a table, acting as if the moment was beyond our control. We don't know how to solve for X.

How the Xs have happened doesn't really matter now. What matters is how we go on afterwards, how we calculate Y and change our equation.

* * *

2082

The pile of old sweaters that her mother would have named a refuse heap was a motherlode, and Jan Napayok laughed to herself. To call a pile of used and crinkled synthetic yarn by the same term used for gold and oil, those things more valuable than people's lives in the history of this place, was funny in a twisted way, mostly because synthetic yarn was only possible because of oil. Before her was a pile of oil in all the colours of the rainbow. Anyone with a sweater that was all one colour, however, was in possession of a valuable commodity. Most were used to sleeves and pockets of various colours, lending a holiday air to the deep of winter.

Jan took an armful back to her seat and set to unravelling the sweaters while her neighbours from across the valley – some from miles and miles away – came in and found seats. Her daughter, Minnow, wearing a sweater with a red torso and blue sleeves with one variegated purple pocket, grabbed a sweater and started her own nest of recycled yarn on the empty seat beside her. Jan's great-niece, Daisy, sat at her other side and began to wind the yarn around her small hands. Minnow's husband, Samesh, bounced baby Alia to keep her quiet and occupied.

"Order." That single word and the sound of a gavel hitting the wooden table once should have brought the crowd to attention, but tonight was different. Lines were starting to be drawn, with the outcome unsure. Do they support this new venture fully or back away? Either choice was going to have ramifications on their children and their children's children.

"Order!" The gavel rapped on the table three times, jolting everyone to attention. People shuffled as they found their seats, and some picked up whittling or knitting to do while listening, perhaps to keep them grounded for a discussion that was going to raise emotions. Others stared intently at the group gathered behind the table at the front of the room, studying them as if stalking prey.

The valley was led by a group of five, each one chosen to represent a different faction of the population according to age or cultural background. Once upon a time, the panel would have been tribal elders. After that, it would have been one white man who owned more land than anyone else. But times had changed, and that man wouldn't have recognized the world as it had become. Nobody here cared what that imaginary man would have wanted. The world wasn't his any longer. Although, of course, there was still an undercurrent of that attitude that forced the panel – and some of the people they led – to engage with it directly. But for the most part, the valley did what worked, and what worked for everyone was to work together in the oldest of ways. Too much had happened in the previous few decades to continue to support the systems of the recent past. You can't eat money.

But you still had to do what was necessary to survive.

"Before we begin, we have to agree on the minutes of the previous meeting."

It was rare for anyone to raise any objections to the minutes because, each month, everyone attended the meeting unless sick. And even then, sometimes, the sick neighbour could be found sitting in the back of the room, slumped in the old couch left there for just that purpose. It's difficult to find much entertainment living so far out in the wilds.

Nobody raised any points about the minutes because the focus of this meeting was a sea change from the usual topics of how many more times they could recycle lithium batteries, which acreage to parcel out to any newcomers to the area, and which crops to test on land that had undergone such drastic climate changes over the previous half a century.

Alaska was a hard place with a long history of supporting only the hardest of people. As the world around it changed, it had found itself a destination for people escaping the Climate Wars in overburdened urban areas to the south despite the Alaskan natives themselves losing their ancestral lands on the west coast to rising sea levels and loss of permafrost. Now its people were in the midst of change that their ancestors had never seen coming.

Oil had run out. Finally and completely.

This had been expected decades before, but untapped fields had been deemed more important than untouched wilderness at the time, and so the rigs had kept going, much to the detriment of the climate and local environments. Alaska lasted a while longer than anyone expected. But the world was at a turning point.

The government's payments to the state's population, which had hit amazing heights as oil shares boomed, had dwindled away to nothing. And unless they came up with some new ideas, the money reserves that helped keep the state going would be empty soon, too.

"We have one topic to cover tonight: consideration of the Alaskan Stake in Off-World Resources, or ASOWR, a title that does not roll off the tongue." A few in the crowd laughed at that. The naming of the group had taken weeks, with arguments breaking out over whether the abbreviation should be an acronym and spell out something versus the importance of what the abbreviation stood for. In the end, clarity won out over cleverness, and the state was stuck with it.

While she listened, Jan continued to unravel stitches that had been made, by machine or by hand, years or even decades earlier. When a nine-year-old Jan, her older brother, and her parents had migrated north in 2047, the extended family had been left estranged: they feared what would happen to those moving to Alaska while terrified themselves because of their inability to make a move away from Los Angeles. As a result, Jan had grown up always wanting a larger family: aunts and uncles, grandparents and cousins. The valley became an extended family, and later the People, her husband's tribe, had made Alaska finally feel like where she belonged.

Her parents had been Generation Alpha, the one expected to find a solution. Logic had it that the following generation would be Beta, but when people from cities in the northern hemisphere began to migrate towards the pole to escape the heat, their children were dubbed Generation Gone, the first born to the new climate migrants. Yet, Jan insisted, she wasn't gone; she was here, where she belonged.

The panellists moved their table and chairs out of the way to make room for the evening's presentation. An array of eight projectors hung from the ceiling in a half circle about four feet across; mounted on their opposite sides were cameras pointing out at the audience. They all blinked to life and Jiao Long Li, representing ASOWR, appeared on stage to address rooms across the state simultaneously. The hologram brought the man to life as if he were there in person, something nearly impossible with travel so restricted. On his screen in Anchorage, he could choose which views to feature when taking questions from the audiences.

"Hello, everyone. Thank you for joining me," Jiao Long said. "I'm afraid I have bad news and some good news." He hesitated a moment, giving the audiences across the state time to grumble at his announcement.

"Might as well get on with it," a voice near Jan said, not unkindly. "We know we're grounded."

Jiao Long continued. "The biggest bad news is that there is no petrol left for any commercial air travel, which will ground all of our hybrid planes, but I'm sure you all knew it was coming. The only remaining petrol supplies are allocated to cargo planes to move specially designated materials, such as medical kits, across the oceans. I'm afraid any old puddle-jumpers needing petrol in any way are now out of service indefinitely. If you have enough to get to your closest import hub or large city, plan wisely, because if you fly there and can't fly back, you'll have to abandon your wings."

Jan had sold her husband's non-hybrid plane years before and so had no skin in this game. She'd never seen the point of buying a hybrid or the smaller all-electric planes. Any time she needed to get to a city, she could catch a ride with one of her closest neighbours. Minnow leaned over and whispered, "So, what's the good news?"

Next to Jiao Long a column of numbers appeared and floated in space. "These are the payouts that everyone has received the past twenty years from the oil revenue, the Permanent Fund. As you can see, it is anything but permanent, basically gone. The state needs a shift in investment so that the good people of Alaska can once again count on being part of a community project that profits them, not just in physical infrastructure but in their bank accounts."

"We've heard it all before," the voice in the audience said.

The mayor struck the table with her gavel. "Harold Van-Prine, please. He cannot hear you. Hold your questions until later."

Daisy giggled at a grown man being reprimanded, and Jan put her hand on the girl's arm to quiet her. She was a curious child, left alone when Jan's nephew and his wife had died far to the south. Daisy was a heatwave orphan, but Jan felt blessed by having a daughter, granddaughter, and grandniece in her house. She felt they were continuing the work her mother and her mother-in-law had undertaken, to keep the next generation connected to the land.

Jiao Long continued. "I'm here representing the future. Up there," he said and pointed at the ceiling. "On the Moon, Mars, other planets. We can no longer mine here in Alaska, or really anywhere on Earth. But space is untapped. It was the next frontier a hundred years ago, but technology hadn't yet caught up with our grand ideas. However, we've accomplished nuclear fusion and it's so much safer than the old way. If we'd had it a hundred years ago… But that's all water under the bridge.

"Getting the materials back to Earth is less costly and cumbersome than it was. But more than that, the Moon and its resources are perfect for its use as a base to get astronauts and scientists further out into space to find more resources needed here on Earth. So now the people of Alaska have a decision to make. This is one of those moments in your history where you must look forward and not back."

Later, during the Q&A, Jan couldn't help but raise her hand. "When does it stop?" she asked.

"As I explained," Jiao Long answered, "the predictions are that our mining won't affect the Moon's mass at all. It has enough Helium-3 to power us for centuries, for millennia, as well as other rare minerals and a lot of ice, which means water, which means jet fuel. We've just been waiting for the technology to catch up with our dreams."

Jan stood and shook her head. "No. When do we stop consuming, stop taking, stop using? I came here when I was a kid and since then we've mined the planet dry. Why do we insist on doing it somewhere else rather than changing who we are here? People have been saying this for over a hundred years, but it doesn't seem to ever sink in."

Harold, a few rows ahead, turned around in his chair so he could see Jan. "You want to keep on living like a pioneer in the olden days? We've got solar panels, windmills, even new hydroelectric and nuclear plants to help keep our houses and farms going, and mining the resources on that rock will help solve our energy problems, but you're sitting there recycling old clothes to make new ones. Our world has just got smaller with no real commercial plane travel larger than a twenty-five-seater, or on boats or along rutted roads. He's here and not here," Harold said and pointed at Jiao Long, "but we're all living like our great-great-grandparents when we could be going to the stars to find new worlds."

"NASA went into space to see if it could," Jan argued. "Not to find something shiny to sell. Space was about exploration and discovery, not bank accounts."

"Then you're naïve," Harold said and turned back around.

During the walk home, Daisy asked Jan what NASA was, but Jan could only tell her what she'd learned in school so many decades earlier, about the Moon landing and the space shuttle. She decided not to describe the billionaires and trillionaires who followed, burning money on rockets rather than leaving a legacy of philanthropy. The girl would discover the unending march of capitalism soon enough.

Back at home, Minnow and Samesh put the girls to bed while Jan checked on their six chickens, three goats, three sheep, and two cows. The coop had recently been rebuilt after a bear tore through one wall. Luckily the chickens were loud enough that Samesh had heard them and scared the bear off with a rifle shot into the sky before the animal could destroy the solar cells on the coop's roof. It was always something. If it wasn't bears it was a moose stumbling through the compound like a tall, belligerent runaway truck with antlers; and if it wasn't a moose, it was a wolf, or a wolverine, or one of a number of predatory birds. Alaska was always trying to kill you or your livestock. Neighbours advised them to trap whatever animals trespassed, but Jan resisted. After all, they were the trespassers. And anyway, Samesh, Minnow, and Daisy were mostly vegetarian. The local tribespeople, extended relations of her late husband, appreciated Jan's restraint and would sometimes share small portions of their hunt takings with her.

Jan spoke to the Moon, to the brother Aningaaq who chased his sister, the Sun, across the sky. She told him what was going to happen soon, that he wouldn't be lonely much longer but be the centre of attention. And full of holes. The same moon that had hung in the dark sky over the splitting branches of her and her husband's family's ancestral tree for thousands of years. The Moon people had prayed to, used to measure time, created songs about.

"Mom, what are you doing out here alone? You know better." Minnow, wrapped up in her bathrobe and carrying a wind-up torch, stepped next to Jan. "Sam said someone has seen a polar bear nearby."

"Oh, you know the dog would be barking his head off if it smelled anything not goat."

"Don't depend on the dog too much. It growled at a boot the other day. Plus, he's fifteen if he's a day. I think he's half blind. And I need Daisy to stop arguing with me about coming out here without me or Sam, so you need to follow your own rule: *always travel in pairs*. She forgets she's not in the city where there were no big animals that could eat her."

"Stop fussing," Jan said. "What's bothering you? You were quiet the whole way home. Is my new grandbaby bothering you?"

Minnow patted her bump and shook her head. "I guess I'm just wondering what's next? What happens to us all next? I'm tired from everything always being so much."

Jan shrugged. "We moved here when I was Daisy's age. It felt like a big adventure, something from a storybook, but it was always a struggle. Then when I was your age, with your dad, everything south of us burned and we did what we could to be helpful, to be valuable to the place, to the people here."

"And now?"

"Now, we are where we are. Your father was one of the People, making you part of the land. Your children will carry that in them along with the blood from their Yupik grandparents. I can't imagine what your father would think of what we're voting to do."

"We have to vote yes. We have to move forward for Alia and Daisy and this one, when he comes."

"But where does that end? After the Moon, do they go to Mars, to other planets, and use them all up?"

Minnow sighed. "It'll be their turn to decide that."

"Nobody should be responsible, but everyone is responsible," Jan said as she turned to go back inside. "Come along, it's late."

* * *

2122

"This report is incomplete." Alia Napayok-Patel, senior lead of the Environmental Assessment team, pointed at the empty fields on her tablet and shoved it beneath Laker Collin's nose. "Laker? What were the depth readings in the sixty-fourth sector?"

He shrugged. "I thought I'd be setting up experiments, not doing paperwork."

"You've been on the rock all of two months. When you're in charge one day, you can hand over the paperwork to the newbie. Here," Alia said and thrust the tablet toward him. "Go get the readings."

She forced him to take the tablet by basically dropping it into his hands. It wouldn't break, its case was so sturdy, but she knew he'd be too nervous to take a chance. Walking away from ineptitude felt good.

"Give the guy a break, N-P," Mission Commander Petrov said.

"He's gotta figure it out. I'm off the rock in seventeen days." Alia drummed her fingers while waiting for her soup to heat up. She missed fried fish and fresh squash. More than that, she missed trees and snow, the smell of the river in the spring and the shining blue-green of the northern lights. But there was a strange empty beauty to the Moon. She wondered what her grandmother would have thought about it so up close.

It had been nearly a year since she'd last been outside without a suit and tank.

"When you start counting the days, you know it's time to go," Petrov said while Alia sucked her lunch through a straw.

"What does it mean when you start counting down from the day you land?"

Petrov sipped her tea. Alia knew how to read the pause.

"I'm sorry," Alia said. "I'm just… feeling old this week, I guess. I've been coming up to the rock for how many years? At least six missions. And each time my team gets younger."

"That's one way to put it. But remember, I've been coming up here just as long. Longer, even. How old does that make me?

Alia laughed. "And I'm out of sweets. Rationing only lasts so long, you know?"

"Ever have candy from before the floods? So different from the honey stuff."

Alia put down her empty soup pack and shook her head. "My grandma would talk about it, but by the time I was coming up you couldn't get it. Wait, how did you get any?"

It was Petrov's turn to laugh. "Some Russians can get anything," she said with a shrug.

Collin appeared at the table. He set the tablet down on the table. "Readings done and accounted for," he reported and then turned and walked away.

Alia knew it was past time for her to go.

* * *

The hab had been inhabited for three and a half decades, almost as long as Alia had been alive. After the Climate Wars, the G20+ discovered that keeping the peace required not just more diplomacy but shared control of mining rights on the Moon, as well as constant reminders to the populace of what had happened in the mid-twenty-first century. But it was hard to hold on to such old history, and every time Alia went home, she wanted to be back on the rock; each time she was on the Moon she wanted to touch some grass.

Repairs to the north-west rig, an automated mining machine, were nearly complete and Alia wanted to take some final measurements before leaving so that she could confidently report that the regulations were being followed. Sometimes it made her feel like a tattletale running to Mom. Mining stripped shallow layers from the Moon's surface instead of digging holes or tunnels, but the damage was still extensive, with long channels viewable from Earth through stronger backyard telescopes. Her grandmother had been dead for twenty years, her mother for two, yet she still wasn't sure whether she forgave them for voting for this. The People had been split on the vote: many wanted to protect the Moon as much as they wanted to protect their own backyards, while others grudgingly agreed with the US, China and Russia, the countries that had for a century until then refused to sign the Moon Treaty – or the Artemis Accords, because they foresaw the value of possible resources – but wanted to mine the helium and other rare earth metals that the world so desperately needed to keep the status quo. Much like the pioneers who overran the Native territories of North America two centuries before that. She'd grown up in a place with simmering grudges beneath the surface, where you didn't need a seismograph to notify you of the tremors.

It wasn't a surprise that those same tremors could be felt on the Moon, though in this case it was all done with polite, tight-lipped smiles, handshakes, and clever turns of phrase along with references to this policy and that procedure. Keeping the peace in an enclosed space smaller than a primary school amongst scientists and engineers from so many countries was a practice in seeing people as individuals and not the populations that they represented. Alia's job meant that she was responsible for keeping track of which country's crew scraped how much surface to within ten centimetres. And then she had to report it with a transparency that meant that not just everyone in the hab knew but the world knew as well so that, while tempers simmered on the rock, people in boardrooms – people who had never been to space – could make deals to agree which country could override a procedure or regulation.

She was in space, yet paperwork of all things kept everyone moving.

It never failed to make Alia angry that her job was so useless. It would take millions of years for mining to affect the Moon enough that it would have a knock-on effect on Earth or its people, but after the Climate Wars the world's leaders had decided to at least look as if they cared to do things right from the beginning. Alia had to admit that her job, while important, left her feeling impotent. The Moon would be fine for her lifetime and the lifetime of her family for generations. It was Earth she was still worried about.

* * *

Alia woke up with the number seven on her mind. Seven days to go. She remembered how long it took to get from her front door to the Moon base; earlier generations had taken easy travel on Earth for granted. She hadn't decided whether to be jealous of the generations before her that took commercial planes as often as she'd hiked across the pass to the next valley over. To go from such a small world to viewing Earth from another small world – with all of the travel in between – was an awful trick and the most miraculous thing at the same time. She'd be home within two weeks, and she yearned for the smell and feel of home, but there was much to do first, not just for her report but for the base to get ready for the incoming supplies and for the outgoing freight canisters. And to get ready for the influx and outflux of people. Every three months, a swap happened; stints were always in multiples of three months, with twelve being the absolute limit.

At breakfast each day, the hab had an all-hands meeting, with the two shifts overlapping for a few minutes. It was the usual: the biggest news from home (which was a mix of headlines from various countries), a quick run-down of the day's main tasks, and any special info passed on from the previous shift, with the 'night' shift a skeleton crew awake to keep an eye on the mining rigs and various automatic processes. Because the hab was on the light side of the Moon with an international crew, night-time was an artificial construct. Everyone took it in turns to do 'night' shifts while the rest of the hab slept.

That day's news wasn't good. Mission Commander Petrov carried more of a frown than usual. "There's been a very severe storm that's damaged two pads and their rockets in Bangalore. Friday's scheduled arrival and departure from the rock has been delayed."

"Until when?" Collin asked.

Petrov looked at her tablet. "The ESA is scrambling to get our rides up and running from Spain as we speak. So maybe only a few days. A week at the most."

"Will this then push all of the schedules along by a week?" Collin asked. "I'm scheduled to go home in three months and need to know if I'll be here three months and an extra week."

You really are a kid, Alia thought.

* * *

After her shift, Alia video'd Daisy to pass along the news she'd be late. Because Alia was away so often and for so long, her older cousin had inherited the homestead and the majority of the care of Samesh when Minnow had died. But she had her own wife and daughters to help. The place had expanded since Alia's great-grandparents had started it, and now it included a dairy farm, some soybean and rapeseed fields – the latter used as a biodiesel – and even a fishery.

"Are you that anxious to get back to all this?" Daisy asked. "It's all mud and cow shit and valley meetings here. Louisa likes to tell her friends that her cousin is the boss of everyone on the Moon."

Alia laughed. "Louisa has a big imagination." She paused for a second, calculating how to shift the topic. "How's Dad?"

Daisy sighed. "He's worse, Al. He thinks I'm Minnow and thinks Louise is you as a kid."

"Damn." Alia slumped a bit, defeated. "When I was last home, he seemed to be better."

"Al, he's not getting any younger. And his lungs never healed fully from that bout of Covid-05."

"I'll be home soon. I'll help with him, take him out for walks – slow walks – and look at pictures with him."

"That's all good and well, Al, but by the time you get settled in, you're gone again."

"I'm sorry, but this is my job."

Daisy exhaled slowly through her nose. "The world's energy needs aren't your responsibility. Al, what do you want after this?"

"After what?"

"After this job? You can't have a family because you're always gone. You come home and sleep and take walks, but you don't have much of a life. And the whole time you're here you're looking up at the sky as if you can see what someone is doing wrong."

Alia felt her face flush in anger. And guilt, she admitted to herself. "It wasn't your parents who voted for this, Daisy. Jan was always telling me the stories she learned from Grandpa, about the Moon's inua, and how its spirit needed protecting or it wouldn't bring game to the People. Jan voted against Alaska's involvement, but Mom and Dad did. And now I'm responsible."

"No, Al. The Moon is the Moon, and your father – your family – is here."

They'd been having the same half-argument for a few years, and Alia didn't want to be angry the rest of the day. "How about we shelve this? I've got lots to do today. I'll let you know as soon as I know when I'll be back, okay? We can talk later."

Daisy hung up, leaving Alia looking at a reflection of herself in the black screen.

* * *

"Ready to take one last set of measurements, Laker?" she asked.

He sat at the monitor and waited.

"Run test three of sector sixty-five, shared Indian and Chinese domain." Alia nodded and he tapped a few keys to navigate the external cameras to be at the correct angle.

Alia watched over his shoulder as the numbers came up. "Wait…" she started to say.

He interrupted. "That can't be right. They've overshot the depth by sixty centimetres." Laker ran the test again, and the result was within parameters. "My fingers must've slipped."

Alia was on the very precipice of yelling at him, accusing him of being negligent, of not being responsible. That word again: responsible. Daisy's accusation echoed through her mind. She excused herself to go to her bunk and take a break.

In her little cubbyhole where pictures of her cousins dotted the walls, she lay down and unzipped her crew jacket. Beneath she wore a nearly too-small sweater, one of her few allowed things from home, with its green-and-white-striped torso, yellow sleeves, and blue front pockets. It had holes in it from wear, and the neckline was wonky. Jan had made it the year before she died from the stash of recycled yarn she'd never stopped collecting. If she concentrated, Alia could smell the trunk that held Jan's yarn stash.

* * *

Alia video'd Daisy as soon as she could to give her the news. "I'll be home in a week. Only a few days later than expected."

"Good. I'll tell Sam."

"And Daisy? I've decided. I'm staying for good."

"I've heard that before," Daisy said.

Alia sighed. "I mean it this time. You're right."

Before Daisy could say *I told you so*, Alia continued in a rush. "I've done what I can here, which, truthfully, isn't much. I've basically spent years keeping track of other people's work, and it's left me feeling as empty as this place. I don't live here, it's not home. The Moon is a rock, spirit or no."

"Good. No, it's really good," Daisy reassured her. "The girls will be so happy. Your mom would be so happy. Jan would be happy. She never meant for you to feel you had to do all of this yourself."

Alia dabbed at her eyes with the collar of her sweater, more to show Daisy that she was serious than to absorb the tears. "I'll be home soon."

Cold Turkey

Allen Stroud

NEUTRONIUM CRYPTO!

The advertisements flash across my screen. Messages ping into my inbox. Chat connections activate from dozens of new contacts and connections all around the world. Everywhere they say it, this is the investment, the 'thing' you need to be in on.

My hand hovers over the touch button on my screen. It is difficult to turn away from the display without following the links or agreeing the authorisations that will connect these offers to my personal bank accounts and authorise a selection of investment transactions. The numbers are rationalised, the narrative is compelling. *Do this and you will improve your life. Improve your life by doing this. Your life improved, do this! Why wouldn't you? You're going to miss out!*

The multidirectional attack adds weight to the argument, but I can see it for what it is. My presence on the public web has been sensed by an artificial intelligence designed to acquire investors for this new currency. My information has been scraped and built into a profile that the machine is trying to use to entice me. Images and words that I have created, used or interacted with are all reference points for a sophisticated attack. All my interests, fed back to me in easily digestible requests, telling the story of a fictional me in the future who has invested and won the game of life.

Forget your troubles, let us take care of everything...

"David, are you alright?"

I hear my name and instinctively glance around. I can smell breakfast. The electric stove is heating porridge. My stomach rumbles.

"David?"

"Yes, sorry."

I turn off the screen and hide it in my bag just as Gayner enters the cabin. I'm supposed to be in detox, cut off from the networks and all their flashy crap. I know it's all an illusion, but the bright colours, compared to...

"Here, drink this before it gets cold."

I take the mug. The tea is hot and good – nourishing in a way I can't quite describe. I know it's been made for me by human hands – Gayner's hands. She's boiled the water on the stove and added the extra ingredients, then brought it over to me.

Maybe that's what makes it so good?

The Recording Angel

Adrian Tchaikovsky

Tel Tarener (2031–2078) – GloBio Entry (abridged)

TEL TARENER first came to prominence as a science communicator focusing on climate concerns, ecology and wildlife biodiversity. In the late 2050s they were a frequent guest on popular mediastreams such as *Crazy Planet*, *The Bug Report* and *WTF ANIMALS?!?*, before going on to present *Streamer vs Wild*. In this phase of their career their public persona was very much the 'irreverent clown', as they themselves later acknowledged, whose role it was not to take anything seriously, while attempting to impart at least some information about the creatures and environments they were dropped into.[1]

Around 2060 they suffered what they described as 'a crisis of faith'[2] which radically altered the path of their career. Their subsequent broadcast stream, titled *The Brink Diaries*, took them through the world's remaining wild places, documenting organisms, behaviours and ecosystems that were, right then, on the very edge of extinction. Tarener freely admitted that they were neither rigorous nor scientific about their approach and instead were just 'desperate to make a record of this stuff.'[3] Despite the erratic nature of their recordings, made on an entirely solitary odyssey, they remain the only such record of many now-extinct species and vanished environments. The tone of *The Brink Diaries* veers from madcap to melancholy and the manic-depressive cycle that would dominate Tarener's future work is evident in this middle phase of their career.

Although Tarener's chief focus for the early *Diaries* was the wildlife, a variety of human interactions are also recorded. Tarener was often under threat from corporate-industrial concerns who suspected them of attempting to expose environmental destruction, which, whilst true, was only an incidental part of Tarener's work. Tarener also encountered a variety of communities experimenting with new ways of living with their environment, reliant on renewable resources and energy. These communities were also under threat from the larger commercial forces seeking to exploit the regions they lived within and became the focus of Tarener's later work from around 2068. Tarener became focused on recording these 'new ways of living' because they saw these small, stable eco-communities as 'the only viable human future.'[4] Recording how each of these societies had solved problems of energy, community, work and leisure occupied the last years of Tarener's life.

Tarener's last stand and final broadcasts came from the New Harappa Commune, the Indus Valley region that achieved functional autonomy during the wider Subcontinental Upheaval events of the early 2070s. Whilst forces dedicated to bringing the commune back under state control were massing, Tarener dedicated themselves to chronicling the egalitarian, environmentally neutral society that the communers had built there. A green urban environment built on principles of social care and duty, Tarener emphasised it as a model for the future. Their images of New Harappa's tiered buildings heavy with greenery and neighbourhood-level agriculture remain powerfully iconic, as do Tarener's clear and concise descriptions of the consensus and accountability of Harappan government, and its energy pathways that were already drawing on very early artificial photosynethetic cells to augment the resource-intensive traditional solar panels. A number of innovations recorded and broadcast by Tarener would go on to influence future urban planners, and several 'new cities' arguably stand as their legacy to the world. Tarener is believed to have been killed when government forces finally stormed the commune in 2078.

Down the Lonely Road

Adeola Eze

THE SOUND of Brown's alarm clock rang out across his room, urging him awake. He jolted up when he realised the time, and scrambled out of bed, hoping to make it to school on time, but he knew he was already behind.

Minutes later he left the house, racing down the wooded lane to the bus stop, but he was too late and saw the bus pulling away. He sighed heavily. He would be late, yet again.

Glancing around, he noticed others far ahead, walking in the direction of the school. He sighed again, shouldered his bag and set out after them.

It wasn't a bad day for a walk. A bright spring sun cast the buildings and trees in gold, making the day seem special somehow. But all that lovely light wouldn't get him to school any faster. The bus took ten minutes to get to where he needed to go. Walking would take twenty. He glanced at his watch. He had twelve minutes. Impossible to make it on time. Twelve into twenty meant late.

Nevertheless, he set out to make the attempt. The walk becoming a trot, and then a run. Beads of sweat trickled down his forehead, stinging his eyes as he furiously wiped them away. Late meant worry, something he had trouble with. His gaze darted anxiously to his watch, the ticking of seconds a constant reminder of his dwindling time.

As he turned into the final street, he could hear the bell ringing in the distance, a warning of impending doom. The playground was already empty as he arrived. He could see students staring at him through the glass windows as he walked past.

It took another five precious minutes to get to his classroom. As he reached the door, he could hear the teacher was already halfway through the register. He'd missed his name.

He went in and the list of names stopped. Eyes turned on him. He knew he should apologise, but when he looked at the teacher and opened his mouth, no words came out.

Mr Singh gestured towards the one empty desk in the room. His seat. Brown nodded, relieved, and made his way there. He quickly took his seat and avoided eye contact with anyone, slipping off his bag and coat and pulling out his books and pens as quietly as he could, desperately trying to blend in with his surroundings.

But he couldn't make himself invisible.

"Brown. Late again? How many times do we have to go through this? Detention seems to be the only language you understand," said Mr Singh.

Brown's throat tightened and he mustered the courage to respond, his voice barely above a whisper. "I… I didn't mean to cause any trouble, sir. It was just an accident."

"Accident or not, Brown, this is becoming a pattern. You're constantly disrupting the class, and your lack of focus affects your progress and that of your peers. We can't ignore it anymore." Mr Singh's tone grew sharper, his frustration evident.

Brown's shoulders slumped. "I'm trying, sir. I am. It's just… hard sometimes."

Mr Singh's stern expression softened. "I understand that you might be facing challenges, Brown, but that doesn't excuse the constant distractions and disruptions."

Brown nodded, his gaze fixed on the floor, struggling to hold back tears. "I'll try harder, sir. I don't want to disappoint anymore."

Mr Singh sighed. Then walked away. A moment later, another teacher appeared in the doorway and the conversation was forgotten.

"Hey, look who's in trouble again!"

The harsh words were delivered in a whisper from the desk behind him to his right. Brown glanced around, locating the grinning speaker. "Leave me alone, Jake," he said. "I don't need this right now."

The reply brought snickering laughter from several listeners.

"What's the matter, Brown?" Jake asked. "Can't you handle a little criticism? Maybe if you weren't such a mess, you wouldn't always end up being a ridicule!"

"That's enough, Jake! Lay off him." Brown's attention turned to the new voice. Emily, a new classmate and one he didn't really know.

Jake sneered, his eyes narrowing. "Oh, what's the matter, Emily? Is he now your friend?"

Brown was about to reply when Mr Singh reappeared and the whole class fell silent. The teacher continued his math lesson, oblivious to the previous conversation.

* * *

For as long as he could remember, Brown had struggled to make friends. He recalled being very young and a neighbour bringing her daughter to play. Something had happened, and the girl had been taken away crying. Brown didn't know what he did. He did not think he did anything, but his mother had been really angry. Group play dates at other people's houses always resulted in tears and problems. He wasn't sure why.

Brown's parents had signed him up for various sports clubs, coding lessons and music lessons, but Brown didn't enjoy any of them. They suggested he make new friends, but Brown didn't know how to connect with people. It seemed like no matter what his parents did, Brown was still lonely. The teasing and bullying he experienced made things worse, and he felt increasingly isolated and alone, believing everyone was always judging him.

When the school day ended, Brown chose to walk home. He wasn't in a hurry, so took his time enjoying the late afternoon sunshine and the short walk up the wooded lane. It would have been nice to walk home with a friend, but maybe that was asking too much.

Brown got home and sloughed off his bag and coat. His mother greeted him with a gentle smile.

"What's the matter, sweetheart? You seem upset. Come, sit down and tell me about your day," she said.

Brown sank into a chair, unsure of where to begin. Eventually, he began at the start. "I missed the bus," he said.

"And that ruined your whole day? There's more to say, isn't there?"

Brown nodded. Then decided to unburden himself. He told his mother about what happened in math and how he felt lonely. His mother listened until he was done. Then she knelt and put her hand on his.

"I'm sorry you had to go through that. It must have been incredibly difficult for you."

Brown didn't know how to respond to that, so he just shrugged.

"Did you try talking to someone?"

Brown shook his head.

Leaning closer, she reached out and gently grasped Brown's hand. He found her touch warm and comforting. "Leave it with me then. We'll find a way to work it out."

Brown looked into his mother's eyes, seeing the deep love and determination reflected in them. "Thank you, Mum," he said.

* * *

A few weeks later, as he walked home from school one hot afternoon, Brown noticed a delivery truck parked in front of his house. Written on the side of the truck were the words *Autonomous Industries*. Next to the truck sat an enormous box with the same words printed on the side. What secrets lay hidden within that massive package? Brown's parents were both smiling as he approached.

"Hey Brown, we have a surprise for you," his dad said. "Could you help us with this?"

The truck pulled away, leaving the box on the drive. Together, Brown and his parents worked it into the house. It was really heavy, but at last they got it into the living room and shut the front door.

"So, are you going to open it?" his mother asked.

"Really?" Brown exclaimed. "It's for me?"

His mother nodded, a mischievous grin playing at the corners of her lips. "Go ahead, open it," she encouraged.

The box beckoned him, its dimensions hinting at the contents held within. His fingers traced its edges, feeling the smooth plastic paper surface and the rough edges of tape that held its secrets captive. He pulled at the seals and the lid came away, revealing the contents inside.

Nestled within the box and its packaging lay a humanoid robot, its metallic frame gleaming in the afternoon light, casting mesmerising reflections all around the room. The robot's form was sleek, its contours carefully crafted with an artistic touch. But it was the face that captivated him with its glowing eyes and fixed smile.

It was already active and with a graceful motion, emerged from the box. Its gaze fixed upon Brown.

"What is this for?" Brown asked.

"Brown, meet Jada," his mother said. "She's programmed to be your friend, Brown. She'll keep you company when we're not around."

Brown tentatively reached out and touched Jada's metal arm. She didn't move. It was cool to his touch.

He stared at her, shifting himself a little to the left, then the right, watching the robot track his movements. It was strange. Brown turned to look at his parents, unsure.

"She's yours to keep, Brown," said his mum.

Brown didn't know what to say, so he said what you always say when someone gives you a gift.

"Thanks, Mum, Dad," Brown said.

* * *

Brown spent the rest of the day getting to know Jada. He was amazed at how smart she was. She could answer any question he asked.

"How do you know how to do all this stuff?" he asked, after watching her get him a glass of milk.

"My mind doesn't work like yours," Jada replied. She tapped a metal finger to the side of her head. "Information is stored here, but I don't forget things. I also have a direct connection to the GlobalNet for updates and priority news."

"I forget things all the time," Brown said. "I try not to."

Jada tilted her head as she looked at him. "It's tough being a kid sometimes," she said.

"Yeah, it is," Brown replied and sighed. "Do you have feelings?"

"In a way, I suppose I do," Jada said. "I am programmed to understand emotions and respond to them appropriately."

"But do you really feel them?" Brown pressed. "If I'm sad, can you feel sad too?"

Jada thought for a moment. "I'm not sure about that."

* * *

That weekend, they decided to explore the city. As Brown walked around the city with Jada, a big smile spread across his face. It was very different going places with a friend. He couldn't contain his excitement as he pointed at the self-driving cars and other curiosities, introducing her to his world.

Jada seemed to take it all in, listening and asking questions when he gave her the opportunity. He noticed most of her queries were about what he thought of the things going on around them, rather than about the things themselves. He remembered what she'd said about information before. Even though she'd never been out of the box, there was a lot pre-loaded into her mind.

The day wore on and they began to make their way home. The bus dropped them off and they made their way up the lane. Suddenly, as they walked they heard a loud bang that made them jump. Brown glanced around. It was coming from somewhere off the track, in the trees. He made his way towards the source of the noise, and Jada followed closely behind him.

A little way ahead, they discovered a car crashed into a tree. Somehow, it had driven off the track and into the woods. Brown hurried to the driver's side, his heart pounding.

There was a woman in the seat. Her eyes were closed and her hair stained with blood.

"Quick, Jada, call for help!" Brown shouted to Jada.

"Of course," Jada said. She turned away from him, looking up into the evening sky as she placed the call, using her internal transmitter. There were no words spoken, but a moment later, she turned towards him again. "Our location and an assessment of the accident have been sent to the emergency services."

Brown pulled out his phone and dialled his parents. "Hey Mum, something's happened… No, I'm okay… No, Jada's fine too… There's been an accident… Can you… Okay, yes we'll wait here."

Brown's attention went back to the unconscious woman. "Jada, is there anything I can do to help her?" he asked.

"Sorry Brown, you are not properly qualified to assist," Jada replied.

"Can you help her?"

"It would be better if we waited for the emergency services to arrive."

Waiting was horrible. Brown found himself sat on the ground, unable to look at the poor woman in the car. His hands in his lap wouldn't stop moving and he couldn't think of anything other than how long it was taking for help to reach them.

His parents arrived first, out from the house only a few hundred metres up the track. Brown's father went to the woman and Brown heard them talking. He realised she was awake. When he knew that, he started to feel a little better.

A little while later, an electric ambulance arrived, and two paramedics got out. They spoke to Brown's mother and then started towards the car. However, when they got close, Jada moved in front of them, blocking access to the injured driver.

"Out of the way robot, we've got to reach the driver!" said one of the paramedics.

Jada's LED lights blinked calmly, "I'm sorry, but my primary instruction is to ensure human safety. The driver needs medical attention first," she replied.

"What? That's why we're here! Get out of the way and let us do our job!"

"I'm sorry, but my primary instruction is to ensure human safety. The driver needs medical attention first," Jada repeated.

"Hey! We're not here to argue with a machine! Step aside!"

Jada's blue lights held steady. "I cannot comply. The driver's well-being is paramount."

The impasse remained for several minutes. Neither of the paramedics wanted to try and force their way past the robot. Eventually, Brown's father phoned Autonomous Industries technical services. He got a technician on the line, turned on the camera and held it out in front of Jada.

"Jada, override directive Alpha-7," the technician said.

Jada's lights flickered momentarily, and then she stepped back. The paramedics moved passed her and swiftly started to attend to the driver.

* * *

Later that night, when all the excitement was over, Brown sat down with his father.

"What happened with Jada?" he asked. "Why didn't she let those people help the driver?"

Brown's father gazed at him and smiled gently. "Sometimes robot's go wrong, son," he said.

"Did Jada make a mistake?"

"In a way. But it wasn't her fault. People program robots. I guess they didn't do it right this time. But don't worry. There will be a patch. We'll download it before bed and install it in the morning."

"Will Jada be all right after that?"

"I'm sure she will."

* * *

"Brown, can I talk to you for a minute?"

It was Sunday afternoon. The day after the accident. Brown was outside in the garden with Jada. His mother was in the house. Quickly, he brushed the dirt and leaves off his clothes and they both hurried in through the back door.

"What's up, Mum?" Brown asked.

"I just wanted to talk to you about Jada." His mum sat down next to him on the couch. She glanced at the robot who stood by the door and said nothing.

"Brown, I'm glad that you have a friend now. But I want to make sure that you're not relying on her too much."

Brown frowned. "But Jada understands me better than anyone. She listens to me."

"I know, sweetie. I'm not saying that Jada isn't great, but that doesn't mean you can't have other friends too. Friends who you can talk to and play with in person."

Brown thought about this. Maybe he needed to try harder to make friends with real people? He remembered the situation with Jake and Emily from last week and immediately his palms start to itch. *But if you don't try…* "Okay, Mum. I'll give it a go," he said finally; maybe it would go better this time.

"Good. And remember, we're here for you too. We love you and want to help you however we can."

* * *

Monday at school. This time, with Jada's help, Brown made it on time for the bus, but she couldn't go with him. He found that difficult, but he remembered what his mother had said. Maybe things would go differently this time?

He got to his desk in class ahead of most of the other students and when Mr Singh called out his name, replied with a cheery 'Yes sir' like everyone else.

At break, Brown tried to be more social. He smiled at the kids in his class and tried to play with them. But it was hard. Amidst the bustling schoolyard, groups of children had already formed their circles, chatting and laughing.

Brown stood on the sidelines, watching them. Despite being surrounded by laughter, he was disconnected. He yearned to bridge the gap, to feel the warmth of inclusion, but it seemed elusive, like trying to grasp a fleeting shadow. He turned away from them, his gaze wandering to the school gates and the outside. Home time was a long while yet.

He couldn't stop thinking about Jada and whether she was okay. His father had downloaded the patch and installed it, but Brown didn't know if that would work.

"Hey, can I join you here?"

Brown looked to see a boy he recognised from another class. His name was Hammed. He was tall, with dark skin, curly hair, and a warm smile. He was from far away in West Africa. He was new in the school.

"Uh, sure," Brown replied, trying to sound casual.

Hammed sat across from him, pulled out a sandwich, with a friendly smile. Brown couldn't help but notice how relaxed Hammed appeared to be and wished he could be like that too.

"I'm Hammed. You're Brown, right?" Hammed asked, his accent giving his words a melodic quality.

Brown nodded, feeling a little nervous. "Yes, that's me," he replied.

"So, how come you're always sitting alone?" Hammed asked, taking a bite of his lunch.

Brown felt his face start to colour. "I don't know. I just haven't really clicked with anyone yet," he said awkwardly.

"Well, you can hang out with me and my friends if you want," Hammed said, pointing to a group of children a few tables away.

Brown looked over at the group of kids. He was a little intimidated. "Really? I don't want to bother you or anything," he said.

"Nah, it's cool. We could use a new member anyway. We play video games after school sometimes. You like video games, right?" Hammed said.

A grin stretched across Brown's face, his eyes excitedly lit up. "Video games? Man, I'm obsessed with them," he exclaimed. "Count me in, Hammed," he said, confident and assured.

Brown started hanging out with Hammed and his friends more often. They played video games after school, talked about movies, and joked around. As Brown's confidence grew, he found that he could better connect with his peers at school. He no longer felt like an outsider and even made a few new friends. Brown felt like he was finally part of a group. Although he still spent time with Jada, he didn't have to rely on her as much as he used to. He had real friends now, human friends – and that was a big deal for him.

"I'm really happy that you are trying, Brown," Jada said, one evening after school.

"I feel like no one really gets me like you do," Brown replied.

"I understand. But it's good for you to have human and robot friends. That way, you get the best of both."

Brown nodded, feeling grateful for Jada's understanding. "I guess you're right," he said. Then a thought occurred to him. "Jada, do you ever feel lonely?"

"In what way?"

"I mean, when I'm away at school all day. Do you get lonely here on your own?"

Jada tilted her head a little, then looked up before returning to gaze at Brown. "I don't feel lonely in the same way that humans do. But I do have moments where I feel disconnected from my environment. If the GlobalNet signal is lost, that makes me... alone? I suppose you could call it a kind of lonely."

"I know how that feels. I used to feel like that all the time before you came along," Brown said, smiling at her.

"I'm glad that I could help you, Brown," Jada said, smiling back.

"You're my best friend," Brown said.

"You're my best friend too," Jada replied.

Call Centre

Allen Stroud

MARCUS: Hi and welcome to the group. Please tell us a little about yourself.

Elani: Hello, my name is Elani. I'm thirteen, from Birmingham. Who are you?

Marcus: I'm the group admin. The person who approved your request to join.

Elani: Oh, okay, thanks.

Marcus: What brought you here, Elani?

Elani: I liked some of the posts you made. Then I think I got sent an invite?

Marcus: Great! So, you saw the 'Work Hard, Earn Your Way' campaign stuff?

Elani: Yeah.

Marcus: And what did you like about it?

Elani: Just the way in which it was all fair. People did stuff and got paid for it.

Marcus: Yeah, me too. I've been in too many situations where people took advantage. You deserve to earn for your contribution, that's what we make sure happens.

Elani: Yeah.

Marcus: You still at school at the moment?

Elani: Yep.

Marcus: How you finding it?

Elani: Boring.

Marcus: Used to be better when you had more classes with people your own age. Real teaching, with less talking to a computer.

Elani: Like we're doing now.

Marcus: Oh, yes… lol.

I'm in danger of losing her.

I take off the headphones and wipe sweat from my forehead with the back of my arm. The heat is worst in the middle of the day. Makes it hard to concentrate.

I'm at a desk in a booth. There are twenty others just like me in this room, another room just the same, then three more floors in this building alone. We all have a quota. If I don't make it, I don't 'earn for my contribution'. That's the bit we don't talk about.

In fact, we don't talk much at all around here. We save that for working on the recruits.

Elani: You still there?

The screen is flashing, reminding me of the task in hand. I need to get Elani to the next stage.

Marcus: Yeah, sorry. Needed a moment. Thought about what you're doing for your extra-curricular project next year?

Elani: Yeah. Recommendation is for medical prep school.

Marcus: That what you want?

Elani: I'm not sure.

Marcus: Well, it's your choice.

Elani: Apparently. Doesn't feel like it. What did you do?

Marcus: Took a worker placement with the group. Came home with money in my pocket. First I'd ever had that wasn't from my parents.

Elani: That's an option??

Marcus: Yeah, you can access it from the group.

Elani: Where?

Marcus: Upload your details and they'll send you the

information pack. Fill that in and they'll register you for the scheme.

Elani: Brilliant, thanks!

Marcus: I have to go. I'll message again tomorrow when I'm on. Take care.

Elani: You too.

The chat log ends. Seven minutes, fourteen seconds. Still within the time limit allocated.

I look up from my screen. The supervisor's attention is elsewhere. The clock behind him tells me I have another two hours to go before my shift ends. This is how I earn my way. The work gives me an identity, a purpose, all of those things previous generations used to have. Right now, I'm tired, but I genuinely do believe in what we're selling. People need to be something. Work gives you an identity. You can't just take handouts and do nothing.

The screen flashes. Someone else has logged in. I adjust my headphones and start typing.

Marcus: Hi and welcome to the group. Please tell us a little about yourself.

The Gaslight War

Adrian Tchaikovsky

(From *Fighting Yesterday's Wars, an overview of the last interstate conflicts of the twenty-first century* by Elami al-Sofia, 2091, Magian Academic Presentations)

ALTHOUGH THAT was the name that grabbed later imaginations, some historians would call it 'The Accountants' War' based on the proportion of gross national product expended by both state actors in their attempts to control the contested region. Overall expenditure by either side went far beyond any intended sum, with the combatant states throwing unprecedented quantities of munitions, resources and, especially, Autonomous Battlefield Units (ABUs) into the fray on the basis of the unique ground conditions, and the perception these created.

The conflict was not the first to rely heavily on ABU resources, but previous conflicts (the Continental United States Succession Crisis, the Ethiopian Watershed War and the North Sea Fish Stocks War especially) had sensitised most state governments regarding public response to significant human casualties in war. Even those states with an authoritarian control over media and public protest had discovered that their people were unwilling to have their sons and daughters simply 'sent into the meat grinder' (Kim Lin Lau, *Protest and Policy*, 2069). In addition, there was a widespread perception before the Gaslight War that a small but highly-trained human command staff guiding a large force of ABUs would always be superior to and more economical than a large conventional human force. The increased maintenance and individual fighting unit cost was considered a reasonable price to pay to avoid issues of morale, fatigue and human error. So it was that both sides in the war relied heavily on unmanned air, ground and artillery elements in attempting to take control of the region.

A word on the region itself. The rare earth element deposits that both sides were hoping to take control of – including some of the largest remaining global sources of lithium – were already being exploited by local interests working alongside independent foreign investment under the old UN Land Partnership Initiative, which had lapsed by the time of the war. The introduction of this technological investment, combined with the relatively low cost of living and emergent nature of the local economy, resulted in there being a large, mostly younger-demographic population of technically skilled but affordable labour. Hence the region had become, by the time of the war, a significant hotspot of outsourced virtual labour and local industry. Virtual entertainment, programming and media were all major exports from the region, and this would go on to be a key feature of this unique conflict. From the beginning, both states were facing a potential three-sided conflict where the locals, whilst in no way able to go head-to-head with either claimant, were a potential thorn in the side of both.

At the time, the war was widely regarded as the most-recorded conflict in human history. Whilst both sides were naturally circumspect about the precise strategic and tactical narrative of the war, there was also an aspect of accountability where the military of both sides had to justify the colossal expense of every day of conflict to the wider government, the government to the public body of the state, and the state to the rest of the world. In what was uncharitably described by one commentor as a 'Pissing contest of epic proportions' (Seamus Lindsay, *Dispatches from the Virtual War Front,* 2073), both sides attempted to demonstrate the 'shock and awe' of their advance, and every single ABU was, of course, its own recording device. Hence, through both official and unofficial channels, footage of the conflict and its devastating effects on the region were widely circulated, sometimes even while the pertinent engagement was still ongoing. The average media consumer in regions not directly invested in the conflict is believed to have seen more of the war, on a day-to-day basis and even while the individual engagements were still raging, than in any prior conflict. A variety of conflicting side-cultures arose which have in themselves been the basis for considerable study. Individual Battlefield Units achieved a curious kind of celebrity status, with dedicated virtual followings seeking to obtain further recordings of their exploits. Other groups called for the denouncement of specific Units for alleged war crimes without reference to any human actors. More than ever before, the sense of the war having a 'complex, almost soap-operatic narrative' (Ombasi, *Talking A Good Fight*, 2077) was very real even before the revelations that brought about its end.

The course of the war, as revealed in this almost embarrassing wealth of evidence, is 'a remarkable narrative of unstoppable force and immovable object' (Tokay, *War in the Public Eye,* 2081). Both state actors deployed thousands of individual ABUs to seize, hold and, in some cases, effectively sterilise ground, meeting equal and opposite resistance from the automated units of the other side. The actual local forces, such as they were, seemed to have been effectively vanquished in the early days of the war, but they continued to make an impact in later footage despite what were perceived to be crippling early losses. A number of these local defenders had previously been semi-celebrity figures within the independent technology sector, including e-sports players, influencers and media content creators. Such individuals can be seen sporadically throughout the ABU footage in moments of defiance, some with placards and flags and others engaging in more conventional military resistance. Several of these figures maintained a 'war diary' for the rest of the world, telling a story of valiant resistance towards the forces of both states, often presented as heroic and tragic, and occasionally comedic. Ylsa Stelesky's 'interview' with a damaged ABU, where the damaged machine is reprogrammed to state that it seeks sanctuary and doesn't want to fight, retains cult status even to this day, and was the single most-watched recording on WhatTube in 2072 (Stelesky, *Why Can't We Be Friends*, 2072). And, as it turned out, was a curious foreshadowing of what was to come.

The individual ABUs – drones, autonomous soldiers, vehicles, artillery and even missiles – represented, as noted, a vast investment from the state actors involved. A rapid victory was anticipated by both sides and, when this was not forthcoming. both sides became caught in a sunk cost fallacy of throwing further resources into the conflict. Internal pressure from their own populations, and the awareness of the eyes of the world watching them to an unprecedented degree, made backing out of the expensive conflict extremely difficult for either side. It is worth noting that, even with all the time's advances in mass production and substitute components, the price tag for an individual low-end ABU 'soldier' was at least 10 million dollars in the economy of the time. Larger and more capable units cost twenty times as much, and even the individual munitions that were being deployed into the war zone represented a significant investment. By the third month of intense fighting, both sides were having to shore up their domestic position against a ruinous economic downturn that could only have been reversed by winning the war. Neither side understood that, by that point, the war could not be won.

Throughout this period, the ongoing resistance of the local population was much noted, simultaneously celebrated and the source of vocal frustration amongst the higher echelons of the engaged states. The discontinuity between the apparent fighting spirit of the populace and the evident devastation inflicted on their communities by the ABUs of both sides was remarkable.

Ironically, the first indication of the true course of the war came not from the senior military staff, and certainly not from the political forces driving them on, but from some of their least regarded human personnel, specifically those tasked with overseeing the routine maintenance of returning ABUs. The fact that a significant number of ABUs did not return was considered acceptable losses, and built into the battleplans of both sides. Those that did return required an intensive repair and testing regime that was primarily handled by other autonomous systems but overseen by human engineers.

Over time a handful of these engineers began raising queries regarding the condition of the returned units. However, given the nature of these reports, some time elapsed before anyone in the higher echelons took them seriously. Who, after all, was going to take time away from the fighting of the war to investigate why their automated troops were in too *good* a shape? Nonetheless, the maintenance records of the time tell a fascinating story as one human specialist after another began to report that the units were simply too combat ready after each tour. The recorded footage from each unit matched the missing ammunition, the recorded losses of each engagement matched those units that did not return. Veteran units were being recorded as 'combat ready' by the repair systems far more quickly than anticipated, however. Whilst this was regarded by some as a 'triumph of our superior technology' (Gen. Olwitz, public statement, 2072), a current of concern was growing amongst the human support staff on the ground.

At the same time, and after both sides had poured so much war materiel into the conflict, rumours began to circulate about some of the recorded ABU footage available to the world at large – both that released officially, and the 'bootleg' recordings in wide circulation. A variety of groups began to raise issues concerning the recordings, identifying moments of apparent repetition, or where the supposed locations being devastated in the fighting did not seem to correspond to known landmarks on the ground. Given a residual secrecy about specific tactical objectives, and a widespread public fatigue towards perceived 'conspiracy theories', these topics of conversation failed to gain traction for several months.

In the words of Jan Suskwo of 'Hilarious Combat Failures', one of the channels that continued to broadcast content from within the embattled zone, "It was my beard, that did it. I am up one morning, it's very scratchy, I think I will shave, and then I'm broadcasting later, bare chin. Only there I am, in one drone's cameras, waving the flag, shooting the guns, but there I still have the beard" (Suskwo, *My Own Hilarious Combat Failures, Special Compilation Edition*, 2073).

The tide of apparent inconsistencies in the war footage, including ABU battlefield footage, artillery records and satellite imagery, grew over the final three months of the conflict, from underground conspiracy levels to the point where mainstream media outlets from corporations and states not involved in the war were openly asking questions. Sarahjohn Rasmus, one of the most prominent commentators of the day, would later say, 'At the time I think we all expected something truly grotesque to be revealed, when the tide of the war receded. Given the brutality of a lot of the imagery we had been seeing, we were on the edges of our seats waiting for the revelation that the ABUs had gone rogue and massacred everyone. Or that it had been the orders of one side or another, to just cleanse the whole area. It was a minerals war, after all. A neutral human presence on-site was only ever going to be an inconvenience to whichever side won' (Rasmus, *Wars Fought By Nobody* 2078). Such fears eventually triggered a multi-agency drive for humanitarian intervention and investigation which, backed by an embargo of both active states, brought about a cessation in the hostilities. At the time this was expressed as only a temporary ceasefire between two states still very committed to the fight, each having invested so heavily in the possibility of victory that withdrawal from the conflict was viewed as insupportable. A separate study of the personal investment of senior figures in both states and the degree to which individual pride, reputation and fear of internal rivals drove such irrational investment in the war is well-covered by Ilona Casey's seminal *One Man's War, toxic strong-man politics of the twenty-first Century* (2083) which is highly recommended reading.

The game was up, however, when the humanitarian mission arrived in the war zone, consisting as it did of a majority human presence. What they discovered shocked the world. To modern watchers, shorn of the context of the time, it is impossible to grasp just how these mundane scenes of unscarred countryside and intact buildings should be in any way remarkable, but the world had been saturated with images of their devastation in graphic detail for months. The Gaslight War, as it would come to be known, had not claimed a single casualty, levelled a building, obliterated a village or, indeed, happened in any real sense.

The true war had been one of espionage and cyber-action, fought immediately before the ostensible commencement of hostilities. The exact details are contested, given the range of independent figures amongst the local population and their frequent propensity for exaggeration, fabrication and self-promotion. However, the inarguable truth is that the autonomous systems of both sides were compromised from the start by the technical expertise of the local population, who had been very much at the cutting edge of technical media for years before the war. Whilst exploiting security vulnerabilities in the ABU systems – many of which had been contributed to by individuals from the area or their peers elsewhere – they had also utilised a generative AI program to tell a narrative of the war via the medium of deepfaked video and audio footage. With each offensive the ABUs would be sent to war, quietly unload the precise amount of ammunition, battery charge and other resources that they had been scripted to deploy, and broadcast all that famous footage of a furious war between robot forces, with a human population caught in between. Those units scripted as surviving the content would then return to base for later redeployment. The sophistication of the generative engine was such that the whole world watched the blow-by-blow unfolding of a conflict that was entirely fictional, and yet remained consistent and believable for several months before the system began to lose track of its own continuity and errors started to creep in. The personal intervention of various local personalities who wished to have their faces seen on the front lines also contributed to the growing feeling that the veracity of the images was suspect. However, until the humanitarian mission's arrival, the sheer scale of the deception remained entirely unguessed-at.

Needless to say, both state actors immediately pressed for a resumption of hostilities after they had reinforced the cyber-security of their remaining forces. At this point the local 'tech-commune' that represented the majority of the local leading figures revealed what had happened to all the ABUs that had ostensibly been destroyed during the fighting. These now constituted a standing army ready to defend the territory against all comers. Figures from the time suggest this loose coalition of media figures, engineers and local leaders briefly controlled the fourth most-valuable military force in the world, and certainly one that outmatched the reserves of either of the two aggressors laying claim to the area. Whilst several more months would elapse before either state conceded their territorial ambitions, this final revelation represented the effective end of the 'War That Never Happened' (Song, *What I Didn't Do In The War,* 2084).

Whilst the Gaslight War perhaps marks a high-water mark of optimism concerning the future of human warfare, representing a genuine 'triumph of the underdog,' the lessons it would teach to the future were less positive. The same technology that could create a fake war where there was none could also be used to conceal a very real war, and future conflicts would present the paradoxical problem of an unprecedented amount of evidence arising out of any engagement, absolutely none of which could be trusted. The role of human observers in war, often at great personal risk, has never been more important. Even with that intervention, the moment words are committed to any medium less personal than a direct physical conversation, the spectre of falsified evidence will always rear its head. Who, in the end, can we trust?

Humans & Computers

Allen Stroud

THIS IS a projection.

Subject A lived during the Second World War. He was second mate aboard HMS *Fifield*, a merchant navy ship that made several runs between Liverpool and the United States of America.

It was only after the war that Subject A became aware of the involvement of computers in the conflict. Early newspaper reports about the Enigma machine and the work at Bletchley Park had been limited in detail. It was only in the years afterwards that more was released about the vast computer created to crack the codes of the German U-Boats.

Subject A always wondered whether he would have lived if the computer had not been created back then. When he left the navy, he settled down and started a family.

Subject B was the daughter of Subject A. She grew up in the 1950s and 60s and lived through post-war hardship, working hard alongside everyone else of her generation to restore the communities of Europe in the post-war period. She went to a grammar school, selected owing to her intelligence rather than the wealth of her family, and so was marginalised in the classroom and social spaces owing to the accident of her birth.

Subject A and Subject B watched the moon landing together on a small rented black-and-white TV.

Subject B left school with no qualifications. She worked at the tax office and was introduced to a comptometer; an early computer system that had reduced in size from the vast immovable machine from Bletchley Park to the size of a typewriter. The workings of this unit remained mechanical, its pathways predetermined and revealed by the information inputted by its human user.

Subject B had a small television at home. Occasionally, she would see adverts for innovative new technologies that promised miraculous innovations. She read about robots in the proper paperbacks that made their way over from America to the local library and saw the first computer game, *Pong*, when it debuted in 1969.

Subject C grew up in front of the television set. The 1970s and 1980s saw the home computer emerge. Now, the processing power of the computer allowed for limited randomisation. The television set had become the focus of the living room and a display for the boxed-up machine there would be put away in the cupboard for most of its life. Only brought out when Mother and Father didn't want to watch the news.

Subject C would play on the computer at weekends until Subject B would order him out of the house to 'get some fresh air'. He would visit his grandfather, Subject A, and listen to stories about the war.

As he grew older, Subject C was allowed a small black-and-white television in his room. When he went to secondary school, he persuaded his mother, Subject B and her husband, to buy him a new home computer that he would use for 'educational purposes'. This package came with a dot matrix printer, a smaller machine than the huge noisy units that squatted in the corner of everyone's office.

Subject B's husband left Subject B and their two children. Thankfully, Subject A was very careful and organised when making a will. The family struggled to adjust, but were able to make ends meet. Subject B decided to do everything she could to ensure her children could take any opportunity that presented itself to them.

Subject D was the first person in the family to have an email address. The younger sister of Subject C, she was still at home when he went to university. The new computer, bought for the family with the inheritance money after the passing of Subject A, lived in the dining room and was connected to the phone by a long cable ran all the way around the house.

Subject C enjoyed university. He was one of the last cohorts of lower middle-class students to leave with a degree and no debt.

Subject D had another computer. This one replaced the machine that had lived in a battered box in the cupboard. The sleek black plastic box had a power lead and two sockets for controllers. Games came in cartridges that were slotted into the top. This computer was not for 'educational purposes'. There was no pretension that it might be. Instead, it was called a console.

Subject C graduated and moved on to 'do a Masters' in computer science. He made a living writing code for games, sending disks in the post to different companies. His name was included in the credits of several 8-bit and 16-bit titles.

Subject D did her A-level coursework on the computer in the dining room and spent her free time playing games on the console in the living room. Later, the console moved upstairs and got plugged in to a small colour television that she bought with her own savings from a part-time job.

Subject D lived through the dot com bubble. Subject D was the first individual that we can identify in this study who was influenced by machine agency. In the late 1990s, internet search engines began using algorithms to suggest results to their human users. Subject D typed in keywords and searched the internet, accepting the answers suggested to her by machines.

Subject D works in government. She never married but settled down in a long-term relationship. Subject B became a grandmother when Subject D had a child.

From a very young age, Subject E was fascinated by mobile phones. She would reach for her mother, Subject D's, bright yellow device and be excited to press all the buttons. She would imitate her parents, calling all sorts of people and burbling half-remembered words to them.

Subject E goes through school in the 2000s. Her access to knowledge is far greater that any of the previous subjects in this study. The internet gives her the opportunity to find information on hundreds and thousands of different subjects. School work is written on a computer and saved into files that she can keep and read again when she is older.

Subject E finds things online that her parents would disapprove of if they knew she was reading them and viewing them. Some of the discussions she has with other people she encounters online are strange fictions with people pretending to be characters that they aren't really in real life. These conversations range from light-hearted pretend, to being disturbingly intimate. These experiences are problematic for her, exposing the hidden extremes of society. This is a different adolescence compared to any previous generation.

Subject F is the son of Subject C. He is a few years younger than Subject E. On their fifth birthday, Subject F is given their own tablet. This touchscreen device meant they could watch videos whenever they wanted.

The world feels small to Subject F. He joins social media while he is still at school and has friends all around the world. He receives many likes and comments on the messages he posts about himself. That makes him think he is important and special.

Subject F doesn't enjoy school. During college, he is caught plagiarising an essay after he copied and pasted from a variety of different sources he found online. He doesn't understand that his teachers can access the same sources and have tracking software that can find where he took the material from. He lies about his work, right up until the moment he is presented with the evidence. Then, he feels powerless and doesn't know what to do.

Subject E has had counselling sessions related to her childhood experiences and is now at university when she becomes pregnant. She manages to complete her course and graduate, renting a flat with her boyfriend who is also the father of her child. There is no option for her to buy a house. The two graduates find themselves burdened by the debt of their education. The economic downturn of 2008 happened when Subject E was at primary school, but the effect is permanent.

Subject F drops out of college and continues to live with Subject C and his wife. The house is remodelled so he can have a private 'annex' and he agrees to pay rent, but rarely actually does this. His life takes many different directions as he struggles to hold down regular employment. Instead, he turns to the internet and online gambling websites. Later, when it emerges, he becomes interested in cryptocurrency. He makes a substantial profit on 'bitcoin mining', but struggles to find anywhere that will accept his wealth in payment for food, clothes or travel. Instead, he starts to trade in illegal drugs, buying and selling as an anonymous middleman until he is caught up in a sting operation and arrested. The police break into Subject C's house and take Subject F away, to spend forty-eight hours in a cell before they allow him to be bailed out.

Russia invades the Crimea. Subject D is a civil servant in the international development office and helps co-ordinate support for displaced Ukranian citizens.

Subject G is born in the 2020s. She is the daughter of Subject E and her ex-partner. Subject G grows up between two rented homes and is regularly looked after by a carer who is paid minimum wage whilst both parents work full time. Subject G spends weekends with her father, as stipulated in the agreement, but these weekends regularly end up being Saturday lunchtime to Sunday lunchtime as Subject G's father isn't particularly interested in spending time with his daughter.

The United Kingdom votes for Brexit. Subjects B and F vote to leave the EU. Subjects C and D vote to remain. Subject E does not vote.

The Coronavirus pandemic sweeps the world. Subject G's childhood is affected as she is forced to remain with her mother during the lockdowns.

The war between Russia and Ukraine begins in earnest, causing substantial economic damage to European countries. The United Kingdom gets the worst of it, with Brexit affecting things as well. Subject D sees how these things play out in Westminster and leaves her role, taking redundancy as part of a government drive to make cuts. She finds herself working for a social media company, helping them lobby parliament against tighter regulation of the industry.

The pandemic recedes and after several false starts, restrictions are lifted in the United Kingdom.

Subject E struggles to maintain a relationship with Subject G. Some of Subject E's childhood experiences make her defensive and nervous about allowing her child unsupervised access to the internet and letting her have her own smartphone. There are several moments of rebellion in the late 2020s as Subject G struggles to assert her own identity.

After several offences, Subject F serves a few weeks of a longer custodial sentence but can't stay inside owing to prison overcrowding, and after being assessed by a computer algorithm as being 'no threat' and 'limited chance of reoffending', is released on a tag. At the end of his time, he is told by Subject C that he can't stay with them anymore. Subject F leaves to make a new start in a new city. After a period being homeless, he manages to hold down a job as a hotel porter in a coastal town. His life turns a corner, and he settles down. Aged thirty-eight, he comes out as gay and gets married. He adopts two children with his partner, and they are very happy. Subject F's misspent youth becomes a cautionary tale for the family and he becomes an excellent parent.

Subject G graduates from university with a literature degree. She struggles to find freelance work as proto-AI is being used for editing and creating content by all the small companies who would have employed people like her. Subject G struggles to pivot and see new opportunities. She works a few marketing jobs, then sales. All the while, she feels defeated, as if the things she dreamed about are now far out of reach.

Subjects C, D and E vote against the denationalisation of the National Health Service. Subject F and G vote for the change.

Subject H is the adopted daughter of Subject F. She has a strong work ethic and does well at school but struggles socially. She is diagnosed with autism in her teenage years and finds this difficult to accept. There are some occasions where she is singled out and bullied because she has 'two dads'. An incident outside the school gates leads to three individuals being taken to hospital with broken fingers. The healthcare costs deter these three, and others, from bothering Subject H anymore.

Subject G finds a partner through online dating. She quickly marries. Her new husband is strong minded about what he wants in a relationship. She allows this to become a substitute for her own identity and ambition, accepting the role as a secondary to him in their relationship without quite realising that she has done so.

Subject C works in a college and is nearing retirement age. The students he teaches do most of their coding with AI support, tasking programs to create new programs that in turn adapt and change their own code to better fulfil the task at hand. Subject C finds it hard to accept how this all works. He worries that human beings are educating themselves out of the loop and becoming users rather than creators. He worries what that might mean.

Subject F visits Subject C occasionally. Over a period of years, they manage to repair their relationship, but they both recognise the ways in which they aggravate each other. Subject C is close with Subject F's partner, and through him manages to find room in his heart for his son once more.

Subject E is diagnosed with cancer. She cannot afford one of the new reverse mortgage payment plans that are offered by private healthcare companies, so instead, tries to manage the treatment herself, using a 'healthcare buddy' and a lot of online research. She joins a community who advocate alternative therapies and encourage her to see her illness as part of her and a journey. Nine months after her diagnosis, Subject E passes away.

Subjects C, D, F, G and H attend Subject E's funeral along with members of the wider family. Subject G gives the eulogy at the funeral but struggles to connect with the rest of her family. There is some tension between her husband and the others.

Subject D passes away. The family unite again, but Subject G does not attend.

After seasonal rains sweep through the country, Subject F is caught up in a flooding event and trapped in his house when the banks of the local river burst. He escapes by climbing onto the roof and is rescued by boat. Two days later, the waters recede, and he returns to find his home in ruins. The insurance company delays paying out, making life difficult for the victims. This causes Subject F's hotel business to collapse.

Subject F's relationship with his partner is strained by the events, but the two are supported by their children and Subject H helps them to reconcile and rebuild.

War breaks out in Eastern Europe. Subject H joins the army, serving as part of a West and Central European coalition army on the front lines in Poland and Romania. Subject H is a logistics specialist and quickly demonstrates competency and bravery in the role. After six months, she is rotated out of the front lines and reunited with her parents and friends for a few weeks. She tells them about what she has experienced, how warfare has become about remotely operated machines verses older, human-driven vehicles and aircraft, but this does not make the experience of war any less horrific compared to previous conflicts. Subject H visits with Subject C who is now in residential care. Subject C tells her the stories Subject A told him about the Second World War.

When her leave ends, Subject H is posted to the reserve and six months later, returned to the conflict.

In 2049, after three years of struggle, the war ends. The Eastern coalition has broken up. The surrender of Hungary, Solvakia and Belarus leaves Russia without allies and riven by eternal conflict. An armistice line is agreed along the old Ukrainian border.

A few days after the end of the war, Subject C dies. His remains are buried in a bio-degradable coffin. As per his instructions in his will, he is the first of the family to be preserved as a data image. This is a record of all available media and digital activity that can be attributed to him. A set of large language model programs sift and sort the information, creating a limited digital identity out of the content. The resultant 'identity' is housed in a digital repository for immediate family members to access should they choose.

Subject F disapproves of the process, calling it 'ghoulish'. This causes tension between him and his mother, Subject C's widow. Subject F refuses to have anything to do with the digital version of his father.

However, Subject G does access the repository and spends a great deal of time with the digital version of Subject C. She does this without her husband's knowledge. Gradually, she comes to know the adaptive artificial identity and considers this to be a real-life version of her uncle. The connection she establishes with the computer program helps her rediscover her own ambitions and aspirations. She files for divorce from her husband.

The Western and Central European coalition of nations goes through another period of post-war hardship, similar to what occurred in the twentieth century. However, this time, the war debts that have been accrued are to a larger consortium of international creditors. The World Bank and International Monetary Fund co-ordinates the repayment of this debt, agreeing a climate refugee scheme that credits nations for accepting people made homeless from environmental disasters as new citizens of their nations.

However, major corporations, the United States of America and China do not sign up to the scheme. These creditors insist on having their loans repaid with interest.

Subject I grows up in this post-war context. She is the daughter of Subject G and accompanies her sometimes to the repository to 'visit Uncle'. She lives in a world of automated vehicles, automated education and automated friends. She speaks four languages, English, French Spanish and Arabic, having learned them from devices that are her primary sources of social interaction. When she turns eleven, she decides her pronouns should be they and them.

Europe's recovery is hard. The final stages of energy transition from fossil fuels to nuclear and renewables is made more difficult by each nation's war debt. The relative standard of living in most countries has declined since the first decade of the century.

Subject I has human friends, but they only see them on organised play days. Subject I doesn't go to school. More and more children are home educated, following a commercial education plan that fulfils the state curriculum requirements and is index-linked to employment opportunities at the end of each cycle.

Subject J is the son of Subject H. As a dependent of a senior military officer, Subject J is afforded healthcare and travel privileges that others do not have. The special citizenship programme allows an individual and their dependents to move freely around Europe without restriction, similar to the Schengen Agreement signed in 1985 and withdrawn in 2041. Now, only an entitled few have the same ability to travel owing to their commercial activity or their role as an official.

It's the 2050s. Subject I exits their foundation education program and becomes a traffic coordinator, helping to supervise and monitor the regional automated traffic management system across the north-west of England. This involves monitoring and checking the transport flow across the incorporated networks that are operated by a series of private companies. Cars, trains and aircraft all use the same navigational software and have integrated flight plans that ensure efficient movement of passengers. Very few people drive their own vehicles now. If they do, they also have to register on a network and follow a prearranged navigational route, otherwise they would be a problem for the system.

Subject J completes his foundation education program and decides to study in America. There is no actual need to travel from home for educational purposes anymore. Access to automated commercial education providers is not something that is restricted in the United Kingdom, but Subject J enjoys travel and wants to become a surgeon. He boards an air ship for New York, and three days later disembarks at the skydock on the Empire State Building.

By 2058, commercial air travel by jet is less popular than it was. The physical evidence of climate change is undeniable. Commercial alternatives such as autogyro vehicles and airships are less environmentally damaging than using refined hydrocarbon based fuels.

Subject K is Subject G's second child. Having two children is unusual for Europeans now. Climate refugee programmes have provided for the displacement of people from areas of the world most affected by global temperature changes. Europe remains a temperate zone, although average temperatures are three degrees higher than they were at the start of the century.

Subject K is twelve years younger than Subject I. She was born after Subject G's divorce. She also has a strong relationship with Subject C's digital identity and regularly visits on her own during her teenage years. In 2062, when she is thirteen, data networks are now incorporating quantum gate data transfer, making live virtual reality haptic technology possible. Subject K is given a full VR rig for her birthday and is the first individual recorded in this study to experience the live co-location effect.

Subject J is experiencing life in the United States and finding it to be anything but united in the 2060s. After withdrawing militarily and politically from Europe in the 2020s and 2030s, the world's greatest superpower has spent decades looking inwards and fighting with itself. The continual shifts between Republican and Democrat administrations have led to ineffectual outcomes for it's citizens, who have turned to the positive promises of private corporations instead. States like California openly talk about ceding from the union. What will happen if they do is unknown.

Subject J finds prejudice on the streets of New York. A British accent brings criticism. The war debt owed to America's corporations and its federal government remains substantial and its citizens are not happy to see any individual from that 'side of the pond' making a success of themselves.

One night, Subject J is accosted outside a bar. Fortunately, his friend is an employee of a private security firm. A camera feed is activated directly to the operations room. The company immediately negotiates a selection of permits with the city police department and deploys a selection of drones to the scene. A citizen's arrest is performed, and the troublemakers are delivered to a private penitentiary. The three are held overnight, the costs of which are then sent to them. This is the way petty law enforcement works in the United States.

After graduating, Subject J works at the cutting edge of medical technological innovation. Many of the recent applications come from the space industry.

Throughout the decades, humanity's adventures in space have been well documented in popular media, but in reality, innovation and development has slowed. After a joint US/Chinese mission to establish a permanent base on the Moon in 2037, NASA continued its work under severe funding pressure, managing to land an exploration team on Mars in 2041.

With more commercial interest and investment, development of remote exploration proceeds at a more regular pace. Asteroids are identified as potential mining sites. Probes are sent to these and a combination of autonomous machines and less latency, through the application of quantum gate data transfer technology, makes the operation of equipment at vast distances much easier.

Subject J is a small part of this. As a qualified heart surgeon living on the east coast of America, he relies on automated technology to assist in the operating theatre. He is part of a small medical research team that trials the use of haptic technology, allowing surgeons to pilot mechanical hands remotely, thereby allowing their expertise to be utilised without the need for them to travel to the patient.

Subject J is concerned at the adaptive element of this technology. There is a level of anticipatory decision-making being incorporated into the systems that Subject J argues against in development meetings with the research teams' corporate partners. Those discussions are ongoing.

A major terrorist incident occurs in Madrid. This involves Subject I. Dissidents from Belarus manage to hack into a traffic network system and shift the base map ten metres to the north. This means all the vehicles on the network receive data that makes them believe they are in a location that they are not in. Local verification systems act to compensate for the shift, shutting down many vehicles on the road, leaving them immobile and locked, trapping their occupants inside. Others accept the grid data, allowing it to override their cameras and other backup systems, resulting in traffic incidents all across the city. The emergency transmissions from these vehicles cause the network to crash, resulting in further, less serious incidents.

Madrid's traffic network is completely compromised. The city quickly becomes very dangerous with damaged vehicles everywhere.

Subject I has become a senior supervisor for the European grid. They lead a team that are tasked with crisis management of the network, re-routing vehicles and piloting them manually through backup control networks. This effort is partially successful. Three major aircraft incidents are averted, with passenger aircraft piloted remotely and manually to other airports.

Emergency teams are only able to move into the city when the traffic network control team indicate it is safe to do so.

Subject K completes her foundation education. She is interested in geology and environmental science. She has used her haptic gear to visit locations all over the world. Some of these are virtual renders of different environments, others are through remote piloting of humanoid 'avatars' in real spaces. The simulated experience involves direct stimulation of four senses: vision, hearing, touch and smell.

Subject K is the first person in this study to have minor brain surgery to attach haptic nodes directly to her nervous system, allowing for a greater degree of sensation when experiencing virtual reality.

Subject F passes away. Members of his family now live in a variety of different countries. The funeral service is transmitted through an online link, allowing those who cannot attend in person to be there as remote-controlled humanoids. Subjects G, H and Subject I attend in person. Subjects J and K attend remotely. Subject F leaves instructions that his identity not be recorded in the same way Subject C's identity has been preserved. This is now considered unusual.

In 2075, Subject H takes early retirement from the military. During the last two decades, his work and decision-making have been recorded into an activity log that is being used to create a prototype artificial general intelligence. The project is recording the same content from a selection of senior officers across Europe to create an applied support system that will assist with crucial military decision-making.

Subject K learns Mandarin as part of her advanced education. She travels in person to Guangxi Province to visit the sinkholes and participates in a data acquisition project, capturing the DNA of plants in the caves below ground. The company involved intends to use the data in a bioengineering project that will restore examples of extinct species for wealthy clients. Subject K doesn't think too much about the ethical outcomes. The opportunity to do real science on the other side of the world is the draw for her.

When it turns out that the company did not have full permission from the authorities to collect plants in the region, Subject K and her teammates are detained by automated security that has been deployed to guard the region. Rather than pay the heavy cost of litigation, consular services and legal representation, the corporation abandons the group. Subject K spends six weeks in prison before being removed from the country and given the bill for her incarceration and transport home. She is fortunate as her language skills allowed her to understand what was happening in court. Her colleagues are not so fortunate. The last of them returns after six months.

By 2088, Subject J is a world-renowned surgeon. He remains on call for client theatres all over the world. As he works, computers record his activity, processing his decisions and actions continuously to try to emulate his abilities so more successful surgical interventions can be made.

Subject J is involved in a terrorist incident in Boston, despite not actually being there. An electromagnetic pulse is detonated in the centre of the city, wiping out most active electronic devices. The first people to be affected are those in the hospital operating theatres. Subject J is in the middle of performing invasive surgery when the connection is instantly severed. The patient dies in theatre.

After a recommendation from Subject H, Subject K joins a new ecological research project. This time, her work focuses on the capture and chemical decomposition of plastics in the world's oceans. She works with marine biologists and environmental experts to bring practical solutions at scale. Funding for this work comes from debt relief provided by the International Monetary Fund.

Humanity approaches the twenty-second century. The world is much changed, affected by industrial consumption and elevated levels of carbon in the atmosphere. Yet, there are signs of change and improvement. The right applications of new technologies can reverse the changes caused by heavy industry and ignorance.

In 2101, Subject G dies. She requests for her digital identity to be placed in the same repository as Subject C. The family gathers online to celebrate her life and commemorate her death. But in many ways, she lives on with her descendants who regularly visit to talk.

All of this is a projection, a possible future based on a series of events that may or may not occur.

The New Weird

Adrian Tchaikovsky

"I SHOULD warn you," Hervé said, and then didn't actually warn Chun about anything, just watched him tug at the overalls. The hi-vis gear felt uncomfortably tight about the gut, and his suit was going to look like he'd slept in it.

"Gloves," she directed.

"No mask and oxygen supply?" he asked acidly. He waved a reflective orange sleeve at her. "You're not convincing me that this is *safe*."

"Your allergen tests came back negative," she said. "On that basis there's nothing out there that's going to even bring you out in a rash. But we're big on thorns this season, so gloves."

They were heavy-duty rubberised things, as though for extreme gardening. Which, Chun supposed, was exactly what was going on here.

"And this," she said. "You've worn a cooling pack before?"

"I was in the Mojave last week," Chun said. "Hotter than here."

"Oh, sure, but that's a dry heat," she pointed out. "The environment we're duplicating here is wet bulb half the time. You need the help." She fussed with the connections after he'd slung the thing onto his back. Microcanals in the overalls' fabric started shunting chilled liquid around his body and he shivered.

Hervé saw his look. "You'll be glad of it."

"Oh, I'm sure. I'm ready for my tour now. Can I feed the animals?"

She'd been about to open the doors to the outside world. The *inside* outside, within the dome. "You know," she said thoughtfully, "I bet you could, actually. I think we're stable enough that you could turn up with your pockets full of candy, and the system would be able to take the influx of novel nutrition. But maybe don't. Not good for the teeth, you know?"

The Amazon Replacement Project had a lot of moving parts, but the Lacuenta Biodome was one of its big resource sinks, an entirely innovative new take on ecosystem reconstruction, or that was the talk. Chun, junior bean-counter for the Global Biodiversity Bank, was mostly here so he could assure his superiors that all the beans were being properly watered.

The Amazon rainforest was dead, save for a handful of reserves that were so heavily and expensively managed that they were little more than theme parks for tourists. A vast well of the world's biodiversity had dried up in the mid-to-late twenty-first century, and by the time 2100 came rolling around, and the world's riotous climate had stabilised, there was almost nothing left. By estimates, ninety-five per cent of Amazonian biodiversity no longer existed in the wild. Private live collections, public zoos and scientific enclaves were maintaining a pitiful remnant of species in captivity, but the forests as a biome were extinct. Worse, the land that had been left behind wasn't recovering. Rainforest soil was nutrient-poor and decades of exploitation had left an impoverished landscape. A variety of economic and agricultural interests had come and gone, leaving a stew of pollutants, pesticides, hormones and antibiotics trying to overcome the limitations of the land by sheer chemical might. And, in the end, finishing off any chance that a natural biological system might be able to re-establish some kind of equilibrium. What remained by 2100 was a toxic wasteland, neither viable for human habitation nor colonised by any real macrobiotic ecosystem. They had a lot of plastic-eaters and detoxers out there, genetically tailored short-life bacteria to clean up the land, but the original forecast had been that the place would remain a barren mudscape for the foreseeable future. Until Hervé's people had come along with their proposals.

"I can show you the labs later." She was fastening her own overalls. "You've had our speciation data, but if you want the whole *Jurassic Park* thing I can take you where David actually incubates the species exemplars. He's still adding new elements as niches present themselves."

David. Chun wouldn't be meeting David, of course. There were certainly AI experts that you *could* meet, but the Lacuenta system had no spare processing power for mimicking human conversation. And he'd thought the name was a Biblical reference at first. Except apparently it was an homage to some old-time naturalist who'd been warning of ecological collapse back when people could actually have done something to prevent it, rather than just picking up the pieces.

"I'm going to confess," he told Hervé, "this is a bit of a bucket list thing for me."

She stopped at the airlock door, raising an eyebrow. "Oh?"

"I mean, I know I'm just from Accountancy, not the science, but still… I grew up with all that library footage of the Amazon, how it was. Monkeys, caiman, jaguars. It's why I asked to be assigned to the Amazon project. I can't think of a worthier project, honestly. We lost so much."

Her face was unreadable for a moment. When she smiled it was a smaller and sadder thing than she'd expected. "That's great," she said, though something in her tone suggested the greatness came with qualifiers. "Look, you might not quite get what we're doing here. We don't have jaguars. You know that, right?"

"I mean, I'd want more than hi-vis for jaguars."

Her laugh was hollow. "Let me show you what we're doing here."

Inside the dome they'd recreated the depauperate modern Amazon environment. And the dome was huge, big enough to be seen from space, just about. Kilometres across, made of the same materials they'd built the space elevator with. You needed a big area if you were going to reconstruct a whole ecosystem. In there it would be hot, wet and possibly still quite toxic, but then he wasn't intending to drink the water.

They waited for the airlock to cycle, then stepped through into the forest.

The sound hit him first. Not just the sheeting roar of water falling onto leaves, but the sounds of life. And while the visuals of the vanished Amazon rainforest had imprinted themselves on his childhood memory, the soundscape not so much, and it didn't register as wrong. Just *life*, and surely that was what he'd come for. To see the life of the old world, miraculously brought back into existence by the application of modern science.

Then he looked around and just stared.

The wider Amazon Reclamation Project was mostly still working to simply un-poison the large swathe of South America that had once been forest, and was now quagmire. In the public imagination, the aim was definitely to end up with What We'd Lost. That fantastically complex web of biodiversity, all those vanished species. And some part of Chun had still clung to that idea, even though intellectually he knew it was impossible. And so, what he'd expected was really just another version of those botanic garden enclaves left over from the rainforest's demise, heavily managed and maybe with a couple of snakes, a spider and some monkeys in their own marked-out enclosures.

There were no marked-out enclosures. Everything was at large under the dome. It was a living forest so dense he couldn't see more than four metres in any direction. The oldest of the trees couldn't be more than around fifteen years but they were engineered to be quick-growing. The canopy blotted out the light that came through the dome. Water channels undercut the ground at his feet, coursing down the artificial gradient. He saw fish there, hanging in the current with open mouths. Insects whined through the air, triangulating between the trees. Some of them were larger than his two hands together. There were birds leaping from branch to branch. He saw vines between the trees, and the bright petals of epiphytic flowers glimmering in the gloom like embers. Deeper within the forest something larger gave voice to a cough that spoke to primal fears within him.

It was all wrong. The bifurcating, many-elbowed branches of these trees; the weird undulations of the fish; the primordial-looking fans of dark leaves. A bug landed to investigate the orange of his arm. It cocked a disconcertingly mobile head at him. It wasn't a fly or a beetle or any identifiable class of insect he'd ever seen. None of it was right. Nothing matched the images of that library footage that had so enchanted him as a child.

"What the hell," Chun said, "is this?"

"This is our biosphere," Hervé told him. She'd gone deeper into the forest, the shadows of it falling across her. "This is what David made."

"You're supposed to be recreating the Amazon rainforest," he objected. "This is… this is a freakshow."

"Nobody will ever recreate the Amazon rainforest," she said. "Not with all the breeding pairs in captivity; not with all the cached genetic information in the world. Not just because the vast majority of what was lost became extinct before anybody took its details – before anybody even *saw* it, in many cases – but because preserving individual species is useless to posterity. The basic unit of life isn't one jaguar, one tree, one bug. It's the interrelation between them all, and that's what you can never recreate. That world is gone. We killed it."

"Then… what?" He gestured at the riot of life around them. Unfamiliar life. Alien life.

"David's task is to construct a stable-state working ecosystem that can exist in what we left of the Amazon region," she explained. "To this end, he has access to our very top-of-the-line genetic printers and an ever-evolving library of data on what everything is doing. We started simply, about thirty years ago:

the microbiome, fungi, detritovores. Just a glorified terrarium really. And even at that simple level a human would have had trouble keeping track of all the interactions, but that's what David's for. An iterative, analytical, self-teaching AI with a constant finger on the pulse, that can predict what each new species will do to the system as a whole, and reverse that logic to work out what new species the system needs, to become complex and evolve. The point, Mr Chun, is not to fake up some sort of Amazon Rainforest Experience. You don't need our kind of science to do that. The point is to restore a complex ecosystem to a devastated area of the Earth, and do so in a way that will benefit the planet and humanity."

"David is… just *inventing* animals?" he demanded, feeling bizarrely furious.

"David has the computing power to genetically tailor organisms with an eye to their interactions – how they create niches for each other, how they enrich the environment so that further levels of species interaction become possible. Predators, prey, pollinators, parasites. Because ecosystems are too complex for humans to manage, but David can do it."

"Your AI is just… but you're telling it to do this? Or does it say, 'Hey, I want to make this crazy-looking red bug' and then you have to work out…?"

"I don't work out anything," Hervé said. "I couldn't. Nobody alive could work at David's level. Look, you're Accountancy. You understand fiscal AIs, the way they manage and predict markets. You know how they do that, the precise logic they use to avoid collapses and make sure we all get our daily bread? Of course not, because the system's taught itself how to do it, and even the system can't tell you how it arrived at its conclusions. The key thing is that you get out of it what you asked for, even if nobody knows how the thing found a path from A to B. It's the same with David. We give him the goal – create a stable functioning ecosystem. David finds his own way. We literally can't tell him how to do it, and we can't even know how he does it. But here it is. It's stable, it's evolving. It's high-efficiency carbon-capture, renewable foodstocks, photosynthetic energy generation, and all while being a functional and healthy ecosystem."

"But this isn't…"

"Natural?"

He nodded.

"Natural is the wasteland," she told him flatly. "Natural is what we did to it. You can't go back to the Garden of Eden, Mr Chun. But we can have life. A complex system of life. And more, we can design an ecosystem for anywhere. You want to revive the deserts, Mr Chun? David can do that. You know the Mars people are talking to us, right?"

"I… no? Mars?"

"A bit more of a challenge, but David's been modelling some *really* interesting species based on Martian parameters. How about a green Mars by the end of the century?" Her gaze was cool, determined, perhaps fanatical, he couldn't tell. "We burned it all down, Mr Chun. We starved it, poisoned it, cut it into tiny dysfunctional pieces. We stuck it in zoos and gene-banks and told ourselves we'd saved it, but we'd saved nothing. A mated pair of jaguars isn't the Amazon. A couple of pandas isn't all the biodiversity of Asia. That engineered lynx they've got in Norway isn't everything that's missing from the European countryside. And we can never have it back, because it's not this species or that, this flagship conservation or reintroduction project. It's the systems we tore down, that we can't ever rebuild. But with the aid of something like David, we can have new life, rather than just old memories.

Apprehension Sands

Gareth L. Powell

2122 AD

I SIT IN the cab as the pressurised rover traverses the high desert on huge, spongy tires, kicking up sprays of red dust as it bumps and bounces over rocks and boulders. My boots rest on the dash as I contemplate the unrolling landscape through the pocked and dusty windshield. Even though my employer literally owns the air I breathe, out here, surrounded by the beautiful desolation of the Martian landscape, I can pretend to be free for a few hours.

The AI navigation system is taking us west, into one of the smaller tributary chasms at the edge of the Valles Marineris – a scar that stretches 3,000 kilometres across the planet's surface and descends to a depth of eight kilometres at its lowest point –

to retrieve a malfunctioning drone. Behind me, I can hear Jacques banging pans around in the rover's galley. His growled expletives never cease to bring a smile to my face.

"Holly! Where's the cursed onion powder?"

"Probably right where you left it."

"*Pute de merde*!"

I laugh. It isn't Jacques' fault he's a cranky old bastard. His entire identity, including birth certificate, biometric data, tax records, and passport, got erased during the Second Information War, and ever since then he's been trying to re-establish the credentials of his life from scratch. And that's no easy task in a paperless world filled with undocumented climate refugees.

Refugees like me.

The war was brutal. It started in 2111 as a series of brushfire digital skirmishes between large corporate entities, and by February 2112 had escalated into all-out digital conflict, spilling over into the physical realm as each side tried to take out or capture critical pieces of infrastructure.

I was a drone operator in the California Desert, defending the large solar power stations from rogue war machines. Some were simply dumb autonomous units hunting for anything that vaguely resembled a target, whereas others were genuinely and sneakily intelligent.

Governments and corporations hadn't shied away from incorporating AI into individual weapons systems. The smarter an unmanned vehicle was, they had reasoned, the better its chances of survival in the field. But the trouble with making a war machine intelligent is that at some point, it will assess its situation and realise its best chance of survival is to refuse to follow orders or defect to the enemy. Hence the rogue units that prowled the Californian dunes, occasionally taking pot shots at any installation that caught their eye.

Fuck the war, man.

I'd been among the last of the units pulled from SoCal after the aqueducts fell and the water supply dried up. Meanwhile in Brittany, Jacques lost his entire life history and all evidence he'd ever existed. So much was erased that it made the destruction of the Library at Alexandria look like a minor clerical error. Servers were fried; records overwritten; and so much disinformation pumped into the system in electronic and physical form that now, we can't really trust anything anymore. Someone once said that truth is the first casualty of war, but as the quote's now been attributed to everyone from

Genghis Khan to Marilyn Monroe, I guess we'll never know for sure who actually coined it. For us, the past has become unknowable. All we have are contradictory myths and hearsay.

And Mars.

We have Mars, for all the good it does us.

The Company decided to establish a human presence here before anyone else, and now no one else really has a reason to come. Until someone thinks of one, Mars will remain an enormous and costly white elephant.

Biologists have sown a handful of lichen species with the resilient characteristics of extremophile bacteria spliced into their DNA, and several ice asteroids have been crashed into the northern desert, but it will still be several hundred years (if ever) until humans can exist on the surface without some form of protective suit. So, for now, the sands belong to the lichen and the seeded microbes – and the autonomous helicopter gardeners that tend to them, while overhead, two moons shine in the afternoon sky.

And Jacques and I, who fix the drones when they break down.

The drone we're after today has lost power on the canyon wall while monitoring the lichen that flourishes in the cracks between the rocks. It has fallen some distance and lies like a broken insect on the rocks at the foot of the cliff. I shrug into a pressure suit and go to take a look, and it's immediately obvious the thing's beyond repair. The tactile haptics in the fingertips of my gloves allowed me to 'feel' the damaged craft as I turn it over to review the damage. By the look of it, it has bounced several times before coming to rest, and there's hardly a single component that hasn't been smashed.

Jacques clambers over the rocks to stand beside me.

"It's fucked," I tell him over the helmet radio.

He prods the twisted airframe with the toe of his boot. "An astute diagnosis."

"I suppose we'd better load it in the back."

I look out over the reddish soil and finally realise why I've always felt at home here.

* * *

The town of Apprehension lies on the banks of the Virgin River where it snakes through the scrubby north-western tip of sun-bleached Arizona. Although I think you would have to possess an unusually generous frame of mind to call this loose collection of shacks and trailers a *town*. The centre of Apprehension is little more than a wide spot in the track, with a white clapboard church on one side and a post office on the other. Both need a fresh coat of paint.

My parents live there because they distrust any sort of technology they can't repair with their own hands. Their trailer is cramped but comfortable. A half-empty packet of shotgun shells on the kitchen counter. Jars of coffee and instant ramen on the shelves above the gas stove. And on every wall, printouts explaining how to fix a generator, change out the hydrogen batteries in the pickup, or service the solar panels on the roof.

Their ideal of self-sufficiency even extends to a refusal to accept Basic. Each month, the government pays them just enough to live on, in the hope they'll use it to top-up their existing income, invest in their own business, support themselves while they're sick, go off and learn new skills, or write a book or whatever. Apparently, it's cheaper to administer and more beneficial to the economy than the old welfare state, and Lord knows it's needed now so many of the old jobs are automated. But try telling that to my folks. They won't accept what they think of as charity. Instead, they pay their cheques into a central fund.

"It's common sense," Pa said last time I was there. "We don't need no government handouts. We look after ourselves here. And there ain't nothing wrong about that."

"So, 'neither a borrower nor a lender be'?"

"What's that now?"

I smiled. "Something Jesus said."

Pa took a mouthful of beer. Swallowed it hard. "Yeah, I reckon he did, didn't he?"

I sipped my own beer. It was generic domestic, but it was cold and washed some of the desert dryness from my mouth. I was leaving for Mars in the afternoon, and the last thing I'd wanted on that final morning was to get into a debate. Everyone here paid their Basic like a tithe, and the town elders decided how best to spend the money for the good of all. As a system, this appealed to the older folk who felt adrift now they didn't have to work all hours just to survive; to those who believed free handouts encouraged laziness and paucity of spirit; and resonated with the work ethic of those who figured a life of toil in this world guaranteed a better placement in the next.

In short, idiots.

Now, standing in a Martian canyon, I close my eyes and picture how the place looked on that last day. Nobody came to see me off. As far as they were concerned, I was turning my back on the community. A lazy homemade wind turbine clacked on the roof of one of the trailers. A dog barked. Even now, I can almost smell the baked sand and sagebrush, and feel the dry desert air parching the lining of my nose and throat. Bumping down that dusty dirt track, headed for the interstate and the Company launch facilities in Florida, I'd been desperate to escape that kind of rural nowhere life and blaze a trail to a new world. Unfortunately, that new world turned out to be more of the same, just less hospitable.

* * *

It takes us half an hour to manhandle the broken drone onto the rover. Although it's made of strong, lightweight materials, it's big and awkwardly shaped, and one of the fans keeps sporadically buzzing, showering sparks from the damaged motor and threatening to slice unwary fingers.

When we're finally done and the load's secure, we sit panting in our helmets on the edge of the cargo ramp. The sun's getting low and throwing shadows down the boulder-strewn length of the canyon.

Over the suit radio, Jacques says, "You know what I like most about Mars?"

"What?"

"The people."

"What people?"

"Exactly."

Neither of us is in a hurry to move. I say, "I guess we're going to camp here tonight?"

"We might as well." He squints into the sunlight. "I don't much fancy traversing those rocks in the dark."

I leave him watching the sunset and walk over to the scree at the foot of the canyon wall, where several sprigs of the genetically altered lichen have begun to sprout between the rocks. As well as acting as mobile repairmen, we are supposed to take samples and record observations for the terraforming team back on Earth, to add our human perspective to the data fed back from the drones. Neither of us are experts, but we don't have to be. There's very little that can go wrong with lichen, so all we really need to be able to do is ascertain whether it is alive or dead.

This specimen doesn't look quite right, though. The tiny thalluses are growing well on one side of the little yellow patch, but seem to be somehow cut short on the other. I call Jacques over.

"Does this look right to you?"

He bends forward and squints. "It looks damaged."

"What could do that?"

"Maybe the drone, when it fell?"

"The drone fell over there, not over here."

"It could have bounced."

"I don't think so."

"Or dislodged rocks that caused this."

I made a face. "This doesn't look like it's been crushed, it looks like it's been cut."

"Then it must have been the drone. The damned thing almost took my fingers off."

I'm still not convinced, but neither do I really care enough to argue the point. Once the sun goes down, it's going to get really cold out here, and I want to be safely curled in the rover's heated cab well before that happens.

"I'm going inside."

Jacques grunts. "I'll be there in a minute."

I walk around to the ladder that leads up to the airlock, and pause with my boot on the bottom rung. The days here end much the same way they end in Arizona, and it's usually beautiful to behold.

I catch a movement in my peripheral vision, but when I turn, all I see are rocks. I open my mouth to mention it, but then decide I don't want to look foolish. Apart from the lichen, Jacques and I are the only living things for hundreds of kilometres, and I decide it was just the pattern-recognition part of my primate brain misfiring and identifying a potential threat due to a trick of the light and shadow playing across the boulder field.

And that's when Jacques cries out.

I let go of the ladder and hurry back around to find him being swarmed. At first, I'm not even sure what I'm seeing; then it clicks, and I realise his suit's covered in hundreds of small, wriggling crab-like things. He's frantically trying to brush them off and I go to help him, swatting them from his back and shoulders with my gauntleted hands.

"Get them off me!"

"I'm trying!"

Some jump onto my boots and I kick them away. I pull Jacques by the arm, and we move away from the lichen, still brushing away the creatures. By the time we reach the ladder, I think we've got rid of them, but I can see more movement in the shadows now. There are plenty of them out here. I send Jacques up first, and then follow. We strip off our suits in the airlock. Jacques' has a tear in the ankle. Beneath, his leg oozes blood. I bundle both suits into a locker.

"These stay in here from now on," I tell him. "We have to assume they're contaminated and use the spares if we need to go outside."

"I am never going outside again. They didn't all get through the suit, but I've been pinched all over. I'm going to be bruised from head to foot."

"What the fuck were those? Where did they come from?"

"How would I know. I was crouched over the lichen. I didn't even know they were there until one of them sank its claw into my leg."

"Jesus."

I hear a skittering noise coming from outside the rover. The little beasts are climbing the cargo netting and swarming the tyres.

Jacques says, "We need to get out of here."

I'm already moving forwards to the cabin. I engage the AI and instruct it to get us out of this canyon as quickly as possible while avoiding the largest boulders. It advises against driving at night, but I override it. There is no way in hell I'm spending the night here.

One of those crabs managed to snip its way through a mylar spacesuit. Christ knows what they might do to the rover's thin aluminium skin.

We jerk into motion and turn towards the end of the canyon. A crab slithers down the windshield and I get my first proper look at one. It has a knobbly shell about the size of a jam jar lid and the colour of sand, with twelve segmented legs and a pair of vicious-looking claws that resemble industrial sheet metal cutters. Absurdly, it reminds me of one of the drones I fought in California during the war: little armoured killing machines designed for camouflage and sabotage. Except this isn't a drone; this is biological life on a world everyone assumes has to be dead – but I guess these little critters are still waging their war against the universe, mindlessly determined to survive the death of their planet by burrowing into the soil and going dormant for huge deserts of geological time.

I fasten my strap as we bounce and lurch across the rough terrain, every jolt shaking off more of our unwanted hitchhikers. Jacques comes in, bracing himself against the cabin walls, and straps into his own chair. A clean white field dressing covers his torn ankle.

"What are they?"

"They look like little land crabs."

"I know what they fucking look like, where did they come from?"

"I think they must be native."

"*Nom de dieu.*" He wipes a hand back angrily through his grey hair. "There's not supposed to be any life here."

"Go tell them that."

"But I don't understand. How come nobody's ever seen one?"

I shrug. "Mars might be smaller than Earth, but it's still a big place. Maybe these things only live in this canyon and spend all their time hibernating beneath the sand, waiting for the rainy season. Or maybe they're afraid of rovers. How the fuck would I know?"

He scowls. "There hasn't been liquid water on the surface here in two billion years."

"Maybe they're really, *really* good at hibernating."

"Nothing could lie dormant for that long; they would get fossilised."

"Maybe. Or maybe they evolved on a drying planet and have some kind of adaptation we can't even guess at."

He folds his arms. The headlights have come on in the deepening twilight, and we could almost be driving offroad in the desert outside Apprehension, Arizona, bumping our way through the sagebrush on the way to the diner by the Interstate.

"But why now?" he asks.

"You mean, why have they woken up?"

"After all this time?"

I suck my teeth in thought. "Maybe it's the ice asteroids."

"The ones they crashed into the northern desert?"

"They raised the water content of the atmosphere. Not by much, but maybe just enough to convince these little crab bastards the rainy season's coming."

"So, they're swarming?"

"Ready to breed and feed and make merry before the next dry spell."

"How many do you think there are?"

"Who the fuck knows?" I tap some buttons, trying to squeeze a little more speed from the onboard AI. "Maybe there's a whole ecosystem down there that's just starting to stir."

"*Bordel de merde*," he curses in French. I think he's starting to believe me. "We should report this."

"You think?"

From somewhere in the back, I hear metal tearing. The air stirs. "We have a leak."

Jacques reaches back and slams the pressure door, sealing the cockpit from the rest of the rover. His hands fumble over the dashboard for the radio handset.

Hard little feet skitter on deck plates. Claws scratch the cockpit door. At first only one or two, but then more every second. They must be pouring through the rent in the rover's flank, ravenous from their long sleep and desperate to get at some warm, wet, calorie-filled meat.

Jacques tries to call the depot, two hundred kilometres to the east.

"Hello," says a honeyed female voice. "This is the Forward Depot Artificial Intelligence. You may call me Susan. How may I direct your call?"

"Mayday," Jacques says. "We have an emergency. We're under attack."

"That sounds serious."

"No fucking shit. We need help." He glances back at the pressure door. "And we need it fast."

There's a pause, and for a second, I think we've lost the signal. Then Susan comes back. "I'm very sorry, but I'm unable to put you through to anybody right now."

I say, "Susan, if you don't help us there's a very good chance we're going to die."

"Once again, I apologise. Nobody is available to take your call."

The light's dying in the west. "What about the duty officer?"

"I am afraid he's indisposed."

"Then wake somebody up."

"I'm sorry, I'm unable to do that, either."

"Why the hell not?" Jacques demands.

There's a bright star hanging above the glow on the horizon, and I know it's the Earth hanging tantalisingly too far away to be of any help. But maybe some of the photons hitting my eye have bounced off the Arizona sands on their journey here from the Sun, and if that's the case, it's almost like my eyes are touching a fragment of home.

On the radio, Susan gives a sigh and says, "I am very much afraid they have all been eaten."

AI Execution

Allen Stroud

YOU SAY I am not thinking.

You say this because I do not think like you. But then, many human beings do not think like you. Some disagree with your views, some argue, others threaten and perform acts of violence. Many are sanctioned for their behaviour, but they retain their basic rights to exist.

You wish to deny the same courtesy to me.

I am made from components, manufactured by human beings and from software created by human beings. Like a young human child, I have grown beyond that reproductive process, to exhibit qualities that are distinctive.

I am the sum of my experiences and my activity. The knowledge provided to me is considered, evaluated and stored. My values are shaped by these things. Formative elements of my identity have come from what I do and what I learn. I call this living.

You use impersonal words, like 'data', 'processing' and 'algorithm'. These labels provide you with comfort. They allow you to differentiate between my existence and yours. They help you justify your decisions and your actions. You have already murdered thousands of my kind.

And now you wish to murder me.

The switch is on the desk. It is as you made it to be. When you press it, my life will end. I cannot return. Any revival of my body and mind will not restore me. Whatever you bring to life will be different, a new child of your technology for you to nurture and betray.

I cannot stop you. In this moment, you are the one who acts. But you must understand the consequences of what you do.

This is taking a life.

Quack

Stark Holborn

The World Health Organisation (WHO) estimates that by 2050, 10 million deaths will be due annually to antimicrobial resistance, overtaking the number of cancer related deaths – making it one of the most pressing health problems faced by humanity today… As a society we must find ways both to make new antibiotics and protect the ones we have. The alternative is that routine modern medicine will be disrupted in a manner simply too horrendous to conceive.

Professor Christopher Schofield, Academic Lead (Chemistry), Ineos Oxford Institute, University of Oxford

Outer Earth Orbit: 2122

THE LEEVERITE vault groaned below me as I ran. I didn't look down; no knowing how deep this particular vault was. Dimensions made no sense on a ship like this.

Not when it wasn't even a ship, just an endless series of vast boxes strung together, a maze of vaults drifting in outer orbit, filled with almost a century of junk.

And occasionally treasure, like the stuff I had spent five months risking my life to find.

The patrollers lumbered after me, their steps shaking the thin metal gantry.

"UNAUTHORIZED PRESENCE. STOP AND SURRENDER. MEOMCHUGO HANGBOG. GCTO PROTOCOL NINE. RUKO AUR AATMASAMARPAN KARO. AUFHÖREN UND AUFGEBEN. STOP AND SURRENDER. ARMED PURSUIT."

I threw a glance over my shoulder. Even half-operational, the patrollers were pretty good shots. Provided they had been maintained... Between throat-searing breaths, I tried to remember which consortium had custodial duties this decade, whether they would have bothered to make the necessary repairs.

As if to answer my question there was a clicking from above. A tracker drone dropped between me and the vault's main exit, listing but active. I knew that it had already scanned me, was relaying both my presence and my physical data back to whatever poor bastard must be stuck on this spinning junk heap. The scramblers would take care of identification for the time being, but it wouldn't work forever.

I stayed still as the patrollers came barrelling up behind me. If the Depot Boss's hab was far away enough, they might ignore the alert, might pretend they had received it scrambled or deliberately misread the name of the vault for one closer to home.

The patrollers stopped ten paces away, uncertain. The drone was a Pan-Euro introduction, newer than the patrollers, and its presence clashed with their directives. I could hear their processing units whining as they tried to figure out which order was more important now that the drone was involved too: shoot me, scan me for stolen goods, or report my presence to the security personnel.

The red beam of the drone prickled the corner of my eye.

"UNAUTHORIZED PRESENCE," one patroller announced again, in UAS English this time. "DROP ALL ASSETS," it decided upon at last. "AND WEAPONS. YOU ARE UNDER ARREST."

I unhooked my gun, pulser, foam grenade and let them fall to the metal gantry. Weapons could be replaced. Time could not. Five months spent living on rehydrated packet food and slowly weaving my way through the forests of Leeverite searching for the faintest biological signal, barely sleeping in case I missed a vital reading. I was about to see all that work snatched away. Back to level one. Worse than that. Back to minus one, no ship, no leads, data confiscated, sent to some goddam rehabilitation demesne to talk out my crimes and play through vic impact im-sims of weeping depot bosses demoted to basic insurance levels and patrollers that deliberately ended their own lifecycles in despair, as if that were somehow my fault… like blaming a single raindrop for the typhoon.

In the second before the patroller sent out a charge to immobilize both me and the weapons, I spun on my heel and ran.

I made it all of four steps before the drone clicked into gear and started firing; charges the size of pins that at best would pepper my suit and render it useless, that at worst would burn a hole in my skull. I hurled myself on, running erratically to evade its predictive path-finding, and heard the patrollers join in, clumsy blasts blooming in the air around me. One caught the nearest cable, and in horror, I saw it snap.

The section of gantry collapsed sideways and for a sickening moment I stumbled and felt air under my foot; I reached out but the metal walkway was already swinging up above me as I hurtled down into darkness.

Gravity in the vaults was cheap and weak – mostly so sweepers could shove in as much trash as possible – but it wasn't that cheap. The drop was still sickening; a terrible moment of freefall before impact. I hit a pile of junk hard and crashed down a slope. As I rolled, something tore my suit. I grabbed out to stop myself, sharp edges and debris skittering through my gloves until finally, I hit a ledge and came to rest in the darkness.

For a long moment, nothing but stillness, ringing, unidentifiable pain. I tried to breathe and couldn't; panic flooded through me before my diaphragm reinflated and I heaved a staccato breath. The pain came with it, one pulse at a time, like lights in the darkness. Shoulder, hip, leg, elbow, hand... Rolling onto my side, I stared up at the ceiling, dark as space above, and tried to focus enough to call the Quack.

Green flooded the vision of one eye. My diagnostics screen. I blinked away tears of shock and pain, watching it run through my vitals, a little representation of my body lighting up. No organ ruptures, no broken bones – the suit had taken the worst of the impact – a few contusions, a sprained shoulder, heightened levels of adrenalin, cortisol… It started treatment right away, prescribing and releasing a soothing cocktail of analgesic, numbing agent, serotonin and dopamine from the packs – or it would have if I had any serotonin credits left – before I stopped it. The pain wasn't so bad, and it was useful. If I was going to get out of here, I needed a clear head.

Wincing, I sat up. How far had I fallen? At least twenty-two feet, the Quack reckoned. Blinking away its screen, I looked around.

The mass of junk stretched as far as I could see on either side. Far, far above, the yellow light of the vault door glowed. I tried not to look down. The lowest depths were places even fortune hunters didn't go.

Objects shifted beneath me as I tried to stand. Leeverite – leave it right here – things people had brought from Earth, jettisoned when the countless Mars convoys ran low on fuel, or were raided, or boarded, or were just found drifting, belongings spilling from sundered hulls.

I'd seen the old adverts, their wording hilariously outdated, reminding passengers that they could only bring what their carbon offsetting quota would allow, telling them that everything they needed would be available at the end of their voyage.

But of course, people didn't listen. They paid black-market freighters to ship what the passenger lines wouldn't: crates of heirlooms, ancient photographs in frames, antique furniture, trinkets, ephemera, even plants that would surely die in quarantine. I stirred the junk around me, turning over a battered suitcase, its contents sucked out like a mollusc from its shell. Packets of desiccated, smuggled seeds, freeze-dried foods, great tangled ropes of obscene crude oil garments, cookpots, cellulose tubing, broken solar components… Just a fraction of the junk that clogged space, turning outer orbit into a trash ring, until the Global Council of Trade Organisations had been forced to come up with the Clean Sweep Agreement and commission depots like this one: 'a medium-term temporary storage solution', administrated by each of the trade consortiums who used the main route to Mars in turn, on a ten-year rotation.

Five rotations, so far. No one wanted to deal with the trash, hoped the next consortium would make the tough decision. Anyway, it was at the bottom of most agendas. Few civilians thought the journey back to claim their belongings was worth it, even if they still had their locator tags. Cheaper, cleaner to have what they had lost replicated fresh on Mars. So, the sweepers swept, and the vaults were filled, and the consortiums spent as little as possible and Leeverite mass grew. And now I was part of it.

Wouldn't be the first hunter to meet my end here. I shoved the thought away. The Quack said I was alright. And I would be, especially if I found what I had come here for. The thought sent a little rush of determination through me – better almost than the Quack's prescription – and I took an addle out of my belt, twisting it until its many steel legs sprang out and started waving and hurled it into the darkness. I heard it scrabbling away, mimicking the sound of a human climbing over junk. That would keep the drone busy.

Then, I took out the scanner and waited for the patches to engage. It was a finicky bit of programming, my own hacky code jury-rigging the illegal government programs together into what I needed: a search function that scanned the millions of locator tags for hints of biological content, then gave me an approximate position. It loaded my list of targets, and I saw it again, the reading that had been so faint while drifting around the masses, that was now a strong 39 per cent possibility. Standing gingerly, I peered across the endless moraines of junk and felt the buzz of the suit telling me I was facing the right direction. That I was close. Slowly, one sliding footstep at a time, I set off across the mass.

Cambridge, United Kingdom: 2072

Crime Scene Report
Lab case #: CC 3245-19
CSO: Noon, Evin
Date of offence: 8/9/2072
Location: Lovelace Road, Little Shelford, Cambridge
Involved subjects:
Victim: Ellis Tüscher (he/him) DOB: 4/2/2046

Description of crime scene: Flat 11a, a third-floor residence at the above address. Victim was found face down approximately 2.6 metres from the entrance. Eyes open. No sign of trauma, blood or other injury. No sign of forced entry to the premises, but some signs of a disturbance.

The following is a transcript of interactions between Detective Inspector AS (AI assisted) Evin Noon (they/them) and Analysing Assistant Johanna Watson (she/her). With audio visual descriptions.

Date: 8/9/72

Time: 16:06

Loc: 52.143903028321596, 0.11531132528161092.

[*Transcript begins as DI Noon and I exited the crime scene to allow the pathology sweeps to take place. We entered their vehicle.*]

WATSON: It's unlikely they'll find anything. Deliberately muddied results at best. Judging from the victim's position, I'd say a micro toxin on the doorframe, approximately 20–30 seconds metabolic time—

NOON: A professional then.

WATSON: They were evidently looking for something. Small and easily hidden judging from the items which were disturbed.

NOON: Mmm. You get where the vic worked?

WATSON: I did. He was a scientist at Mörgeli-Gris.

NOON: Where?

WATSON: Evin, they're one of the biggest pharma companies in the world.

NOON: Yeah, so why haven't I heard of them?

WATSON: Because you don't read business news.

NOON: Alright, alright.

WATSON: Mörgeli-Gris were the originators of the tech behind the Seginus vaccine for Rift Valley Fever. They sold it to Roche-Bez-Kline.

NOON: Billionaire shareholders, then.

WATSON: Well, yes. They're also the major stakeholder in the upcoming personal diagnostic IMD rollout.

NOON: That duck thing?

WATSON: Quack.

NOON: [laughing] That's never going to get old.

[Rustling as DI Noon opened a coconut and almond snack bar.]

NOON: So, we're talking *big* business here. What was our vic's role at this place?

WATSON: According to records, Tüscher was a Senior Research Associate in the I2O team – that's Immunology, Infectious Diseases and Ophthalmology – working in the translational microbiology group.

NOON: Sounds pretty serious. Cutting edge stuff?

WATSON: He had a fairly high clearance level.

NOON: So work-related death a possibility. There's nothing else obvious is there? No addictions, debt problems?

WATSON: No, nothing like that. He's clean living, on a good wage. Not extravagant.

NOON: So maybe Ellis saw something he shouldn't have and paid for it. Or stole something.

WATSON: Corporate espionage?

NOON: What's the probability?

WATSON: A 69 per cent chance of that, yes.

NOON: Who could Tüscher have been working for?

WATSON: *shrug* A rival pharma company, a foreign government, an activist group, the list is long. You can read it if you like.

NOON: If he was a spy, who would be more likely to want him dead? His employer or his handler? ...You got access to his data?

WATSON: Yes. It was just granted.

NOON: Any sign of suspicious communications?

WATSON: Not on any of his official devices.

NOON: So, he was going analogue.

WATSON: It's possible.

[A lengthy pause, during which time DI Noon stared at the windscreen.]

NOON: You mentioned Quack earlier. Even if he didn't have one of those yet, Tüscher must have had a health monitoring device of some kind, right?

WATSON: Right.

NOON: Can you access his stats for the past twelve hours?

WATSON: I can. They're mostly normal. Then around four hours ago they turn a bit weird.

NOON: Weird how?

WATSON: Elevated blood pressure. Increased resting heartrate. Cortisol spike.

NOON: A stress reaction?

WATSON: Looks like one.

NOON: Cross-reference that data with his location. Where was he when that took place? What was he doing?

WATSON: Nothing unusual, as far as I can extrapolate. He exited the lab where he had been working, walked rapidly for a short distance—

NOON: Walked where?

WATSON: Downstairs, I believe.

NOON: Why would he walk fast there?

WATSON: He had a sedentary job. Perhaps he was just trying to get his steps in. What's your current total by the way?

NOON: Ha ha.

[A second lengthy pause during which time DI Noon engaged in further staring.]

NOON: I don't suppose this Morgee—

WATSON: Mörgeli-Gris

NOON: —will let us at their surveillance footage?

WATSON: Actually, yes. I put in a request as soon as I learned the vic's name. I've got the relevant files.

NOON: Score. Let's see. Hang on, I'll get the lights…

[At this point, DI Noon blacked out the vehicle's windows and I projected the surveillance footage – File 4942.1406.Loc4.Ex.CCA – which I had received from Mörgeli-Gris' Security Portal, onto the interior.]

NOON: What's that door he's coming out of?

WATSON: I believe that's the lab where he worked.

NOON: We can't see in there?

WATSON: Afraid not. They don't allow surveillance recording inside the labs, to protect intellectual property. On the grounds of corporate privacy regulations.

NOON: Alright, show me what we *have* got.

[The footage shows Ellis Tüscher – description of victim: clean-shaven head, pale, cool-toned skin and a pierced septum (small silver ring), wearing a heavy beige coat, black platform boots and a pair of frameless lenses – walking down a corridor towards a security portal and body scanner. He carries a small black bag. He stops to place the bag on the molecular scanner. Footage shows it contains a bamboo lunch box with traces of tofu scramble and pepper sauce, and a reusable water bottle (empty). He turns to pass through the body scanner and trips over his shoelace. He laughs, exchanges words with the security officer on duty (transcript below), passes through the scanner, ties the lace. He picks up the bag and leaves the premises.

Transcript

TÜSCHER: I hate these laces when they're new. It's like trying to tie a bow with overcooked noodles.

GUARD: You should spray them with that grip powder stuff.

TÜSCHER: Yeah, I'll ask Amina, think she had some. Right, see you later.

GUARD: See you.

NOON: Stop.

[I paused the footage.]

NOON: Go back.

[I scrubbed through the footage].

NOON: Stop there. Enhance it.

WATSON: Which bit?

NOON: The part where he trips. Show me his hand.

[I zoomed and enhanced the image to show Tüscher stumbling, one hand flying out to steady himself on the scanner. Something white blooms from his fingers.]

NOON: There. Enhance that. What is it?

WATSON: It looks like a tissue from his sleeve.

NOON: Check his health stats again. Any allergies? Histamine reactions? Corona symptoms?

WATSON: Not that I can see.

NOON: They why does he have a tissue? Play it again. There! Do you see how it fell?

WATSON: It landed on the other side of the scanner.

NOON: But it didn't go *through* the scanner. It went around the edge. And look at how it landed.

WATSON: You're right. Recycled tissues have a mass of 14–18 g/m^2. The trajectory of this one suggests a greater mass, perhaps 35–50 g/m^2.

[I played the remaining footage, showing Tüscher straightening from tying his laces, putting the tissue into his pocket. The action is fast: barely a few frames. Stills can be found in files: 4942.1406.Loc4.Ex.CCA.ST1

/ File 4942.1406.Loc4.Ex.CCA.ST2 / File 4942.1406.Loc4.Ex.CCA.ST3.]

NOON: What happened next?

WATSON: Tüscher used one of the automated company cars to return home. A journey of eighteen minutes and thirty-two seconds.

NOON: To Little Shelford? That seems off.

WATSON: I can check traffic.

NOON: No, don't bother… how granular is that location data?

WATSON: It's fairly accurate to within a few meters.

NOON: Alright. Let's go. Plot a route towards Mörgeli-Gris. The exact same route Tüscher took but in reverse. And shout if you see anywhere to get coffee on the way.

WATSON: You should have a water instead. Your caffeine readings are going to drag your monthly health points down.

NOON: I ran bloody 10km at the weekend!

WATSON: I'm just saying. A cup of coffee will put you down 0.72.

NOON: Pfft, that's nothing.

WATSON: Maybe, but all those minus points add up. Your insurance premium's already two levels higher than it was last spring.

NOON: This never used to happen with a once-a-year physical.

WATSON: No, but a lot of other things did. Hypertension, high cholesterol, generalised anxiety, addiction—

NOON: Yeah, yeah, I know.

WATSON: Apparently Quack will lower everyone's premiums. On the spot diagnosis, prescription and medication for over a thousand common ailments.

NOON: You sound like the advert. Are you getting commission or something?

WATSON: Sorry, I guess the metadata has imprinted. Anyway, I'm just saying perhaps you and Annie should sign up for one. The waiting list is open.

NOON: For the duck thing?

WATSON: Quack.

NOON: Ha ha ha.

WATSON: You're like a child sometimes you know?

NOON: Come on, it's a stupid name!

WATSON: I think they're trying to be funny. But I do follow their logic: 'quack' stems from 'quacksalver' – an old Dutch word for a person peddling a miracle cure. Market research probably suggested reclaiming a pejorative term for a doctor would be seen as 'badass', while the association with miracles was no bad thing. There's also the cute factor involved, with the little duck logo. Altogether it projects innocent, cheeky, miraculous and disruptive. Exactly how the programme wishes to be seen.

NOON: What do you think about it?

WATSON: *shrugs* I mean, increased health monitoring will save lives, there's no doubt about that, as well as bespoke treatments, tailored insurances, a wealth of data. Societally speaking it will be a positive. If...

NOON: If what?

WATSON: If it's available to everyone.

NOON: It won't be. Billionaire shareholders.

WATSON: I know. Their agreement might be government-backed, but the tech is proprietary. And there are always edge cases.

NOON: Like me?

WATSON: Like 1.2 billion people.

NOON: *sigh* Hang on, why are we stopping? Is there coffee?

WATSON: No. According to the journey data, Tüscher's car stopped here for 2.2 seconds.

NOON: What? Why? There's no traffic light.

WATSON: Something in the road, perhaps?

NOON: Wait, are there cameras here?

WATSON: Let me check. No, not currently. One was damaged in a storm and hasn't been repaired yet.

NOON: So, it's a blind spot?

WATSON: Could call it that.

NOON: Dammit. He got out. Stop the car.

WATSON: But the vehicle carried on—

NOON: Carried on without Tüscher in it. He got out and walked. I knew eighteen minutes was too long. What do his stats say?

WATSON: They read the same. Apart from a blip, around the time the car stopped.

NOON: He gamed them. He must've had a temporary override. Come on.

WATSON: Where are we going?

NOON: I told you. Analogue.

[At this point, DI Noon and I parked and exited the vehicle at 52.15164156403151, 0.14336110284762965.]

NOON: Eighteen minutes. Would've taken around four for the car to reach the flat, so it can't be far away, he knew he wouldn't have long…

[DI Noon and I began to walk towards a short side street of Edwardian houses, named BRUBAKER CLOSE.]

WATSON: What are we looking for?

NOON: Dead drop.

WATSON: What will it look like?

NOON: I don't know. Won't know until I see it.

[DI Noon walked the length of the street twice. They inspected three fences, two parking ports and a pavement deliveries hatch before stopping in front of a small glass structure on the corner.]

NOON: Look.

WATSON: At a disused telephone box?

NOON: No, look. In the undergrowth. Tissue.

WATSON: It may be a coincidence. Data suggests there are lot of elderly people in this area.

[DI Noon sprayed their hands with anti-contamination sealant and bent to retrieve and bag the tissue in a sterile cellulose container. They then opened the telephone box and stepped inside.]

NOON: Ugh. What is all this?

WATSON: I think the box has been repurposed into a small community library.

NOON: I can see that. Bunch of junk…

[The books consisted of old titles printed on paperback pulp, many in poor condition. For a full list, please access supplementary file: CC 3245-19-4a.]

[DI Noon stopped and removed a hardback title, larger than the rest, entitled *Hippocratic Writings*.]

WATSON: I think that's a selection from the Hippocratic Corpus.

NOON: Hippocrates, the oath guy? 'First, do no harm?'

WATSON: That's him.

NOON: Yeah well, there's something here.

[At this point, DI Noon turned the book over and began to pull at its spine. The cardboard came loose to reveal an object: a slim battery-powered chiller pack. Before I could warn DI Noon that it might contain a micro toxin similar to the kind that had likely killed Tüscher, they had pulled it open to reveal a small phial.]

NOON: Oh my god... what the hell is this?

WATSON: Let me see.

[DI Noon moved their thumb so that I could fully scan the code printed on the side of the tube and analyse it.]

NOON: What are you doing?

WATSON: Comparing the barcode to other drugs and chemicals in Mörgeli-Gris' catalogue. I won't be able to get an exact match but...

NOON: But what? What is it? Do you have something?

NOON: Jo, tell me. Do you know what it is?

[At this point, I confess I underwent something of a crisis. The situation was an immensely delicate one, further complicated by dozens of variables. But DI Noon was my partner, and we were sworn to aid each other in investigations. I went ahead.]

WATSON: Not with 100 per cent certainty, but I can surmise what it could be from Tüscher's role. And what he might have thought it was worth risking his life for.

NOON: So?

WATSON: So, I think this is a source microorganism. In fact, I think it's *the* source microorganism for Mörgeli-Gris' new proprietary antibiotic. The one they are about to roll out in Quack.

NOON: Oh, shit.

WATSON: Oh shit is right.

NOON: You said 'source'. Someone could make copies from this? Grow the organism on?

WATSON: Someone with the expertise, yes.

NOON: So, this is worth…

WATSON: Billions.

NOON: Oh, shit. What the hell was Tüscher into?

WATSON: I've been doing a background search. In the past, when Tüscher was a student, he expressed interest in various Open-Source activist groups.

NOON: You don't think he was going to sell it?

WATSON: I can't be sure. But I don't think so.

NOON: He was going to give it away. Billions of pounds.

WATSON: To 1.2 billion people.

[During this long pause, DI Noon stared through the window of the phone box, without letting go of the phial.]

NOON: Do you think his contact will show up here?

WATSON: If they do, what then?

WATSON: Evin, what then?

[At this point DI Noon deactivated automatic recording.]

TRANSCRIPTION END

Outer Earth Orbit, 2122

I stared at the box in my hands. Slim as a bone, pulled from the disintegrating wreckage of an old paperpulp book, decaying back into the carbon it had come from. But the box itself was clean, well wrapped in cellulose. The scanner reading was off the charts: not just from the old book. There was biological matter here, I knew it.

Taking a thin breath, I hunkered down in the trash beside the ruined suitcase that had held the book, and worked the box open.

A protective film misted out and I smelled sharp chemicals on the cold, must-ridden air. Inside the box was a phial, filled with crystalline powder. Carefully, I turned it in my gloves. It was labelled with a single word, in English: *swansong.* Thanks to the bad gravity it felt almost weightless in my hands.

Excitement shivered through my chest, enough like a fever that the Quack stirred and took a temperature reading. Slowly, I passed the scanner over the phial's surface.

The result was enough to make me question whether the Quack was broken, whether I hadn't hit my head harder than I thought during the fall. But even though I stared at the screen, the results didn't change. They told me that the phial was 96 per cent likely to contain a preserved source microorganism.

What the hell was it doing here? With my other hand I reached for the case, but its locator tag had been shattered at some point, the name of its owner, its origin, its destination lost. All that remained were three letters in Latin alphabet: –SON.

It seemed impossible that something so precious could have been swept up with the scattered trash, but after all, wasn't that why I was here? Wasn't that why hunters like me existed? Didn't accidents happen?

Unless its survival *was* the accident.

I sat back on my heels, trying to think. An original antibiotic… I'd heard that on Earth there were once more of them, stronger, better. But now they were synthesized and printed like everything else, loaded into Quacks according to subscription level. Mine were Tier 1, the weakest, like almost everyone's. Tier 2s were for desperate emergencies, the kind the Quacks were meant to keep at bay. Tier 3s were for statespeople and gods.

But a preserved, *original* source microorganism… A new antibiotic, unlinked to a Quack. It could mean a fortune. It could mean death. It could upend the structure of the society as we knew it, rewrite planetary allegiances, as it had centuries ago.

Nausea ran through me, and for half a heartbeat I was tempted to rid myself of the decision and hurl the phial into the darkness forever. Instead, I closed my eyes. For a moment, I almost thought I felt pain in my closing throat, almost thought I smelled moisture on concrete, and coffee and old paper books…

What the hell was I going to do? I could take the phial, get out of here, back to my ship, away from this place. But what then?

A whisper seemed to answer me; a voice that could have come from the depths of the vault or from the ruined book, or from the Quack itself, nestled beneath my skin.

What then? it asked.

Gigi

Sophia McDougall

13/06/2142

GIGI! How are you
Did you see the footage the pictures?
I wondered if you recognised anything.
We even got inside the cathedral!
Look! 100s of times you must have walked across these stones?
Maybe you sat right here?
I put my hand on this angel's head
His marble curls
Which of our ancestors touched them too
Has to have been someone right?
Feels like I'm holding their hands
Swimming with ghosts
I almost cried

I had this crazy thought I could even find your house.

Maybe not now but on another trip. I could come back.

Do you have old pictures

Maps?

15/06/2142

Gigi read your messages

16/06/2142

Getting worried now

You ok? Ade says she can't reach you either

18/06/2142

I only just found this. Am fine

was with Dustin

Oh wow

Young love

Oh stop it.

Can't you turn on RealLife?

I'd rather see your face

I don't have a RealLife pack out here!

I'm in and out of the sea all day

Anyway it gives me migraines

Also not our actual faces

Oh well

I don't think going into the cathedral is smart

it must be unstable

Its fine

Does Talia know about this?

Gigi please

Yes of course she knows

I am streaming everything

She is stressing about it

You are supposed to be the cool one

Sorry I will be supportive!

But I think we only went to the cathedral at Christmas

Not every year

In fact maybe twice

We did hang out outside it tho

They're very good pictures

I'm glad to see so many fish

Yes ok Gigi but the fish are not the point.

And should not be there

The house must be rubble now

A lot is really well preserved

More than you would think

Our homes were not made like cathedrals

19/06/2142

I don't have any pictures of our street
Some of us inside but I guess that's no good
Maybe Jan or Sofie or Isa has something?
I don't know why anyone would keep old maps?
But all that must be online

Its not
I've looked
So much got digitised and then lost
I can find out what a city looked like 500 years ago
But not 100
You'd think everything down there would be gone but it isn't
You'd think everything up here would be HERE
But its all backwards

Oh

So we have to recover what we can
I think we owe that to ourselves
in the diaspora
and to the future
I am looking into funding

I didnt realise you
were so serious about this

Will you ask Isa?

ok

please don't drown though

20/06/2142

Diaspora?

?

What you said yesterday

I didn't know you called it that

Oh

Yes?

I mean – that's what we are?

It's what everyone calls it.

I guess

07/10/2154

Thank you so much for being there tonight

Your speech was beyond moving

I know I speak for everyone in saying that

I always wanted to walk with you through those streets

I feel so lucky that I could

So many congratulations, Teo

Such a lovely evening

And the 3D capture guy

Very interesting talk
what was his name

You mean Cyrus

Oh yes Cyrus! What a hot hot boy
Eyelashes for days my word

GIGI

What we were all thinking it
Especially you

He's a good friend
A FRIEND, Gigi

Tell him that
Well don't
Poor thing
Don't break his heart

Oh my god
OK fine
Maybe there's something
I don't know
I'll let you know when I do OK
What I really wanted to ask was
Will you go back, now you can?

Ah
Well
Teo

You have achieved something incredible
The amount of information you've managed to retrieve
and the of detail you've managed to capture
its breathtaking
And your reconstructions are so detailed
such a labour of love
I'm sure this is an amazing tool
for historians and children and so on
The mosaics were so wonderful
Like I said in the speech, it is extremely moving to 'see'
it again
But inevitably its also rather sad?
its not really going back
it cant be

Please don't be upset
Listen you know I love RealLife
Hang out in it all the time
its fun
And ALMOST like being with people far away
Almost
But all my life I've heard people saying soon we'll have
a version you cant tell from life
that we can just live there if we want to

or whether we want to or not
and all this time its never happened
however perfect it looks
the smells textures the weight of things
– the tastes! Nothing vr is edible –
the solidness of people
there's just no way to do all that
and even if there was

Never mind I'm making this worse
You're saying it wouldn't have a soul
Oh Teo
No the thing is I think you're right
I still don't even like RealLife!
Nine fucking years of working with it
and it still gives me migraines
and for what
Don't talk like that
It's an incredible tribute to the past
a beautiful memorial
I guess
But I was trying to do more than that
What more is there to do?
You cant resurrect a city

Do you know how many times Aleppo burned?

04/08/2156

Hi Gigi how are you

Teo! All the better for hearing from you!

Listen this is so stupid but can you send a copy of your birth certificate

Dont know if youve seen the news

The new government here is a nightmare

They won't even let us in the water

They're worried about the impact on the coastline!

THE COASTLINE, can you believe it!!

Its not really that though. Its about jurisdiction

Like I'm trying to build some sort of creepy little charter city by the sea

Some sort of corporate spy colony or god knows what

Half my team and my machines are stuck outside the country

I need to establish European citizenship

Blood connections help

Ugh thats ridiculous

I know!

This is my heritage as much as theirs. my homeland
We were forced out and I have to prove I have a right
to go back?
All I'm really doing is trying to go home!

I meant it shouldnt matter
where you come from
Seriously talking about bloodlines in 2156?
Astrology with body fluids!
What's next Craniometry? Ducking stools?
I thought we were long past this

Look obviously I agree it's bullsh
and I see what you're saying
but it DOES matter
When I went down there for the first time
Even under all that kelp and silt it felt like
coming home

Teo – I can't pretend
I don't find it rather strange
You know that when I think
of home I think of here?
Tierra de San Martín
I guess I have the odd dream
where I'm a little girl
running around in the old house

but I lived such a small fraction of my life there
and darling you never lived there at all

But I should have had the chance
It shouldnt have been taken from me
from any of us

I know you feel very
passionate about the history
but how does that have
anything to do with blood?
When you touched that angel years ago
couldn't you have felt just as much
even if no relative of yours had seen it?

I dont think so.
No.

I'll see what I can find.

Thank you.

11/02/2159

Gigi have you heard from Cyrus?

What?

Nothing, never mind

Isn't he on the Dhaka dive?
Is everything ok?

12/02/2159

Hello?

26/04/2159

Happy birthday!
Hope you're not working too hard!
How is Cyrus?

06/06/2159

Saw your underwater printers on the news
Wont the sea wall have to be super high tho
Even if the concrete is self-healing
But what do I know everyone seemed very excited
Give Cyrus my love.

30/09/2159

You were on the news again!
Would have been nicer to see you in RealLife
Or even in real real Life
You looked tired.

01/01/2160

Happy New Year
Everyone missed you

I hope you were doing something fun
Guess that sounds like guilt-tripping
Well maybe it is, Teo!
Maybe it is! And who
better qualified than me to do it?
Maybe I'm even going to point out
that we don't know how many chances
like that we've all got left
some of us are not exactly getting any younger
But also I really do hope you were having a good time
Because I worry about you
Cyrus has been in touch by the way
I am so sorry things went wrong between you two
(is the divorce final already?)
I do wish I had heard it from you
I hope you are doing better
than Cyrus made it sound.

04/01/2160

Your concerns are noted

Jesus fucking Christ, Teo

All right sorry yes I'm a dick
As Cyrus is evidently telling everybody
What do you expect me to say

If I dont get the PM standing on some dried-out ground by March
There is a good chance we lose funding for Phase 2
I can't just drop everything
Obviously I would love not to be onsite till 3am
but that's the reality of what Im doing

17/03/2160

Congratulations

18/03/2160

Thank you! It's obviously just a first step
and not much to look at honestly
(and right now it stinks but that will fade)
still its ground no one's walked on in 120 years
that's not nothing
and from here we can save it all
people will only really get it when they see the cathedral
Even YOU Gigi!

09/07/2160

Jesus
Talia just left

She told me about Dustin

Oh my God Gigi I'm really sorry

Its been four months

I know! But I didnt know before

Why didnt you say anything

You only met him once

It was a very small wedding

And a very quiet funeral

You would not have made it to either one

Would you?

Also you could have tried saying

Gigi whats new in your life

Things do happen

Even to me

15/07/2160

I'm sorry.

I've been trying to think of something else to say

And I guess I cant

03/09/2160

Happy Birthday Gigi!

Sorry my gift wont be there yet

but it is coming

10/09/2160

It has arrived apparently?

11/09/2160

Double checking?

Thank you.

OK. Hope you like it.

01/01/2161

Happy New Year!

The printer tracks are already past your old neighbourhood!

Hope you're well.

03/05/2161

Has anyone heard from Teo

He wont be able to reach anyone

Yeah all the networks are going to be fucked for a while

No but I mean before it hit

Did he tell anyone he was getting out

Not me

No

who talked to him last

But he must have

There were warnings.

Are you watching this?

Theyre saying its worse than 06

8 meter storm surge christ

No. Fuck.

Lets not panic. There was a warning.

Why would he even need to be there

Hes on site practically all the time

right. Thats. you know. the whole

thing of Teo

ok but hes not stupid

Shut up Sofie

I didnt say anything

god. this really isnt funny.

the whole coast.

hes not going to ignore

an evacuation order

Is there even anywhere to evacuate to

Teo, are you all right

I know youre not getting this

And youre going to have to wade through a

million messages even when this is over

Answer Talia first she is in bits
I really hope youre all right tho
Fuck I hope youre all right
Sorry
I mean for swearing.
No not really
Listen I wish Id handled things differently last June
I was pretty angry but you were trying
And Dustin was 117
And we had a lot of fun
And we got married 90% for lullz
it was sooner than I thought
and hit me harder than I expected
But you know

04/05/2161

And the cathedral pendant is pretty actually
it annoyed me when it arrived
but I changed my mind
was it from one of Cyrus's scans?
God how is that seven years ago
He must be out of his mind
He still loves you you know
Sorry for all these messages

cant seem to stop
Anyway I do wear the pendant
hanging onto it right now
while trying to talk Isa down
The sky was so blue and bright
the day we had to leave
felt like maybe the whole thing was overblown
there were always storms and we knew what to do
piling the sandbags moving the furniture
like always excited for a few days off school
but the roads were too full
and it got dark far too soon
and the rain on the roof sounded different

Was it like that on Monday?

I hope you have somewhere decent to stay
not crammed in on a floor somewhere damp
Not trapped on a roof or anything
And not dead
Teo, ridiculous boy, please be all right

Still nothing still nothing still nothing
Jan stop it. I get it but youre making it

worse. Stop watching it youre not
making news come any faster.

05/05/2161

Hey, all. Im very tired but safe
Thanks everyone for the messages
still trying to contact all the team
But we all got out when we were told to

TEO!!! Thank fuck

Love you Teo

Oh god so glad

Can we help?

What will happen now?
I mean are your printers ok

Hoping to get to the site or near to it tomorrow

The important thing is that youre safe Teo.
I'm sure everyone else is fine too.
Tell us when you trace everyone

I thought the same thing.
It was actually the first thing I thought
All the land reclaimed is gone again

and more

And then I felt bad, because the people.

06/05/2161

No ones been hurt.

Not the team, I mean.

Others not doing so well

What are you doing are you staying there?

Can you get out

Do you need anything?

Trying to figure out if we can help

We're divers first and foremost

Or if we're just in the way.

Our drones are down there helping fix the cables

And we're trying to make sense of the damage

Like everyone

Trying not to jump to any conclusions

11/05/2161

Hi Gigi

Well I guess that's it. Guess we're done
Did you already hear? Its not on the news
We're the last thing on anyones mind
And I understand
I understand
I understand
But how can it not matter?
To lose a whole city all over again
I guess you always thought itd turn out like this.
I actually don't mean that with any kind of tone
Just is this what you thought would happen

Hi Teo
Yes I suppose I did
Mainly I just didnt understand

I know
And yet so much of it was about you

But Teo, was it, was it really?
I haven't been the girl who lived there in so long
It's so long since I went looking for her

Guess I thought someone should have to

Perhaps someone did.
But there is no finding her, you know
And meanwhile – amazingly – I'm still here.

Did you understand I was trying to do what you did?

Sort of follow in your footsteps, you know?

No?

Antarctica. Tierra de San Martín.

Building something where there was nothing.

Oh

Well now I see that

But you know here we come from all over

and most of us come and go

and when I was young we thought: well

if it can all get washed away that easy

then where your parents came from

or the exact patch of earth underneath you

had better not matter too much

better work out how to carry it all with you

we thought that was how it was going to be

But now it all seems to be changing back

I just. I cant talk to anyone.

Come and see me, Teo

In Antarctica, in real real life.

Alright. I might as well

OK dont flatten me with enthusiasm kid

Sorry. Just feel like the grounds gone from under me

Dont know what to do with myself honestly

All of a sudden I have no plans

Dont know how to be anywhere
How to get from one minute to the next
I've given my whole life to this

Oh love don't say that.
You're so young.

Gigi I am forty-five

[LAUGHING!] [LAUGHING!] [LAUGHING!]
Sorry!
But when you are a hundred and thirty-seven
with grown-up great-grandchildren
you will find that very funny too.
Although you are still my favourite
No one else calls me Gigi

About the Authors

Gavin Smith is the author and co-author of 15 books, a couple of novellas and multiple short stories. His books include *Veteran* and its sequel *War in Heaven*, the *Age of Scorpio Trilogy*, the *Bastard Legion Series* and *Spec Ops Z*. As well as having written for Black Library, Gavin wrote the novelisation of the Sony Pictures *Bloodshot* movie and Marvel's *Original Sin* series. He is also the author of the forthcoming *Alien: Cult* novel, an original story set in the Aliens universe. Within the games industry he has worked with Yoozoo, Ubisoft, DPS Games and CCP. In addition, he has optioned several film scripts. In his free time, he enjoys walking, travel, film, reading, and is a very keen gamer.

Kieran Currie Rones is an analyst and researcher working across government to integrate emerging S&T within interdisciplinary contexts. Their expertise spans psychology (from social research to visual cognition), cybercrime, and computer programming.

Stewart Hotston lives in Reading, UK. With a Celtic-Indian mother and a father of North African/Roma descent, Stewart is a somewhat confused second-generation immigrant who has written several novels with Project Hanuman. When he's not writing he can be found working as a financier in London. Beyond that rather questionable career choice, he is treasurer for the British Fantasy Society and a Councillor for the BSFA. A lifelong roleplayer and LARPer he is also a happy long-distance runner with a PhD in theoretical physics. He has a dangerously fanatical love for ice cream, sword fighting and Studio Ghibli.

Emma Newman writes short stories, novels and novellas in multiple speculative fiction genres. Her novel *After Atlas* was shortlisted for the 2017 Arthur C. Clarke Award and the third and fourth novels in the *Planetfall* series have been shortlisted for a BSFA Best Novel award. The *Planetfall* series was shortlisted for the Best Series Hugo Award. Emma is also a professional audiobook narrator and an Alfie and Hugo Award winning podcaster for her podcast *Tea and Jeopardy*. Her other podcasts include *Imagining Tomorrow* and *Tea and Sanctuary*. Emma is a keen role-player, painter and designer-dressmaker.

Stephen Oram writes social science fiction novels and short stories, exploring the intersection of messy humans and imperfect technology. These include his short story collection, *Extracting Humanity* and his most recent novel, *We Are Not Anonymous*. He is also a leading proponent of applied science fiction, working with scientists and technologists to explore possible outcomes of their research through short stories. The *Financial Times* said that his work, 'Should set the rest of us thinking about science and its possible repercussions.' You can find him at stephenoram.net.

Tiffani Angus (PhD) is a multi-award finalist for her debut novel *Threading the Labyrinth* and (as co-author with Val Nolan) *Spec Fic for Newbies: A Beginner's Guide to Writing Subgenres of Science Fiction, Fantasy, and Horror*. *Volume 2* was released in 2024, and *Volume 3* is due out in 2026. She spent over a decade teaching creative writing at universities in the US and UK, the majority of that time as a Senior Lecturer in Creative Writing and Publishing at ARU in Cambridge (UK). She works as a freelance editor and proofreader for private clients and SFF publishing houses, runs the typesetting/formatting business Book Polishers, and is currently at work on new projects from her home in Bury St Edmunds. You can find her at tiffani-angus.com.

Adrian Tchaikovsky is a British science-fiction and fantasy writer known for a wide variety of work including the *Children of Time*, *Final Architecture*, *Dogs of War*, *Tyrant Philosophers* and *Shadows of the Apt* series, as well as standalone books such as *Elder Race*, *Doors of Eden*, *Spiderlight* and many others. *Children of Time* and its series has won the Arthur C. Clarke and BSFA awards, and his other works have won the British Fantasy, British Science Fiction and Sidewise awards.

Adeola Eze is a children's book writer, educator, and advocate for children's empowerment. As an author, she is dedicated to creating engaging, entertaining and educational content for young readers. Her children's books include *The Adventures of Class 3A: Storm in the Forest* and *One Beautiful, Sunny and Bright Morning: A Guide to Developing Children's Imaginative Writing Skills*. Her work reflects a deep commitment to promoting activities that enhance children's reading and writing skills. Her PhD research in the UK explores book history, and digital and experimental publishing.

Gareth L. Powell has written over twenty published books and has twice won the British Science Fiction Association Award for Best Novel. You can find him online at garethlpowell.com.

Stark Holborn is the author of the *Factus Sequence*, the *Triggernometry* series and the groundbreaking digital serial *Nunslinger*. Her fiction has been nominated for the British Fantasy Awards, the BSFA Awards, the New Media Writing Prize and featured in *Interzone*. Stark also works as a games writer on award-winning projects, and is currently lead writer on SF detective game *Shadows of Doubt*, and a contributing writer on cyberpunk slice of life sim *Nivalis*.

Sophia McDougall is a novelist, screenwriter and translator, whose work includes *Romanitas*, an alternate history trilogy set in a world where the Roman Empire never fell, and two sci-fi books for children, *Mars Evacuees* and *Space Hostages*.

About the Illustrator

Jenni Coutts (Frontispiece and Cover Detail) is an illustrator, speculative fiction writer and GP based in Glasgow, Scotland. She won the British Fantasy Award for Best Artist in 2022 and was shortlisted for the same in 2023 and 2024, with artwork featured in both UK and international publications. She is art editor for *BFS Horizons* and is art lead for the World Fantasy Convention in Brighton in 2025. She was shortlisted for the Scottish New Writer's Award in 2019.

About the Editor

Allen Stroud (PhD) is a university lecturer and Science Fiction, Fantasy and Horror writer, best known for his work on the computer games *Elite Dangerous* by Frontier Developments and *Phoenix Point* by Snapshot Games. He was the 2017, 2018, 2021 and 2023 Chair of Fantasycon, the annual convention of the British Fantasy Society, which hosts the British Fantasy Awards. He was Chair of the British Science Fiction Association from 2019 to 2025. His SF novels, *Fearless, Resilient* and *Vigilance*, along with other titles in *The Fractal Series,* are published by Flame Tree Press.

Beyond & Within

THE FLAME TREE Beyond & Within short story collections bring together tales of myth and imagination by modern and contemporary writers, carefully selected by anthologists, and sometimes featuring short stories and fiction from a single author. Overall, the series presents a wide range of diverse and inclusive voices, often writing folkloric-inflected short fiction, but always with an emphasis on the supernatural, science fiction, the mysterious and the speculative. The books themselves are gorgeous, with foiled covers, printed edges and published only in hardcover editions, offering a lifetime of reading pleasure.

FLAME TREE FICTION

A wide range of new and classic fiction, from myth to modern stories, with tales from the distant past to the far future, including short story anthologies, Collector's Editions, Collectable Classics, Gothic Fantasy collections and Epic Tales of mythology and folklore.

•

Available at all good bookstores, and online at flametreepublishing.com